S0-AUK-967

Unknown Friend

Other books by William A. Luckey

Fiction

The Death of Joe Gilead
Cimarron Blood
Bad Company
Texas Soldier
Unknown Friend

Unknown Friend

William A. Luckey

to Betsy, who loves horses—
Belinda E. Perry
(William A. Luckey)

Santa Fe July 2003

BETANCOURT
& COMPANY
Doylestown, Pennsylvania

Unknown Friend
A publication of
Betancourt & Company, Publishers
P.O. Box 45
Gillette, NJ 07933-0045

www.wildsidepress.com

FIRST EDITION

It was Melissa's simple question; "Who is this, Gramma?" which reopened the shame I'd thought long since buried in time. Minutes had to pass before I could get enough breath to answer, and my granddaughter waited impatiently beside me, seated on the dusty trunk, the hand-tinted photograph clasped in front of her small body like a precious trophy. Then the story erupted inside me, and I began to tell it from beginning to end, edited of course for the innocence of the listeners. But it was the telling of the story, hearing the words spoken from my own mouth, that brought me to conclusions neither perceived nor understood at the time the photograph was taken. Now I could look at the events in their entirety, from a distance of those intervening years, and accept what had happened, although I found I still could not forgive myself for my own foolish behavior.

The day began peaceably enough. Kept indoors by unusual rains, we were in the attic, me, my granddaughter Melissa, and her friend Amy, both just ten. They were digging through a trunk filled with what I had assumed were harmless treasures. Until Melissa offered up the troubling photograph and asked her simple question.

I am Cornelia McKendrick Herrera, known for most of my life as Neelie. I was named after my great-grandmother from Kentucky, and the name was both honorable and old-fashioned. Grandmother Cornelia, so family legend had it, fended off a band of renegade Indians while her husband was out hunting. From the family stories it sounded like a narrowly averted massacre, but when my husband, Mickey, and I were visiting Kentucky and did some research, the truth emerged. All Cornelia had done was to tell a curious party of Indians to leave her and her small children alone, and after she had given them sugar and coffee, they politely did as she asked.

She had ten children, the first born when she was barely sixteen. Like her, and my own mother, I started my family young, and at forty-nine have a granddaughter who is ten. My own mother was blessed with me when she was twenty-one, but at sixteen she had given birth to and lost her first child. I proved only slightly more patient and had my daughter Constance one month after I turned eighteen. There are no regrets for these early conceptions, but the history leading to Connie's birth is part of the photograph and runs deep in my mind, a blending of tragedy and passion.

I will explain about the picture and its troublesome history, but first let me describe the photo and its two subjects, let me show you their shared portrait since individually and together they formed the foundation of the life I now lead. It is of two boys, one much bigger in stature than the other. That this size difference turned out to mirror their hearts' capacity for love is coincidence and nothing more. They stand close together, arms around each other, a rare gesture in those times when males did not touch except in anger or sports. This was the fifties, in rural Colorado, where we each stood isolated while trying to reach our dreams.

Despite the photo being hand-tinted, a process now used mainly in art photography, the colors have faded to a sepia tone. Since Melissa is a precocious child, she asked me what was wrong with the smaller man, while Amy looked at him and said he was cute and the bigger one looked goofy. Melissa became impatient with my wordless remembering, and prod-

ded me; "He is sort of cute, Gramma." I could feel the reservation in her voice. "Was he a boyfriend or something? He looks almost...mean."

While her young voice could not soften the comment's impact, the words hung in my mind. How to describe him, how to find the balance of truth and not reveal the family shame required a depth of diplomacy never asked of me before. I was better known for speaking before thinking; even my husband had not heard all the truth about this particular family saga.

'He's cute' was what I had said to my mother more than thirty-five years ago; later I too said he was mean. Both times I had not expected an answer to my shy observations; when once I had looked at my mother, I saw an expression, a restlessness I had never seen in her before. She was watching the smaller, 'cute' boy, seeing him in a way I did not yet understand.

My mother was the center of our small family which was about to expand. We had inherited a cousin no one had known existed until a letter came in the spring of 1957. The photo, still in Melissa's hand, was from a year later when the two boys were life-long friends. It seems so long ago yet with the photo I can remember it too clearly. At the time of the picture's taking, our entire family was completely engaged with the smaller boy. At sixteen he possessed a smile which knew all about women. This knowledge showed in his eyes despite being only a child. And oddly enough I recognized some of the difference in him from my cousin even while I was only a country girl. The smaller boy was beautiful, with dirty blond hair always streaked from the sun, and pale gray eyes which darkened or changed during extreme moments.

At the moment of the photograph we were still tolerant of the boy, including my father who was the pragmatic, silent member of the family. There must have been a crack which preceded the oncoming division, a need no one chose to recognize, which allowed the beautiful young man to invade us as a unit. He was the welcomed wedge which ultimately destroyed our once contented family. In a few years we were never to be the same, missing some members, adding others in natural rhythm but shaken and betrayed. At the time of the photograph, we embraced the laughter and lightness North's new friend offered and were glad of his intrusion, each of us for our own reasons.

I have digressed again; let me try to finish the descriptions. Two faces fill the image: my cousin North is his true self, high and solid, deep through the chest and neck, one hand at his side, enormous for a mere boy, overshadowing his friend. North's eyes were hidden by the twist of his head so the camera did not record them, but he was a simple, honest boy forced by the immensity of his size and the harsh loneliness of his early life to become a man too soon.

Beside him stands the shining one, bathed in all his contrasts, eyes glowing even in the dimmed image. I find myself unconsciously reacting as I trace those eyes and that mouth and remember the work-hardened, skillful hands. I can feel his singular effect even now; such tension of emotion and sexuality has not come to me again, not even with my beloved Mickey.

Right now Mickey is on business in Denver and I miss him as I always do. If he were here, I would not be in the attic with two boisterous, curious, demanding little girls whose inquisitiveness has reached a core of pain hidden by my complacent life.

Again I have detoured. My cousin North was a welcome addition to my young life, a newly discovered kin whose body size had no relation to his gentle heart. As for Key, his story is in his appearance. The given names for each boy are unusual, as if each mother believed in a favored destiny for her son. They both look older than their years in the photo, North because of his size, and Key simply because he never looked like a child once he understood about sex.

My cousin's name was Northern McKendrick, the last name the same as mine even though our parents were brother and sister. This alone tells you of my aunt's private shame, and more than likely explains why we as a family never heard from her. It is also why North came to live with us just after his fifteenth birthday; his mama was dead, my father was the closest, the only relative they could trace. We were now his family.

In the photo there is little hint of North's tenderness, and equally absent is the dark force in his friend. I could close my eyes and clearly remember standing between the boys, awed by my cousin's size while taking in the raw maleness of Key. But a keen observer like my granddaughter saw past the romance of his face, the straight features, dark lashes shading pale eyes, thick, unruly hair, the pure beauty that hid evil. Even the color of his skin was hinted at in the sepia tones although the original hand painting had almost erased this aspect of his heritage. Key's rich copper skin played beautifully against the darkly blond hair; poor North, in contrast, peeled and turned blotchy while Key only deepened in color.

Interestingly enough, Key received little overt hatred for his obvious heritage; that hatred was reserved for his continued, outlandish betrayal of anything and everyone who sought to claim him, to hold him steady while all he wanted to do was run.

I am no better than all those from the past who were enthralled by Key; I have begun to describe North and end up detailing more of Key's charm and power. The story pains me, even distanced as it is by the kind years of my husband's love, the three children we have raised. That the tale with its ultimate effect on our family lives can still wound me is a frightening revelation, one I am not ready to share with my beloved grand child.

So I revert to a story tinged with bits of the truth. But Melissa interrupts me before I can properly begin. "The picture has writing on the back, Gramma, it says this one is 'North' and the other is a friend. How can he be a friend and not have a name?"

The truth comes from many directions; Melissa had found the center of the tale. Now I had to form an answer through lips thickened by awakened memory. "Child, hush. His name was Key Larkin and he was a friend of your Uncle North's back then. I'd forgotten his name, that's all, when I was trying to put these pictures in some order." I had managed to delay beginning the story because of the two girls, sitting, waiting to hear another one of Gramma's funny tales. But this story is not funny, so I will tell them some of the truth and hide most of the reality. But to myself and any listener, I will relate the truth as I understand it now.

It began in the spring of 1957 when I wasn't quite thirteen. We lived in a small Colorado town near the New Mexico border and close up to the Rocky Mountains, yet we were on the flat plains, backed up to a high mesa but still distant from the mountains. I grew up loving those mountains, with rare visits into their heart. Now that I am an adult, with grown children, and have both the time and ability to travel, I find I prefer to sit on the front porch, an activity sadly outdated, and watch the mountains as they change color and disappear or emerge through the clouds and violent storms of our region.

There was no one in my life like North until he came to live with us. Pa grumbled some when he first saw the boy supposedly his nephew, swearing under his breath to Mama that he was meant to be a child not much older than me and not a full growed adult bigger than Pa himself. Pa spoke in that voice of his made you listen hard even to know breakfast was ready and it was corn fry-cakes and wild plum jelly or that he was headed out to Dubble Wells to fix the motor again. My daddy talked in a quiet voice from deep within himself and it made folks listen.

I learned that some people used this softness to control others but Pa wasn't like that. He was truly a quiet man, a, slow and even presence in our house, a hard worker on the ranch. He acted on instinct and generally it was right. As for the soft voice, I think he didn't like noise, wasn't going to make much noise himself. When I learned, as an adult, that he had been terribly ill as a child and lived in a silent, peaceful room for months, the softness made more sense to me. I never heard Pa yell, never heard him curse, except of course about Key.

So the day North came to us, Pa spoke quietly to my mother and she hushed him, chiding him for being callous, hurting the boy's feelings, and then she called to North as he stood to one side while the rest of the passengers got off the bus and hurried away, knowing where they were going. North stood there motionless, holding on to a rotting canvas bag. He did not seem to hear my mother's voice.

Then Papa stepped up to him and questioned the huge child. I was frightened when North took my hand in his big fist for the first time; any fool on seeing North would know that if he lost his temper, there would be broken bones and cracked skulls and neither of those would belong to North. He lost his temper only once with me, and I deserved it, bur that first time I saw him I felt both fear and awe. The awe quickly shifted to worship and the fear disappeared when he took my hand and leaned down to speak my name correctly. His voice was soft, like Papa's, which is eerie when you think on it.

He was big like Papa, only taller and not yet sixteen. When North died he was still big, even after months of the sickness. Laid out in the coffin he filled the box to both sides, the thin wood barely able to contain the full span of his extraordinary body and spirit.

Key was lucky North didn't know his reputation the first day they met in the school yard; Key on his back being pummeled by a bully, North immediately, without thought, hauling the attacker off of Key and extending his hand to the injured boy. Key was smart, he lay still, covered in dust, with a bloody nose and cheek, a long scrape bleeding through the thick hair. He must have guessed that whoever pulled off the tormenter didn't know about him yet.

North squatted down and spoke to Key as if he were a scared and beaten pup, using soft soothing words and gestures.

He wasn't far wrong on the physical but a little kicking and punching never touched Key's spirit. Like I said, North didn't know better then. Even after he came to know Key he insisted he liked him, which no one else ever said. And if North ever hated Key for what he was, or was jealous or angry with him, except for that one time, none of us ever knew. North was loyal to his friends.

And they were friends from the first moment, with North spending his time trying to attract Key's attention while Key spent that same time and more energy deviling North, going his own way certain North would follow. Key wasn't wrong, North was always there, one or two steps behind him, cleaning up the chaos Key engendered. How I felt about Key Larkin privately, how my feelings changed as I went from a child to a woman, had nothing to do with Key Larkin's notion of the goodness and rightness of his life. Or North's championing of him when all others condemned Key's behavior.

Then again, my opinion wasn't worth much; I was a girl cousin, of less use than the runt of our blue heeler, Hazel's, yearly litter of pups or a calf out of the one-horned brindle cow Pa kept up for milk. I was a girl, and not much to look at till I got my full growth and then Key paid attention but so did other boys.

North took a long time to find his way in the sexual rituals of our growing up, but not Key. For him the local girls and some females all the way up to Pueblo and the older women Mama insisted weren't ladies took up his attention early on and he went at them with great fervor and style.

No one learned much about Key, no one except of course North who never betrayed a secret, and finally, briefly, me. But my initial instinct proved correct. I was fascinated by Key as by a wolf cub or caged bear, but I was my daddy's child and I knew it wasn't right for North to run with Key Larkin.

Chapter One

When North was ten or thereabouts, Ma told him about his daddy. That he was a big man, bigger than any other man she'd known. Even bigger than her own brother who was no small child. It was the only time she talked about the man who sired him so North paid attention. Talk was something his ma rarely offered, other than 'mornin'' and 'what'll you have?' She worked at a diner and came home bone tired each night, too tired to do more than hand North a package of cold meat and a loaf of bread, or some leftovers she brought with her.

She couldn't tell him much about his pa, she didn't know anything really important. North guessed maybe she never knew the man's name and didn't want to explain this to her impressionable son. She said nothing about why they didn't marry, she told North only that his pa'd been big in girth and laughed a whole lot, and that one time he told her he'd grown this size when he was real young. She told him this to reassure North that his size at ten was to be expected. It also told North she had been with his pa more than once. That made him feel better despite not knowing the man's given name. At least he weren't a bastard off a one-night stand. She never said if he took after the man in any other way, and North was fearful to ask. He'd learned to watch his ma carefully, to judge her sadness, and he came to be ashamed that he was like his pa at all. It had to be an evil in him from his pa, that made a sainted woman like Lily McKendrick miserable and so alone.

North figured he could go either way; he was terribly strong physically and quick-minded, he could fight and be a bully like he imagined his pa had been, or he could move to a better purpose. No one would ever know the fear buried in him, that he was what caused his mother's deep sadness and early death. That he was somehow to blame, from his huge size and clumsy hands and the need for so much food and that he reminded her of his blood pa.

North grew quickly into his teen years, working from ten on as a man in a succession of menial jobs needing brute strength, caring for his ailing ma and trying hard to keep up with his schooling. He finished his growing above the border in southern Colorado.

They lived in the Texas panhandle, in a town dependent on cattle, feed lots, and grain production. While his ma served burned coffee and watery beans and eggs to red-faced cowboys and truckers, and salesmen eager to sell her whatever they carried in their sample cases, North ate and grew and cost his ma most of her adult life.

He grew up with half-breeds and cast-off wetbacks as playmates, with old, bent-kneed cowhands to tell him stories and no one to answer his few quiet, desperate questions. He didn't know if his pa found Lily in the diner where she worked or in the smaller town where she grew up. He didn't know if there had been courting or where the ultimate act took place or if she had left her home in other disgrace and he was conceived in a nameless dusty town. These questions haunted him, left him older than his physical years.

At fourteen North was three inches over six feet and weighed close to two hundred pounds. He would carry another thirty pounds before he was seventeen and then keep that weight until he took sick. Despite his age, he worked in the feedlot for the year his mother took to die. He attended school when he could, studying in the evenings so he could stay with his grade. His ma died three weeks after North turned fifteen and there was no cash to bury her. The mayor and the pastor of the church Lily rarely attended agreed it was best the boy live with relatives. A Raymond McKendrick in Colorado was listed as her brother. The truth was, no one in town wanted to feed a youngster big as North.

Lily McKendrick was buried quickly, with few mourners, and her belongings were put in a rummage sale at the Methodist Church. North's bus ticket was paid for by the Legion which took two of Lily's prints and her favorite plush chair in payment. Within six months a drunk shot both prints in their exact centers and when the Legion Post was torn down for the highway, the prints and the chair were bulldozed into landfill.

North took a canvas suitcase strapped shut with two belts, filled with frayed but clean shirts from the church and one pair of new J.C. Penney jeans. The only picture he had of his ma was wrapped carefully in newspaper and padded with his extra socks.

North had a pleasant, bland face, with light brown hair which curled in a wayward cowlick across his forehead. He kept his hair up to right before his death and even then it was only slightly thinned out by the drugs and he was proud of that small accomplishment. His eyes were soft hazel, hooded and hard to read within the roundness of his face; his beard never grew more than a few wisps which he shaved off every two or three days when he thought of it.

The soft eyes eventually were lined with their years, but they remained comforting, and the features of his lumpy nose and round cheeks never took on the planed angles of most adults. Even the texture of his skin was baby soft until he was laid out in the casket. But his size and the breadth of his hands, the width of his shoulders, his voice with the undertone of 'do what I say now' got him through the years of brawls with few scars and no broken bones. No sane man, even drunk, would see North come at him and try to fight back. Few ever called his bluff, and those who did often were carried to a doctor or hospital by North himself.

As far as the McKendrick family was concerned, too many of those battles were fought for the protection and reputation of Key Larkin.

The bus ride was long for any man, and more so for the hulking boy who was hunched up against the grimed window, feeling the itch and spasm of his cramped arms and legs, suffering the indignity of his overwhelming flesh for the two hundred and seventeen miles it was from his mother's grave to southern Colorado.

North stared out the window, saw the endless miles of mesquite and sage twist and turn into smoother, bright grassland; in the distance always were the snowcapped mountains. Then the bus turned away from the blue peaks, headed northeast. North shrugged, let his head fall back on the greasy seat as he tried to sleep.

He woke as the bus stumbled into lower gear. North groaned too, and dislodged his seatmate who bit off a complaint and shoved North's left forearm back onto his side. The road narrowed and turned, stunted trees grew almost to the macadam edge. Behind them the hills rose covered in rock and more stunted trees. It seemed the bright sun was shut out by sharp peaks and high ledges. North saw the sign; Raton Pass it said, and then 'Welcome to Colorado.' He sighed, guessed he'd slept through most of New Mexico.

The town itself weren't nothing, excepting for the hills and the narrow stretches of wood houses. Black gravel hills mottled with red and orange intrigued him; his seatmate uttered a few words; "Mining town, son, them's slag heaps." As they got closer to the town's center, the narrow ridge showed them a distant view of the town spread below. High brick buildings with fancied windows and doors were set on streets crossed with railroad tracks. The bus thumped badly and then hissed to a stop.

North got off the bus first, then stepped aside, letting the passengers mill about him. He could see over them easily enough. One man stood out from those waiting; tall, broad, hand raised to shade his eyes from the late sun and North grinned, felt suddenly weak; it was a gesture and stance familiar from his mother. He gulped at sudden tears, shook inside, feeling like a mongrel pup looking for the next home.

Words were passed between the man and a pretty woman; North heard the comments on his size and grunted to himself, already in trouble. Then the man walked up to him, said something North couldn't hear. He shied from looking straight into those eyes and hated the cracking of his own voice as he asked: "Name's Northern McKendrick, sir. You my uncle?" The man accepted North's outstretched hand, shook it hard twice, dropped it, and North stepped back, uncertain, afraid. It was the woman, come up beside her man, who comforted him with her easy chatter.

"Ray ain't use to talkin' much, child. Me, I'm your aunt by marriage, Aunt Claudie. And this here's our daughter Neelie, proper name of Cornelia." North wasn't ready for more relatives; he'd been used to the man, glad to know he had an uncle, but not this tall, lean, polite woman whose eyes showed a bright regard for him already. The girl was puny, too much younger than North for him to take much notice of her. But he knew his manners, wanted to let them know his ma taught him well and shook hands with the child, accepting her as he did the man and woman,

Then, abruptly, the man rested a hand on North's shoulder. For a moment the touch was reassuring, and then it became a burden. "Boy, you come on with us. Sit in back, we come in the truck." It was both command and invite, and North wanted to smile but saw only a retreating back. Again it was the woman who helped; "Come on; boy, hop in, it's time we got home for supper."

North picked up his case and followed. The girl clung to her ma and hung back at the same time, watching North. She had big eyes, kind of a mixed blue and green with specks, cat's eyes. He gave her a quick grin, she stumbled and skipped ahead of her ma and he was alone.

The surrounding buildings were tall, blank-faced brick, with no fancy decoration. Backside of a street, he thought. Then he froze, unable to blink or draw in air, he was going to die right here and it would take a long time for the new people in charge of him to know he was dead and he would die alone. Like his ma.

Tears burned his eyes. He winced, prayed he could wipe out their betrayal, their shame. All he wanted was his own ma to comfort him. Nobody else, just his ma.

Instead he felt the hand of a child touch his wrist and he cranked his head far enough to look down and see the youngster who was trying to nudge him back into the world. "You look kinda funny, North, you all right?" He could speak just barely; "Nothin' wrong with me, just lookin' 'round." He quit, jarred by his lies. The child stared at him, the eyes deep blue-green, surprisingly like his own ma's. They saw into him with her knowledge and knew that he was lying.

It would be the only time North lied to his cousin. Except once when no man could speak such a truth. Even with all the horrible things to come, North learned he could tell Neelie the truth, sometimes a truth he didn't know until they heard the words together. But this time he quit, caught in a trap. "I'm fine, missy. Just tired from the ride's all." She dug her fingers inside his fist and he winced, ducked his head, wiped his face on a shirtsleeve all the time she was talking.

"It's rough comin' to live with strangers, we don't know you either. But you won't be a stranger long. After a supper of Mama's chicken and a cobbler, we'll be family, North." She tugged on his hand, forcing him to squeeze her small, fragile hand in return. "Come on, North, it's supper time."

The truck was older than North, riding on spoke wire wheels, and a rotted wood bed. North climbed over the tailgate and settled, back to the cab, used to riding there. He half-jumped when the girl climbed in over the side and settled in. Her parents didn't seem to mind so he said nothing.

They chugged through the town, sputtering and jerking at each stop sign. The streets cut into each other, loaded at first with fancy storefronts and more tall buildings like North'd never seen. The houses were different too, some close to the street, other square in the middle of cropped green grass. Finally the fine houses thinned into rows of shacks and fenced pens where cows and chickens and even a mule stood around and looked bored. North felt better seeing the animals, it seemed more like home, more like the Texas cow town with its feedlots and greasy diner.

"It's minin' around here, you know. You should see the trains come through, haulin' out that coal all over the place." North jumped, dug his back into the truck's bed. He'd forgotten about her. "We live at the ranch of course, the three of us. And now you. I got no brothers or sisters, Pa says I was so perfect I was all they needed." Then she seemed to recognize what she'd just said and could not look at North.

He shrugged, felt the wood planks scrape him through his shirt. "How'd your Ma die?" North winced, his heart fluttered. She might be a kid but she asked grown-up questions too freely. He half-raised a hand against the questions, then heard his ma's voice chiding him about his size and power and how he couldn't use it against those weaker than he was. He eased back, took that extra breath Ma always reminded him about, and settled himself into having to talk.

"Well, what happened? You can tell me, we're family now, ain't we?" Durn kid was persistent. North gulped, tasted dust and oil, felt the truck begin to pick up speed. Glancing away from his tormenter, he saw grass and hills and narrow gullies and more rocks. Then he relaxed, comforted by the surrounding land and saved from having to answer questions by the rushing wind and grinding metal that made any talk impossible.

The McKendrick ranch was set in a small bowl at the end of a long dirt track, right up under a high mesa. It was isolated and protected from wind and storms, a pretty little place, simple and easy on a Texas eye.

For a brief moment the house was shining as they approached, rays from the setting sun angled in to the polished stone surface of the house, then the sun sunk lower and the house became gray and tired and simply stone set on common dirt. Before the truck ground to a halt, North slipped out of the bed, glad to have his feet on solid ground. Behind the stone house's sturdy shape, North recognized the lines of a familiar building, a melting adobe, more'n likely a sheepherder's hut. This'd been a ranch a long time.

When he followed his uncle up the dirt path to the door, he stopped a moment, laid the palm of his hand on the fitted stone and felt the sun's warmth come into his flesh. Then he followed his uncle and aunt, and the kid, into their home.

There was a room on the back that was just his. It were no bigger than a horse stall but it was his; the rest of the family slept upstairs, in a second floor which was foreign to North. He'd always lived on a sofa or in a corner curtained off for privacy. The bed was narrow in the small room, and too short for him when he lay down at his uncle's insistence. His uncle laughed, a sort of strangled sound. "Guess we'll do somethin' 'bout that for you, boy. Want to make certain you're comfortable here with us." Soft words, spoken easy, holding out a welcome that startled North.

Then she came poking in and stopped North from what he needed to say. "Mama says we got a cold supper all laid out, best come eat. Pa, you come with me." The kid grabbed for his hand and her father reached between them, half-lifted her from one arm, hugged her briefly, put her down for a running start with a spank on her behind. She looked back over her shoulder as if she knew something her father had not yet learned; that she was too old for such gestures, that she was rapidly outgrowing being her father's little girl.

Ray McKendrick turned to North, waited that one moment so the girl was out of sight. "She's our special child. Lots of heart and temper. And real smart. You watch out for her now, she's comin' of age." North heard the words and stumbled over his thoughts: he'd watched out for his mother and failed, but this was different, he was being given a second chance.

"She's a girl, our whole life." Here a strange noise escaped from his uncle and North stepped back. "So you watch her like you would a little sister, your little sister." Thankfully a voice called, female and demanding; "Ray, food's ready. Any time now."

North took a step but his uncle wasn't done yet, his words stopped North, made him tremble as he listened. "Your mother, she was my sister even if we didn't see each other. Took her own road, lived her own life. Now you, you're with us long as you chose."

No one asked him the next morning if he knew anything about ranching or cattle or fences, or the windmill east of the barn. Breakfast got eaten in silence, even the girl did nothing more with her mouth than put food in it. When Ray McKendrick stood up and nodded to his wife, North followed, mumbling a politeness which was accepted without response.

His uncle stood in the new sun; it was just 6:30 in the morning. He stared out to the flat grass. North stood beside him, waiting. "You call me Ray, boy." Said so quietly that North almost didn't hear him; he nodded in mute response. Out to the corrals, Ray let him choose up a horse, watched without judgment when he roped and saddled with a borrowed rig. He chose a sturdy, plain, brown gelding had a good eye, wide rump and enough girth to carry North's weight. "Ain't gonna be easy keepin' you in broncs, boy your size." Nothing was asked or needed from the words. North had heard them all before. "You ride that fence there"; Ray pointed due east. "Up over the mesa, you can't miss the trail. Check wire, and any mama cows you find. Should keep you out till sun hits midday, then we'll take care a dinner. That'll do it."

It was his whole summer in those words: ride fence, repair the windmill at a place called Dubble Wells, dig holes, string wire, curse the windmill, its rotting wood tower. Work hard, eat good food, laugh some with these people, and sleep. There was no fuss or questions, no worry for North, only the promise that when fall came he would have clothes to wear and would go on to school.

He'd never had a friend near his age, never mind a girl with a mouth and mind like this one. Neelie saw everything that moved and had to talk about it. At first North got irritated but he slowly learned there was no hurt to her, it wasn't her nature to be mean, only the desire to understand everything shown to her by the world.

She was a gnat he swatted that first day, tagging along while he saddled the brown gelding and tied on the tools he'd need. It wasn't until he climbed on the bronc and the big horse tried to buck and then quit, snorting, that North saw the glint of acknowledgement in his uncle's eyes. Neelie was right there, asking what was going on, why was her pa smiling? North spat out a rough word about 'nothing,' then regretted the severity in his voice as her eyes got real quiet. But she didn't let him off the hook. "Why're you so mean, North? I ain't askin' for secrets, all's I'm askin' is why Papa's pleased."

Ray had drifted off, leaving North to explain. "I don't know 'bout your pa, miss. But he and I agreed on somethin', didn't have to say a word neither." This was no lie, North felt the space between him and his uncle getting smaller already. This McKendrick family felt as if it had been carved out of rock and pine and there was just enough room for him.

He waved a hand as her face registered disbelief; the bronc snorted, its head came up then the horse stepped sideways against North's legs and put its head down into an easy buck. North laughed and slid his spurs along the brown sides. When the contest was done, with respect on both sides, he looked for the girl and she was gone. No sign of her papa neither.

*H*e was a half-circle east of the ranch when noon came. The high sun told him the time and North was almighty hungry. Too far out to ride in, too hungry to work; he'd have to settle for a long cold drink of water at the stock tank but it wouldn't be enough. He sighed, rubbed his belly when it rumbled, and his head throbbed. Too much sun and wind and never enough food.

A shadow moving from the tiny ranch buildings caught the brown's eye first and North knew to pay attention. He watched and soon enough saw it was a horse, loping easily, a small figure perched on its back. He guessed it was Neelie, and he hoped she had brought food.

Sure enough she had two big ham sandwiches squished in her saddlebags, an apple, and a slice of pie still warm. Almost enough for North's hunger. He tried thanking the child, tried outguessing her while he tore into the food, chewed quickly, letting the bulk settle in his belly. "How'd you know where to find me and why didn't your ma just give me lunch this mornin', save you the ride. Thanks, though, for comin' out." He caught the funny look on her face and was curious as he bolted the last of the pie.

"You're too easy, Northern McKendrick. You think 'cause you're big enough to ride a fence line by yourself that no one can figure you out. Well you had to come this direction ridin' this fence and this's the only stock tank for miles so you'd stop here if nothin' else but to give Billy here a long drink and a rest 'fore you go on. Where else could you go?"

She sat hunched up in a stick shape, a skinny kid not tall enough to reach North's chest. She waved a thin hand out, to include the flat valley she'd just ridden and the tiny house, the paper corrals, and far in the distance the county road to Trinidad. Behind them rose the bulky mesa, shaped by scattered boulders and thin juniper, some piñon and a few mesquite to vary the terrain.

"If you rode all morning with this food it'd be worse flat. And Mama hadn't baked the pie yet, you can tell, it's still warm. You want to complain about fresh ham and warm pie you go ahead, must a been livin' pretty fancy to have any complaints about this food." For such a scrawny child; she kept track and knew where she was going. "And if we left you out here all day with no one to care you could think we don't like you. Mama and Pa never treat a hired man that way, never mind real kin."

North bit into the apple, wincing more from the sharpness of her observations than the tang of pulp and skin in his mouth. He could defend himself but she didn't seem to expect answers. When she got down to eating her own meal, North found he liked the company, liked the shine to the red hair as she bent over her share of the pie, the small eager noises she made as she licked her fingers when she was done. After she rode out, the quiet was no longer so peaceful

He rode in to the yard around six, when the sun hit direct into his eyes. The voice surprised him since he couldn't see a damned thing . "You had yourself a long day, son. Supper's 'bout ready. Neelie says you got up to Dubble Wells this afternoon, good for you. Get use to the place, that Aeromotor gives us a lot a trouble."

He was out again the next morning early, stiff and sore, feelings his knees raw from the too-short stirrups on the old saddle but he had work to do. And again Neelie met him at noon, by two dying cottonwoods tucked in a narrow canyon. He wondered how she found him but didn't dare ask for being lectured on the obvious. He'd rather get through the two sandwiches this time and find out what sweet Mrs. McKendrick sent along. He didn't know how to call the woman, she wasn't kin 'cept through marriage and she was too young for him to be comfortable with a first name like he called Ray. She was an aunt not by blood, and attractive for all of being nearer to thirty than his fifteen. Her presence embarrassed him, especially when he saw the family laundry hung; out, washed by her hand. It was worse that Neelie helped her; there wasn't much a man could hide from a woman washed his clothes, especially when the night brought dreams and fantasies and thoughts no man could control. Mrs. McKendrick made it worse for North; she carried a light step to her and a glow when her husband came near. He envied them, able to raise pleasure from a touch, a soft word or a hand to the back, a squeeze on an arm, a finger laid gently on the face. North was shamed by his interest in these small gestures. He'd never seen such lightness in his own ma, especially when a man came around. Her eyes always held a deep weariness, her body pulled back instinctively from any touch and North was old enough and too aware of his flesh to know his ma did not want any man's attentions.

Yet this woman and wife continued to invite her husband near and the husband smiled at the invite. It was a new sensation for North, to see and share in others' pleasure. He hoped these moments would not stop and equally as much he hoped neither McKendrick parent or the girl would see and understand what affected North at such times.

Sitting outside last night, when it was too hot to remain indoors, he had a flash of knowing; he'd been asked that first day to protect Neelie, to preserve her; it was from thoughts such as his own sinful wanderings, as much as from real physical lust that Neelie was to be protected, it was from any man's lust-filled eye that might damage her person.

Thankfully alone when he understood the task his Uncle Ray had set him, North felt his face grow hot, his eyes blink from tears as he imagined his Neelie responding to a man's offer of temptation. He groaned out loud, bit his lip, felt that long shudder drive through. There was too much he could not protect her from, but he could be her guardian against the desires and imaginings of the local boys. He knew his size, knew its power, and here was a chance to make that power useful.

That private vow of protection would absolve him in some small way of the baseness of his dreams. Whatever girl he might imagine, she would never bear resemblance to Neelie, or her mother. North shook with the strength of the vow; he would not allow any man to touch or demean Neelie, or hurt any member of his new family.

Three days later he rode to a section that sloped over a long slow hill. He was looking for a break in the fence that Ray said was mixing the first bred heifers with the dry cows meant for fall market. North didn't mind the urgency of the ride, or the distance; he liked time by himself, liked it even better when he knew Neelie would appear at noon. Sure enough she found him. She was riding a new dun pony her pa had just taken in trade from a neighbor for one of Hazel's heeler pups. The pony could run; North set his back to a rock and watched. Flat out, ears buried in the thick mane so North couldn't see them, the pony was low to the ground and it happened so fast North couldn't react. A bird flew up under the pony's chest, smashed into the pony's muzzle and the terrified animal went sideways mid-stride, came down on one front hoof and folded. Chest down then sideways and rolling with Neelie clinging to the saddle, disappearing under the solid body as the pony tumbled.

North was halfway up when the pony came full over and Neelie was free. He knew even as he stumbled into a run that at least she was clear, as least she wasn't under the pony's thrashing hooves or rolling belly. He reached her as the pony half sat and then stood, to shake itself and hobble a few steps before lowering its head to graze.

She was so small and delicate that North distrusted the strength of his fingers as he felt the joining of her jaw and neck where a pulse should be. So thin, pale skin with blue veins showing; tangled red hair, finer to the touch than he expected, even the thin cover of her eyelid was tissue soft, far too delicate to protect her closed eyes. Neelie groaned, a child-like tone of growing intensity. North let his fingers rest on the pulse at her neck, let its interrupted rhythm soothe him. Then he sat back on his heels, careful to keep his large hands away from her face. There was so little to her, especially against the immensity of his thumb and forefinger, which could just about circle her neck if he so chose.

She twitched, her eyelids fluttered and North laid a hand as gently as possible on her shoulder to hold her still. "Yeah, lean on me you big lummox like that pony tried to do." It wasn't much louder than a squeak but it was Neelie's mouth and mind speaking, tinny and bright, teasing him even as she groaned again, trying to lift her arm.

Her eyes stayed open; North leaned way forward and stared into them. He could see blood actually pushing through a vein in her forehead. Her voice startled him, his heart lurched; "Am I still all there or are you peerin' at me like some freak 'cause I lost a nose or one ear or somethin'?"

North jerked back, shook his head, rubbed his own face, felt the fine density of his beard. "Don't move yet, kid. Let's see what's broke and what ain't, 'fore you go gallopin' wild again like that. Your pony sure can move out." He couldn't say the words that told her how thin and pale and fragile she looked, he couldn't tell her of his fears so he teased and she gave it right back which pleased him. "You get those hands off me and get out a my sun so's I can see and I'll be just fine."

Then she cried and North felt the cry inside him but her words were a shock; "Your lunch, it's squashed flat. Mine too. And it was dried peach pie." He threw his head back and laughed and she peered at him, her bright eyes furious, her lips drawn back, readied for battle. Then she too laughed, gingerly at first and when nothing seemed to hurt she let out a whoop and sat up, winced and swatted at North's encircling arms. "You better eat it anyway or I'll be mad." She watched North as if knowing she sometimes pushed too hard. North guessed she was scared he'd tell her parents and was trying to get him angry so he'd forget her reckless gallop and the spill. Then she gulped, wiped her mouth and again he marveled at the smallness of her wrist and hand. "Pa'll stop me from ridin' out to met you we tell him 'bout this. I ain't hurt so it ain't like we're goin' to lie."

She didn't ask, there was only a small bit of pleading in her words; "They got enough worry they don't need to fret seein' me ride and I don't want to stay home all the time." North agreed silently, tilting his head and looking away as if the gesture was enough. She cocked her head in question, he shuttered his eyes, shook his head again and the matter was settled.

It was their first joined secret, the shuttered eyes and cocked head to become a signal.

There was little damage done; she'd torn her blouse which could be explained by a low-hanging tree limb or a barbwire fence between her and a bunch of flowers. Other than a few bruises slowly coming to color, she was fine. The pony was a different matter; he held his off hoof raised slightly, refused to put weight down on it. North drew a bucket of water from the stock tank and stuck the pony's leg in it for twenty minutes which must have felt good for the half-broke pony stood with no fussing or complaints.

But the cold water treatment didn't slow the swelling above the fetlock, so Neelie thought up a story to tell her pa and said she'd lead the pony home. North watched her leave, marveling at the straight line to her back and the determined pull it took to get the pony hobbling along. She'd be all right, she'd get her pa to think the pony tripped in the rocks and fell, and North's placid days would go on. Except that North would hold to that small worry about Neelie; he'd not done his duty, he'd not been able to protect her after all.

Towards the end of August, Mrs. McKendrick took North into Trinidad, with Neelie in tow, to shop for school clothes. New jeans that really fit him, three shirts that weren't too bad but hung off his belly while they snugged his neck and were long enough to the wrists; men's shirts, not boys, nothing flashy or in fashion, two red plaids and a blue plaid undistinguishable from what he'd worn all his life.

It was the buying of new underwear and tee shirts that made North blush; to have a woman like Mrs. McKendrick ask him his size and did he prefer jockey or boxer; he didn't know there could be a choice, he'd always worn what was dug out of the thrift box at the local church.

Socks too, white ones that came up past the anklebone so his boots didn't rub. Neelie's rolling eyes told him he looked like a dude but North had no clothes left that could be called decent. He didn't let her teasing rock him, she was just a kid.

Two days later he went to the new school and that first day was a beaut. To start, North had a question but was fearful still of bothering the family to ask. Ray was busy with a sick cow and Mrs. McKendrick, she kept asking him to call her Aunt Claudie but he couldn't fit the words in his mouth, she was making up school lunches and picking at Neelie's dress, telling her to stay clean the whole day.

It was silly of him, dumb, but he wanted to know how they got to the bus, did they walk or did someone drive them. Real dumb, but he'd never ridden a bus before, had always walked to school, hitching when he got older. The Texas town'd been so small only the ranch kids rode a bus. Now he was the ranch kid and he didn't know how to go about this new life.

Neelie seemed to guess his worry and spoke up, just the way he'd learned to expect; "We ride a horse down to the end of the road, turn it loose and it comes on home. Nighttime we walk or Papa's there to get us. We don't walk in the mornin', we ain't got the time, there's chores to be done 'fore we catch the bus."

North was puzzled; "Your ma said to stay clean. For school I mean." Neelie laughed at him; "I ride on a towel, dummy, I ain't goin' to school with horse hair on my behind."

The ride went smooth enough, on a fat-barreled appaloosa already growing a winter coat. They made it on time to the bus but North kept washing his hands down his pants leg, trying to remove any stray hairs. Neelie kept saying he was clean. They'd taken turns inspecting each other's backside until they got plumb silly.

North sat in the bus seat where he was too big and stared straight ahead, kept his face frozen, just like his insides. Too many new faces, all young and small and strangers staring at him; he already hated riding the bus.

Neelie took care of everything once they got to school. She was a step ahead of him as usual, laughing with a group of friends, shying away from any new faces while never letting North get too far behind. He came around a corner and walked into a group of girls all Neelie's age, she put a hand on his wrist. "This here's my cousin, North. He lives with us now. He's in the tenth grade. Ain't he somethin'?" He hated her bragging words even as he trusted her logic.

She paused for effect and North inwardly cursed the dramatics. "He's big and smart and don't no one mess with him." North couldn't stop his blush, then Neelie found a girl she hadn't seen all summer and the fluid crowd of little girls swirled around the two girls, making him dizzy.

The schoolhouse wasn't much, right at the town's north side, a low yellow building painted with brown steps and window trim. He started to go inside but Neelie's command stopped him. "It's too early, only sissies go inside now. Go 'round back, that's where everyone is."

The girls fled in their mass of braids and dresses and squeals, Neelie right up front, and North was glad to see them go, tired of orders and not knowing what he was expected to do. Then he walked slowly towards the back of the high, narrow building, looking all around, curious and still doubtful of his surroundings. Until he heard growls and jeers, sounds he understood. From all over the playground at the school's back, groups of younger kids, mostly girls, had drawn themselves up into a silent barricade.

It was a brawl like so many in Texas, hot and dusty and more push than real hitting. Far behind the mass of legs and arms, North looked back at the distant mountains, at once pleased and comforted by their ragged size. Here, now, in the schoolyard, a bunch of yahoos kicked and cursed each other and the world was no different, yet the mountains gave him a peace he could always find by simply searching for them.

Then he watched a shaved-head jock sit on the kicking form of a skinny kid who cursed and laughed and changed the rest of North's world forever. It was the laughter coming from the smaller kid, despite fists pounding all over him, that caught North's attention.

We all knew about Key Larkin so I didn't feel bad standing there with a group of my friends gleefully watching Stevie Plunkett pound him into the dirt. More than likely Key deserved that pummeling for one reason or another misdeed. Then I looked up at North. I can still see the pain in his eyes as he watched. I remember thinking fearfully that North didn't know about Key. Having a small but clear understanding of my cousin by then, I knew instantly that he was going to mess up his first day by jumping in to save Key and it would be a terrible mistake.

Of course before I could get to North and tell him about Key, he was bending over and picking Stevie up by the back of his shirt and he literally threw him some ten feet or so into the crowd of kids. I mean threw him; I knew North was strong, but watching him pick up Steve like he wasn't more than a mewling kitten I realized how much like a full-growed man my fifteen-year-old cousin was. And I could only vaguely guess then how much trouble that strength could bring him.

Looking around it was easy to pick out the older girls, those who saw in North a quality I was not yet familiar with; they lowered their eyes and several of them touched their mouths, which were half open and wet. Now I understand that such gestures were from an awakening sexuality; then I could only snigger at their foolish parodies of desire as they read about it in the teen magazines. But their feelings were real; in that moment of watching North throw Stevie effortlessly, they were experiencing the raw power of an adult male. Even I felt a quickening of my breath as I saw what North did and how little effort it took.

Key did not hurry to get up and away from the trouble but lay in the dust and dirt and laughed and called Stevie a dirty name. I thought maybe that North would see Key's basic, mean nature, but he was too trusting, my simple, starved cousin from Texas; he leaned down with a big hand extended, expecting to pick Key up from the ground badly scuffed or wounded and weak. Of course Key did not do what was expected of him; he never did.

I have gleaned from my childhood and from marrying a good man often judged too quickly for his color and surname, that my own initial opinion of Key was unfair. Books and educators and prison authorities tell us that a criminal may have been forced into crime by terrible circumstances we don't understand; an abused childhood, a horrible act done to him which he then perpetuates on others. What I also know, from my own experience, is that the individual is capable of making a choice, in the middle of such horror and brutality, to forgive, to love, to help those who would abuse him.

We are all ultimately responsible for the good and evil we create in our lives. I believe this firmly, and Key Larkin, despite his erring mother and no father, his brutal childhood, had no true excuse for the havoc and pain he caused to those who were taken in by his wounded charm and tried to help. Of course I speak of my immediate family, for they are my major concern and source of knowledge.

By the time of the schoolhouse brawl, I knew that North was a fixer, a tilter at windmills, a dreamer despite his appearance. He dreamed he could make amends for Key's beating by holding out his hand and offering peace and safety.

Instead Key rolled over and came up quick on his feet, walked over to Stevie, who hadn't recovered enough yet to move and kicked him once, hard, in the ribs, before North could stop him. Then he turned back to North and stuck out his own hand. "Wanted him to remember me." As if Key had been the aggressor, the source of Stevie's pain. North hesitated, Key grinned and used his magic and I could see North soften. They shook hands, briefly; North towered over Key. "Big sum bitch ain't you." That was pure Key, charming and rough, quick with the truth when it served him. Never had a civil tongue, always talked like he couldn't read a simple page which was a lie, yet despite all of what we'd known, we fell in love with him. Especially at school; there we were silly, dreamy girls who loved the notion of an outlaw. And Key loved us in return, for our innocence, and so he took full advantage of anyone willing to be with him.

This particular time it was North McKendrick who fell in love, in his own male, distant way, willing to take up a new and highly intriguing cause. The protection and adoration of Key Larkin.

Chapter Two

Key and his ma lived in a succession of rented places; brick tenements, two rooms over a pool hall or bar, even for three months when Key was real little, in a new single family home in a nice neighborhood. That was the worst place for Ma, she got crazy with the ladies watching her.

The best time was the four years they lived on a ranch north of Trinidad where his ma couldn't get to liquor easy and Key had horses to ride. But she blew that one and drove Key half mad in the doing.

His ma could cook when she tried, and she was agreeable to housework of sorts and might scrub dirty clothes but there had to be a man and a bottle involved somewhere or she'd quit. She was a pretty woman and knew it, and was always wishing for what she didn't have.

Men found her often sitting lonesome in one of Trinidad's bars. The smart ones would speak softly to her, learn her name was Marie Larkin and then would tell her earnestly what they would do for her, promise her whatever she might want, if she would spend some time in bed with them. She would let the knotted hand touch her thigh or brush against her breast, she would pretend there were sparks ignited and she would put aside her good intentions and the knowledge of her growing child and go home with another salesman or restless cowboy.

Often she moved in with these random men and brought Key along. He wasn't a bother even as a little one; he knew to sit outside on the trailer steps, or if it got too cold he would ask a neighbor woman to feed him cookies and hot cocoa. He heard the words; 'Oh isn't he cute,' and 'how pretty he is for a boy,' and while the sentiments were uncomfortable, he was hungry so he accepted the food with a show of reluctance. And as he ate, he refused to see the pitying smile and Baptist satisfaction of these women doing good for the poor abandoned child of the local whore.

As he grew older, he learned to ignore the men. He rarely heard and remembered their names or cared what they did. The neighbor women began to look at him differently, and the 'cute' became 'handsome' and the hands clung to him as if their notion of his salvation involved some physical contact of his flesh with their benevolent bosoms. He knew instinctively what they wanted, he'd seen too many men climb on his ma and poke her until they grunted liked damned pigs and then climbed off and demanded eggs and hash browns and maybe a fresh pot of coffee before they hit the road, had a new account to Elbert, be back in about two weeks. So they told her and she wanted to believe them.

The churchwomen gave him that same look which taught him just what they wanted to save. He wasn't quite old enough when he figured this out, but in a year or two he took them up on the offer of their peculiar notion of prayer.

Marie moved herself and the boy around Trinidad for years but never got far from its center, except for the one time they lived in Walsenburg for two months with the school janitor and then the four years in Pryor. Key liked Pryor best. He liked the land and the wild cattle, and he liked it more when the rancher put him up on the back of a swayed sorrel and let Key boot the horse into a reluctant trot. Then Key could pretend he was a cowboy and forget about his ma and her stinking men.

His childhood was safe only in pretending. He'd known early that in his mother's world he would not survive. So he willingly sat on the back of the retired cowpony and knew exactly why the rancher set him up there and what he and Key's ma would be doing while Key rode but it didn't matter. Key was the best cowhand in the world for those moments.

He never told his ma any of the dreams. She would have slapped him for such foolishness. As an eleven year old, he knew too much; he knew that the worn-out broncs the rancher gave him and the advice on how to ride better left Key in his own world while the rancher rode Key's ma without her brat watching.

Things were quiet in Pryor; Key rode and learned, his ma had a steady man as she washed and cooked, and held to her own impossible dream. She even swept out the adobe and put clean sheets on the bed sometimes. Her dream was that they married; she told Key this, insisting the rancher was just waiting for the right time to make it legal. He'd be the boy's step-pa, first one he ever had. The rancher had different ideas; with the boy as free help on the small ranch, a woman in his bed, marriage wasn't something he needed to consider.

By the time Key was thirteen he knew the value of

his ma, knew the rancher's intentions, knew instinctively the situation wouldn't never change. When he was fifteen and restless, Marie decided her rancher loved her and began to get fat and sloppy. She worked on the house chores, kept the floor clean, fixed up fancy meals out of ladies' magazines with marshmallows and tuna fish and crumbled bacon. She kind of forgot about sex and the rancher didn't speak much about her passivity but pumped into her every day or so and patted her on the rump when he was done and wanted to know what was ready for supper.

Marie was almost thirty-five and hadn't slept in an empty bed more than five times since she was sixteen. Even if she only lay under the man while he pumped into her, and dreamed of other things, she needed to know she was good for that much at least.

Those four years came to an end the last day of August, when Marie took herself and her fifteen year old son back into Trinidad, to a sagging rental next to a roadhouse outside of town on the county road to Branson. In the Pryor years, her son had gone from being a cute little boy to a handsome young man. His features were fine and regular, his nose straight despite being broken several time. His prominent cheekbones and lean jaw were a hint, but it was the color of his skin that drew attention. Beneath the dirty blond hair he was copper-colored, so his pa had to be Indian since his ma was a faded blond and everyone knew her folks up near Trinchera Plaza. There was a Comanche hung around the bar for a few months sixteen years ago, got fired from the mines, went home with Marie a few times then disappeared. He was the only Indian the locals knew could sire a boy looked like Key.

As for the name, no one knew the why of that either. Marie Larkin might have been pretty and was still easy, but she was never known for the truth on any day. Born in Trinidad as Muriel Tesmer, she went away at nineteen and came back as Marie Larkin with a baby three years later. Worn and hardened but not changed much, she left the baby with a series of lady friends who took him in cause he was cute, while Marie went back to the bars. Finally, her friends wore out with caring for the child for free, she took the boy with her, leaving him in a corner with a book or a puzzle while she sat on a bar stool and went to work.

Key was intelligent; his teachers throughout school could agree on that at least. And it was his smartness that kept him from being a full-time delinquent when he had all the possible credentials. But most folks meeting Key saw only his looks and formed their opinion of his character according to their own needs, leaving not much room for Key himself.

The rancher went south in late summer to an auction in Texas. Said he would be gone a week, maybe more, maybe less. Marie smiled and said they'd be fine; Key would look after the spread. The rancher nodded, gave Key a list of necessary chores; move a small group of dry cows to a back pasture, drag mineral blocks out to the heifers two miles west. Chores that made Key a real cowhand.

And the rancher knew exactly what he was giving the boy, he could read that dreamy look in the gray eyes and grinned to himself. The boy was coming up a good hand for no wages and his ma weren't bad in bed; a good deal for a few more years.

The woman came out to see him drive off; he ran his hands up under her skirt to her soft rump and felt the sagging flesh as he planted a hard kiss on her mouth.

Key was past fifteen and reaching for his full height

of 5'7." Burned by the sun, too lean from his ma's cooking and the ranch chores, he was hard, capable, and strong; hands sprung from the work, blond hair streaked red and gold in vivid contrast to his copper skin. And Marie Larkin wasn't use to being alone. She knew loneliness all the time but she couldn't live with no man beside her. She didn't always like their rutting but she liked the weight, the comfort of the thick, pot-bellied frames and the rasp of rough hands. She hadn't conceived a child after Key, something had torn or twisted the doc said and that was fine by her. It wasn't fun being mother to a restless boy, it was more fun being with her own man.

Now she was stuck on the ranch for a week alone. Until recent months she hadn't look close at her son, he was always there, hanging on her skirt when learning to walk, then running wild, but never running away. He was a good boy, her Key, a good son to his ma. She refused to know that some of the men who bedded her beat on her pretty child, whipped him for their own pleasure or because he annoyed then asking something of his ma when they were busy humping her.

She took a look at the son who constantly surprised her, a long look. He was handsome like his pa only with her blond hair and those pale eyes come from a relative Marie once met. She laughed a bit, he didn't look at her, and so she watched him for a few minutes more. Key kept his head turned and paid her no mind. That suited Marie, she enjoyed the watching.

Key had no idea of what his ma was thinking. She fed him most of the time, left him alone pretty much and never cared enough to ask questions. In return, Key learned to be polite. He said 'yes, ma'am' and 'no, ma'am' and 'thank you' to her. But by late afternoon of the sixth day the rancher hadn't returned and Key rode in tired and still restless. There'd been a barren mare come into season and Key'd stay to watch the rancher's stallion court and mount her like nothing he'd seen before.

Now he had that ache below his own gut, and when he saw his ma at the door he rubbed one hand briefly across his loins, knowing it was a crude gesture but he could still see and hear that stallion and the mare and their eager coupling. The notion of men and women going at each other like the horses had done aroused him in a way nothing his ma and her men ever could.

Key left the old gelding chewing on thin hay and went to the house. His ma was still in the doorway, her eyes closed, her own hands cupping her loose breasts; stroking, rubbing herself, in a trance. She didn't move or speak as Key pushed past her to the old kitchen. There nothing simmered on the stove or waited in a fry pan and he was sure hungry.

So he slammed the fridge door and it sprung open; he stared in, needing food, seeing shriveled meat and stale tortillas, and when he felt his ma come up behind him he knew exactly where her breasts pushed against him and the heat was unbearable. He stared at the unappealing food and held his breath, drew in his gut and felt a pulse drive through his body.

Fingertips brushed the brass buttons of his jeans fly; he shook, drew away, knew it was wrong, her hands touching him so intimately, arousing him when he didn't want the heat. Her palm swept over the rough denim weave, scorched the flesh enclosed there. There was a moment when Key knew he would burst against his mother's touch. Then he stepped back from her temptation and turned to yell at her, to beg her to get away.

The rancher stood in the empty door watching Marie Larkin fondle her own child. Key couldn't bear looking direct at the man; right now he hated his ma, hated himself even more. The rancher was more direct; aroused by her actions, he clouted the boy hard on the neck with clenched fists and when the kid was off-balance and trying to fight back, he smacked the boy in the head hard enough to put him down. Then he dragged Marie into the bedroom and mounted her savagely, cursing and beating on her as he took care of his needs.

Key stayed half-conscious on the floor; able to hear his ma cry and finally whimper, he was unwilling to climb up to her rescue. Later, when the rancher was gone, leaving behind a curt order for them to get out of the house before dark, Key knew he had not wanted to save her this time. The bruises she wore, the split lip and swollen eyes, were much less than what he might have done to her.

Long past the time when the anger and shame of the leaving settled, Key still dreamed of the narrow valley and its bawling cattle, the heady independence of the horses, the ever-changing sky that did not care. He could smell the sparse juniper stunted from blunt winter winds, he could taste the rise of air over a water tank, he could feel the wet of a rare early dew when he rode out before the sun.

She found another run-down home for them, this time next to a saloon, no more hiding from her choice of life. The place had once fancied itself with wagon wheels and steer horns but now it was a dive of sawdust and spit, blood and piss. They could have half the bottom floor of the old mansion next door, its upstairs wasn't safe, the owner said. He himself used the rest of the house for storage, and kept good track of the number of bottles of whiskey on hand. He didn't want none of them gone missing.

It held a sagging kitchen, a rectangular room that

might have been a front parlor once, a small back room where Ma put her bed. Key got a corner of the kitchen where he'd slept often as a child. It was Key who went and registered himself for the Trinidad north school. The new principal had been his teacher in fourth grade and she allowed him the liberty, having had Marie Larkin in school as well.

The first day of school he got there early, preferring its chilled silence to the sounds of Ma and a man. He waited, leaning against the fence and playing with smoking one of the cheap cigarettes the new man gave to Ma. It was a habit Key was considering.

By seven-thirty there were four girls and three boys in the yard. The girls giggled and looked at Key too often. They held their young bodies close, twitched their braided hair and did not understand what they were doing. Key knew, but these recent teenagers stubbornly remained children and pretended they didn't know at all.

The biggest of the boys was Stevie Plunkett, Key had known him before. Grown large and ugly; by himself the boy was dull, with girls to watch him he acted like the world fit into his hand and he could beat on anyone he chose. And right now he'd chosen Key. The girls giggled and looked away, acting out their supposed horror, thrilled with the coming bloodshed.

The kid's mouth matched his feet, size twelve and clumsy; "Hey, Larkin, heard you been screwin' your own ma this summer. 'Bout time, ever'one else got into her." No beat of time, no hesitation, no dance; Key went full force, cigarette stuck to his dry lip, eyes cool, hands fisted and seeking any part he could hurt. He knew Plunkett would beat on him badly, and that he'd be punished later by one of the teachers, or his old friend the principal, but he could not and would not let Stevie's words escape unchallenged.

Key hit Plunkett's jaw hard as he could, the boy

shook his head, grinned, grabbed Key's right ear and twisted him to the ground but that didn't let Key quit. He kicked high with his knee, heard Plunkett groan, cry out. Key kicked up again and Plunkett backhanded him, enough to spin Key's eyes, spit blood from his mouth. He took several more blows meant to kill but was able to kick at Plunkett hard enough the boy went weak below the knees; Key grinned through the blood, saw the fury in Plunkett's eyes. Then Stevie fell forward on Key and laid all that weight on him, nearly crushed the breath Key fought to keep.

"Bastard." Stevie's voice was in his ear, then the weight was plucked off and Key stayed quiet, let out a breath and knew he had no cracked ribs, only a sore mouth and some cuts on his face. A new voice intruded on his imagined revenge; "You all right?" Only then did he look up at his rescuer. He was used to being beaten unconscious and saved by a teacher or the librarian, but this bulk leaning over him was neither. Key glared at the face, then flinched at the size of the hand reaching down for him.

Instead of accepting help, Key rolled over and was up and headed towards Plunkett before anyone thought to stop him. One good kick to the ribs, like the rancher did him, to keep the memory alive. Then he turned back to size up his protector. "Big sum bitch, ain't you." He held out his hand, watched it disappear in the boy's huge mitt and shook his head in admiration. Which was a bad idea as he got dizzy and knew he was falling and then two of those damnable-sized hands caught and steadied him and he found his footing and stood square again, head thrown back, eyes bleeding into the whites, wild hair tangled and filthy. He wiped at his mouth, spat out a gob of bloody mucus.

Then he spat again, driving back the circle of worried kids, twisting his face into the grin which always worked unless it brought a punch from a man whose woman found Key more appealing, too dammed handsome never mind he was still a kid.

Yeah, the grin usually worked but right now he needed to seduce the ox with the big hands, too much grin would set the boy walking. Key wiped his face again, grimaced, then shut down all expression except that of admiration. "Bet you ain't been picked on much, the size of you." He waited, that instinctive beat, wiped his bloodstained hand on his pants and held it out again, a gesture of truce and appeasement. "Somethin', ain't it, comin' to a new school an already in a fight." That beat again, to let the word sink in; "Friends?"

They shook, the bigger boy careful not to squeeze tight. Despite the disparity in their height and breadth, Key held his own. His hands already looked too old for his boy's slight body, knuckles sprung, one finger broke and healed bent, heavy calluses across the palm. Key squeezed, bearing down with his wiry strength to make this monster gasp.

Then North grinned, a wide, awkward opening of the round baby face and ended the contest abruptly by closing his fingers hard, just once, before letting go.

Key showed none of the startling pain from the final grasp. Instead he looked away, nodded, started to the schoolhouse and the drifting groups of children. It was set, bound and confirmed. "You got a name friend?" He liked this, asking first.

"Yes, ah...right...my name is North McKendrick." Key looked at him, actually startled. There weren't many McKendricks around Trinidad, a few cousins and that one man had the daughter with the tough mouth. Neelie, that's right. Wouldn't know what she looked like now, but Neelie, that was her name. Had a pretty mother, a stern father and no other kin named McKendrick that Key knew of.

"You kin to those McKendricks work for Charlie Rushton?" The big boy nodded, "Yes, I'm a cousin, living with them now." Key wondered about how that happened, and, knew he would find out in time. "Okay."

Key never thanked North for the rescue, he never thanked North for anything except for that one awful time when they met as enemies. Even then he could only whisper the two unfamiliar words through raw, wounded lips and most likely never knew if North heard him.

It would make sense to explain some about my family. Papa was a rancher, from a long line of ranchers. In fact that's why he married my mama so late; he was working for an uncle, from whom he would inherit, and wanted to offer ownership of the spread to his chosen wife. The uncle took a long time to die, and papa waited.

He ended up cowboying for an old man who let him run the family brand on a few head, and every time he saw the Rafter M on a mixed breed cow eating grass claimed by another man, it had to hurt. Papa gave full value to his word and was tireless as foreman for Charlie Rushton's CR, as careful and thoughtful as if the land belonged to him. It wasn't bad choices that ruined Papa, it was luck turned back against him, like it turns for a lot of us. He and Mama had to live with the results.

I learned about their history long after Papa died and we all had scattered and the knowledge had to come from my mama. When he was alive, Papa would shake his head and say there's no going back, that the past was there and done, and he never answered one of my childhood questions. I couldn't disagree with him, not out loud, not against those quiet eyes and the big hand that patted my shoulder and spun me around to head me back to another chore.

Since there was no getting facts out of Papa as a child and he died before I could try as a reasonable adult, I had to ask my mother, and had to plan the asking so she would not see the course I'd set. It took a few years to get the story; even then I had to grow some and learn from others before I could appreciate what happened to my folks.

North came in on the last of the details and helped me accept what all the tears and grim silences meant. North was like that, he could see the other side, the differing perspective. With of course the exception of Key Larkin.

It was a friend who put me on the notion that my parents had their own lives and personalities, both before my birth and even as we shared the ranch and the hard work. Inside those tired faces and worn bodies lay dreams and hopes and desires that were not part of me, of my existence. I believe now that the realization of my parents being individual humans was the beginning of my journey from eager child to wary adult.

The friend had come to spend the night, supposedly to study for a big test and incidentally to giggle and talk and make the casual observation which at first shocked me and then started me wondering.

While we shared our family supper I saw her stare at my father too often to be excused as polite attention, especially when I don't think Papa said more than two words the entire meal, his usual manner of supper conversation. When we went upstairs to my attic room my friend blushed and coughed and through her stammers I learned she thought my papa was awful good-looking for an old man. He couldn't have been much more than forty-nine at the time but to us he was old. Real good-looking she said, kind of like Gary Cooper.

Finally I came back enough to feel the angle of my dropped jaw and the whisper of air in my mouth; immediately I needed to get a pencil sharpened which meant going downstairs to the room where Papa did his accounts for old Charlie Rushton.

Papa was stabbing bits of stained papers and mouthing

what I guessed to be curses and he barely noticed me as I slipped in to sharpen the pencil with his flat-blade knife. He never cussed around the family but I could guess what he might say outside where he belonged, with cattle and horses and had only the vigilant ravens to hear him. Here, indoors, stifled and confined, he could only think in unsaid words.

I was quiet as I worked, staring at him when I thought he wasn't paying me any attention. I memorized his eyes and the shape of his nose, the set of his mouth, as if I had never seen him before and expected to see him only this one time. I was looking at my father through Doreen Spinelli's eyes and she was right, he was a handsome man.

The concept was frightening; it meant that others saw and appreciated my father in a way I never had, as a male who carried the appeal which had drawn my mother to him. Thinking about Mama charged me; I coughed and Papa looked up and I waved the pencil and fled the room.

If my father was handsome, attractive, then my mother had her own wants which were met by his presence, she had her own looks and appeal. She once saw him not as a provider and father and companion but as a virile man to romance her. This choked me.

I ran upstairs where Doreen lay belly down on the single bed, legs waving in the air, pretending to read the assigned work. I put my hand over my mouth when she sat up and cocked her head; we began talking together, then stopped as suddenly. It felt that for Doreen to say she thought Papa handsome was acceptable; for us to giggle over his looks and discuss them like in the magazines brought to mind the older boys and girls in school and their actions, their gossiping, which was too intimate and personal and overwhelming for both of us. We were much too immature to allow parents their own lives.

Instead, much to our mutual surprise, we chose to study. We must have absorbed enough from the night's effort to do well in the test. For Doreen this meant a B-, for me an A. Papa looked at the lesson when I brought it triumphantly home and said 'good enough' and went back to the endless bits of paper and the reworked figures that haunted him. I never looked at my parents quite the same again

From that time I also became aware of the male sexuality surrounding me. Poor North, who came to us looking for safety and a home, and found a cousin suddenly too curious about his male feelings and dreams. His huge presence, his enormous physicality, his lumbering body confined in the schoolrooms alerted me to other male personalities. Each boy was examined privately, as to the worth and value of his possible physical ability and use. And then I began to see what the girls wanted from Key.

For all that I loved North, I could not imagine him with a girl, holding hands and dancing or sipping an over-sweet fruit punch while watched by eager chaperons. North was unique, himself, my friend and blood cousin, exempt from the uncertainties of growing up. Later I came to realize he was so filled with need that he gave up himself in his devotion to others.

Key, however, came to work for Papa and Charlie Rushton, and life was never the same.

Chapter Three

The alphabet put them together in the small class: Larkin, McKendrick. Over the endless first day noise of names being called, boots scuffed on wooden floors as the students found their assigned seats came the labored sound of Key's disturbed breathing. The teacher barely bothered to look where Key and North sat; it was only the first day back and already the Larkin boy had caused trouble. But the teacher had dealt with him before. Eventually she allowed him to soak a kerchief in cold water to wipe over his crusted bruises but that was her only concession.

Key made her pay for the privilege of ignoring him; he pressed in close as she allowed him to come to the desk for a hall pass, he rested a hand lightly on her wrist then drew it back as if burned. All the while he was shy, barely raising his eyes to see her but knowing, watching, waiting for the inevitable spinster reaction. Slowly her skin paled above the high tight collar of her dark dress, then two bright spots highlighted her cheeks and Key's eyes blazed quickly before he lowered them again, sweeping away any residual anger at her indifference while he played out the familiar game.

When he did leave the room to soak the kerchief under the water fountain, he left a pulsing, awkward, slightly moist teacher who could not easily return to the task of calling out her students' names.

As he reentered the room Key tuned in to North, cramped in the student chair, flesh hanging on either side of the desk arms, knees up past his belly and if he didn't stretch into the aisle he'd pop the slanted desk top off its base. Key laughed, didn't look once at the teacher as he sat in his assigned seat, which fitted him just fine.

At recess Key stayed inside on teacher's orders while she left the room to monitor playground activities; North stayed with him and no one questioned why the shy newcomer would choose Key as a companion. North himself wasn't certain except that he recognized another outcast, a rare double for his own loneliness. So far Key had said nothing about the brawl except to roll his eyes shut and offer a clown's smirk when his nose started bleeding again during a question period on local history.

North hung with Key every morning at the school yard but in the afternoon the boys separated, North to go home to the ranch and his chores, Key to a saloon to check if his ma was drunk and then on his rounds of odd jobs and neighbor ladies who kept him in hot stew and pie and well practiced in his proper manners.

Two weeks into the fall, North found Key braced on the school fence, shivering and holding his body in private embrace. North said nothing as he leaned on the same fence; they both grunted when the fence creaked. It was a long moment of nothing until Key could not bear the watchfulness in North. He wiped at his burned lower lip, then shook slightly.

"Fella livin' with Ma did it. Said I talked too much." He knew better'n to try a grin, instead he looked towards the mountains and as usual envied them. It was tough to focus; his head throbbed, his bruised ribs hadn't been improved by a night sleeping on the ground back of the school.

North discounted the light tone of the words and read the wisps of grass in the dirty blond hair, judged the damp wrinkles in the shirt and no jacket and wanted suddenly to hit something. He dropped his hand gently on Key's shoulder but his friend ducked from the gesture and kept staring up at the mountains, giving North nothing to confirm any suspicions.

"Key, he hit you anywhere but that eye and your mouth?" Still nothing. North sighed. It was like trying to deal with his ma when a bully came on to her; she wouldn't look at North but shake her head and asking about school or tell him a storekeeper downtown who came in for coffee too often was looking for a new stock boy, had to be big and able to work alone. Anything she could imagine to keep her son from taking care of her.

North's hand clamped down hard on Key's arm and the boy cried out as he pulled away. North persisted; "You tell me." The words were strangled and wrong, a challenge to Key but they were all North could manage around his fearful anger. "Ain't nothin', North, just tired. Got to get me a job, some bucks of my own." A common enough goal among the schoolboys, wanting to buy a truck and work as an adult while still in school. A mark of their new status as almost grown-up.

But Key was different, and North didn't trust the way he looked right now, the tight mouth and bruised face. The throwaway words that didn't match the eye under a glaze of fear and pain. North could take care of the fear at least.

"Let me see." North scrubbed his jaw, felt the miserable softness of down and stared deliberately way past Key's shoulder to give his friend room. "Unbutton your shirt, let me see." Key pulled back, gave North the look he knew was coming. "You turnin' queer on me?" North wagged his head, wouldn't let go of watching Key. He saw the defiance leave, saw the pale eyes go blank as Key looked down to the schoolyard dirt, scuffed his boot toe in the dust.

"Ain't you goin' to protect me. I'll do it, done it all these years 'fore you." Useless talk, North thought, the remains of how Key scraped through life. He took clear estimation of his buddy, the spare frame even more lean now his ma had a new lover. The copper skin had gray edges, the eyes red-rimmed. The years of tending his ma taught North the signs.

"I ain't askin' again. You shed that shirt here or we go inside and I'll pull it off your hide." North stepped in, using his bulk to force his words. And where most folks listened when he got like this and did what he asked, Key snapped back; "You son of a bitch." No slurring over the curse, no polite kidding. North hunched his shoulder to accept the blow. Key swung as North drew his head back but the fist still caught him along the jaw and he heard the snap.

"Darn it, Key, I only want to help." Nothing. No warmth in the pale eyes, only the glare of unfocused hatred that warned North he was trespassing. Key spat the bitter words. "You're a stupid son of a bitch, ain't you. I don't want your help, I don't need it, ain't askin' for it. Made it this far without you, you son of a bitch."

North grabbed the shirt collar, yanked hard and the shirt came off. Torn pieces hung from Key's neck and both wrists. The exposed flesh now revealed was dark with welts and raised scabs, and there was a long, fresh cut across the right ribs. North swore. If he didn't know better, he'd bet there were tears in his new amigo's eyes.

"Happy now, you damned queer." Key raised his head, his light frame shook and North read the glazed eyes turned brilliant stone and wished he knew it was fear but guessed he was wrong.

Anger fueled Key; the taste of betrayal from one he thought could be a compadre. The one person he had counted on; now he was exposed to the whole damned world, he felt the gathering of stares flay him, touch on his back and belly and shoulders and the laughter they would not yet allow would kill him even more. Damn North McKendrick, damn the whole world.

A teacher came to check the sudden quiet of the schoolyard yet she made no attempt to approach the two boys. Key's flesh rippled in the cold, he ached but could not back away, would not soften and ask. He knew now, again, there was no help.

North unbuttoned his own shirt, feeling the quick cold as he undressed, and blessed Mrs. McKendrick for the heft of the flannel, the clean, dry warmth of the gray tee shirt he wore underneath. He had to force Key's arm down the too-long sleeve and it was extra hard to wrap the collar around his neck, jam that other arm in; Key was mute, motionless, only his eyes showed a hint of feeling, turning from their black stone to a lighter gray, a kinder softer glow which still worried North.

The warmth shattered Key, he could not move, could not help the shaking that rocked through him, his throat ached, his eyes pounded in his skull. The thick flannel was more than cloth and warmth, it was the birth of something terribly frail. He shuddered hard, once, then forcibly straightened and grinned at North. "I'll look darned sight more a fool in this." He figured the words would be enough to skip past unfinished business but North wasn't deterred.

"I want his name, Key." Key shook his head, shivered then looked directly at his once-again would-be rescuer.

"You can't save me. This's happened before, will again 'til I get out a her life. You can't mother me, North, no one can."

North hated the statement, as if Key knew what he had yet to learn. "The bastard's name, Key." Key laughed; "Swearin' don't sound good on you, North. But I'll tell you, just to see what'll happen. It's Merle Summers over to Blanchard's Esso."

Then Key tried to explain; "You can fight him for this but it won't stop. No need bustin' a knuckle or gettin' in trouble for me." He waved a hand across his chest, his ribs and belly visible under the loose, unbuttoned shirt. "There'll be another when Summers leaves."

North made a bold statement; "Live with us then, after I settle with Summers." North knew those were big words but he trusted the McKendricks enough to believe they would take his word for Key's trouble. Especially if Uncle Ray saw those scars, old and new, and read what was behind the glittery eyes. Key was just a kid for all his experience. And a man like Ray McKendrick would not let a child suffer. North wanted to be like his uncle so he too had to follow through; he would find and punish Merle Summers.

Key interrupted North's fantasy; "Yeah, sure, I'll come with you out to the good folks who took you in, barely making ends met as it is and they'll be delighted to see me, another mouth to feed, and one with a doubtful past. Good folks like I know they are, right after you mop up the station floor with Summers they'll surely be proud of all that blood and guts and you fightin' just for me."

North fumbled a book, dropped it, bent down and twice couldn't get his fingers to close around its covers. "Kind a gets to you, don't it North? What you been sayin' to me, makin' your tough promises about revenge. Like what I want don't count, like I can't handle my own life. Hell, boy, you don't know half a what's gone on before you showed up."

Then he grinned, a full, true smile which broke open his dark face and rekindled the fire in his eyes. The cheer in his face had to be false, North knew Key could not show what he felt. "Sure, then, I'll come to your uncle's place, bet he's got more room for an extra mouth, sure he's got lots a food for some cast-off 'breed no one else wants."

The grin stayed, to take all bite from the words, but North knew as true as he'd learned anything the false bravery of those words and the ugly grin were exactly what Key felt about himself.

The school bell rang, both boys started. They joined in the line of students, carefully ignorant of the eyes that followed them, the girlish heads close together, the loudly whispered speculation. Key began to shiver inside the damp red and gray flannel shirt and North felt naked in the cotton tee. A long day lay ahead. Before they squeezed into the classroom, North had his final say. "You come to the ranch after school. Today'll be that Merle fella's turn, then you'll come home with me.

I wish I had known all this when I first saw Key at the house. I knew, of course, all about North's shirt and that Key was banged up; everyone at school had talked about it all day. But we had no idea what lay behind the bruises, so everyone had their own version. All I could comprehend was that North was late getting home and had a friend with him and Papa didn't seem to mind too much. Mama, however, was badly agitated which in turn upset me.

I will admit that on that one night Key was almost a romantic figure to my inexperienced heart. Still wrapped in

North's huge shirt, the best one Mama bought him for school, Key was a lost, beaten, sweet child, carrying a swollen eye and mouth and a hesitation in all he said. It was probably the only time Key was so off balance with any of us.

By the time he got to the house his bruises had turned bright red and dark blue, and later I accused him of using that display to his own end, that he earned our collective sympathy with pity while never speaking a word as to why and how he'd been hit. He did an admirable job, but the worst was, all the speculation between my parents, which I overheard later, was correct; he had been beaten by his mother's multitude of lovers, and he was still only a child.

I was ugly about Key. Torn between the shock of his beauty which was made more beautiful with the beating, and angry that he could demand so much attention and compassion, I became furious at him for shattering my visions of knights in armor and bullies and a glorious battle for right and against wrong. In reality he was a statistic of drink and sex and a wayward parent. Here it was, when I was too young to recognize one of my favorite arguments and beliefs of later on; Key had the intellect and ability to chose a different life for himself than what he had been given by his whoring mother. But he chose nothing, made no choice which was in itself to make one. He let nothing get to him, he wanted nothing, he loved nothing. All this came from his early life, all this would have changed if he had wanted something badly enough to fight for it.

This is a sermon I can repeat by rote now, years later, after all the events and their aftermath are dissolved; then I was only furious that he could enter our life, and madder still at North who brought him there.

What actually transpired was more ordinary than I wished, where I saw dragons and heroes, North had to deal with a drunken mechanic who was beating on Key and screwing his mother, both for private amusement. Yet this is where our true heroes lie, not in grand deeds but in the daily caring of one soul for another.

It makes sense now but no one knew then exactly what had happened or offered any caution when Key came in the door. I guessed that the boys had been fighting before school and when Key so obviously was the loser, North felt such guilt that he brought him to us for healing. What a poor guess, how little I understood, how much more I can see now when it does me no good except to soothe my memories.

North got on the school bus and pulled Key off and the driver didn't question why. Key tried to object and North simply held him in the air with one hand and waited until Key quit flailing around and then set him down. North tried to explain that it wasn't right to ride a school bus to go beat up on a man and Key laughed and slapped his leg. "By God, North, you're right."

North had sent his books and jacket home with Neelie, and gave her no explanation except he and Key had some business, he'd be back soon as he could and please tell her folks not to worry.

As he and Key walked, North noted that Key carried no school books and thought that was wrong; going to school meant reading and studying otherwise why go through the motion, especially for a maverick like Key. What he didn't yet know was that Key could read a book once and know most of what was inside without having to ponder over the words and their meaning. Key scanned a page and was bored waiting for the class to catch up, which didn't endear him to the teachers or the other students either. North knew one thing about Key so far; being liked or disliked meant little to him, it was freedom and movement that held Key's interest.

It wasn't more than two miles to the Esso station.

For North it was nothing but a steady push and pull of his muscles and the raw bruises on Key's face to keep him focused. Key was silent, had been silent most of the day, even in school, didn't answer any questions in class, and whatever showed in his eyes kept the dumbest student or teacher from asking what happened.

North glanced over at Key when the battered, leaning Esso sign showed up ahead. His friend was staring, moving in jerks, his eye almost closed now, the lip badly cracked and crusted with blood and dirt. North didn't need to see the scars under the shirt. No one should beat a dog that way, never mind a human being.

The saloon was next to the Esso station and shared the parking lot, which held two trucks, one a 3/4 ton GMC flatbed filled with rough cut lumber tied down badly with unraveling hemp rope. The other truck was a Studebaker past its prime five years ago, dented fenders, bald tires, cracked headlights speaking everything about its owner. Key nodded at the Studebaker; "Yeah, that one belongs to Summers." North snorted. Rubbed his tender jaw, thought he needed a moment to get up some anger. "I bet he's inside the bar, braggin' on what he done to you."

Key leaned on the front left fender, wished his feet didn't hurt and his head would quit pounding. "You still don't get it, do you? He's in there." Key waved towards the shabby mansion stuck behind the broken wagon-wheel fence. "In there, fucking Ma."

The word stopped North, baffled him. Key's face was dark, a lop-sided grin meant to show toughness tortured his face. North knew even Key's heart had to be twisting within the single ugly-spoken word.

North needed to decide; go in the bar and ask for Summers, or knock on the house's warped door, then call Summers out to the fight. North rubbed his jaw again, caught up in something he couldn't imagine.

But Summers made it all easy, he stepped out of a side door to the house, pulling on his belt, barefoot., and shirtless, tall, with the corded arms and big hands of an out-of-work miner.

The man stopped, looked back to the house. His voice was high and annoyed; "I'm gettin' smokes, Marie damn it." Then he started towards the truck and saw Key leaning on it and his face broke into a wide grin of anticipation. "You ain't too bright, like your ma said. Boy I'm gonna beat the shit out a you this time." His stride lengthened despite the bare feet, his fists were clenched in anticipatory pleasure, his shoulders jerked high to strike.

Then North stepped into his path. His belly twisted with a baby's fear but he couldn't not do this, couldn't offer the respect he'd been taught for his elders. Summers stopped, he had no choice because North blocked his path. The man's eyes stayed glued to Key. North smelled the whiskey, watched the wet tongue lick at white scum stuck to the coarse lips. "You're a sorry son, that you are." Absently he pushed at North, "Get the hell outa my way."

North pushed back, gently, hitting Summers on the chest. Finally the man looked at him. Despite the baby face and bland eyes, he recognized a stronger opponent. "Hell, that kid pay you to fight his battle? Get outa my way 'fore I kick your ass too."

Drink did strange things to a man, made him think and act against his better nature. North only smiled and grabbed Summers by the forearm, waited, and caught the blow aimed at his jaw with his other hand. Now he and Summers were locked together and Summers finally had a real good look at North; his size, his smile, the breadth to his chest, the strength holding his two arms like they was kindling wood. That easy to snap.

Summers struggled, North hit him once on the

point of the jaw. The man went backwards, arms windmilling, falling hard on the gravel, and had the good sense to stay there. A flick of blood dripped from his mouth, he licked at it, wiped his face, kept his eyes on North.

North spoke up, his voice shaky at first, then gaining authority; "You quit beatin' Key. You ain't never goin' to hit him again. You hear me." No threat, no high fearful voice, no needless promise of mayhem. Summers didn't need any of that to recognize North's power. The two watched each other, Summers looked away, nodded once. Loud noise interrupted the confrontation, laughter getting close. North glanced up, saw that the bar must have emptied, now men watched and laughed while one of their own was being humiliated. Then the laughter stopped and five men closed ranks to stalk North.

Key slid off the truck fender, calling out names, detailing what each man had done to his ma. As a group the men turned, went for Key. North saw Key's eyes go dark, his mouth widen in that manic grin, his hand clench. There was nothing menacing about him, a thin fifteen-year-old boy already beaten. Easy prey, easier than the size of North.

Then the group dissolved; moving as individuals, a mob no longer, they scattered back to the bar door. North shook his head, confused. "We better get goin', Key. Ray'll be mad enough I didn't come right home." Key came around on North's left and he saw the silver flash of a knife blade being folded and understood. Key with a knife was a wild card not even a drunk would bet against.

They walked in the dark, separated by the width of

the road. Key's knife was hidden and North's knuckles hurt where he hit Summers and each was lost in their private thoughts.

Finally Key crossed the road. and pulled North around to face him. They weren't more than two feet apart. "How're you plannin' on gettin' home? It's more'n seven miles from here. Me, I ain't goin' with you. I'll find me another place for the night." Key grinned that ugly grin which told North too much about his plans. Then Key lifted a hand; past the tips of his fingers were the miles of grass, the swells and dips of gullies and rock evened out by a false perspective of evening light and distant towns.

"It ain't like you can fly. By now your uncle'll be madder at me than you but he don't know that yet. He will once your homely face shows up to the door, me behind you. I'll save myself from that at least." Key's face split into a genuine smile; "By God North you are somethin'."

North waited for the thank-you, Key filled in the time with a low growl. Then as North tried to accept Key's bad manners, an old truck rumbled towards them and Key raised his head, watched as the truck slowed and then came to a drifting stop. The horn honked once, then twice. It was Ray McKendrick's face that showed through the window glass.

I need to finish explaining about my parents. Theirs is a story still happening to many couples who live too far out for medical attention, especially in the plains where small towns huddle around a gas pump and a general store and advice and consolation is offered, but there is no doctor on call.

Claudie Mitchell fell in love with Ray McKendrick when she was fifteen and still in school. Ray was in the process of dealing with the reality of his uncle's death and the debts needing to be paid before inheriting the ranch. Ray was thirty at the time, exactly twice Claudie's age. I saw a photo of them together and he was indeed a handsome man even given the oddities of his period clothing. Clear-featured, rugged, with a shy and honest gaze as he looked off from the camera, too shy to put his arm around his new bride. From the slight but visible bulge under Claudie's loose frock it would appear they married for necessity as well as love.

Their ranch was way past Branson on a thin road impassable in any bad weather except by horse. I drove up there once after I married, it's a county road now, graded and with signs telling you how far it is to someplace else but then, in 1938, it was a road best left to the four-footed and clever.

I don't mean to over-emphasize these few facts but what follows is so painful unless I can distance myself; words are useful this way, they can remove the speaker from what is being told.

I don't even have to provide details for any imaginative person to guess what happened. The baby started to come early one morning while a high wind and heavy rains flooded the land. Her husband tried his best to help, for without speaking they knew the child would have to be born at home. He got the water boiling, he pulled out the clean cloths and sterilized a knife, for he had attended births of horses and cattle and had some idea of what might be needed.

They'd been married five months and the entire time had passed in planning for the coming event. The birth was fairly easy I was told, a slip and a push and the small bundle flooded from between her legs, passive and tangled in the cord. Ray knew what to do; he cut the cord and bound it with alcohol, then slapped the baby gently to get the lungs pumping and nothing happened, no cry, no wrinkled face furious at its entry into the world. Nothing. Their baby never drew breath.

They cried together and then separately, grieving for the small dead being and perhaps for themselves and the hurry of their act which finally had produced nothing but pain and tears.

The rain turned to snow and then hail. By late afternoon the sun blazed a long shadow streaked with fading light. Ray fed the few horses he kept up to the barn and took longer than usual to finish the chore. When he got to the house, she was sitting in her grandmother's rocking chair, a thick padding of towels wadded under her. He saw the bright red stains and heard her small voice; "Ray, I need to get to the hospital." That was all she said for over a week; by then her life had been saved, but the debt for her existence could only be met by selling the ranch and moving in closer to Trinidad, where Ray finally got a decent job working for Charlie Rushton, and Claudie was told she could not have anymore children. Then I came along five years later and made liars out of the medical profession. I was very healthy, squalling as soon as I saw light and kicking up a fuss all night long. As a child, having learned some of the story, I wondered if they ever regretted my living, since I kept them up for hours every night until I was well over a year old

I know from having my own children, that in a moment's exhaustion there might be a wish or curse about a colicky child, but when all is well and the child smiles again, there is only love, at least from the woman's perspective. I will never know how my father felt about those dreadful years, but I can guess how he must have yearned for his lost chance. Mama gave me sketches of her feelings, stock answers to the initial tragedy and then the ranch sale, but she never retreated so far as to give me the current religious babble about the Lord wanting their child and taking her to His bosom. For all of my mama's toughness and her distance from me, and what she did to us later on, she was never a hypocrite, never dishing out pap as an easy answer. I bless her for that, it has allowed me to come to my own sense of religion and faith without any disgust or anger left over from those useless and I believe harmfully appalling phrases of regimented religious grief.

And I can always hear my father's voice telling North that when I was born I was special, and enough for them. I know the meaning behind those words, but that Papa wanted to let North know immediately how much I meant to them was an expression of love from my father I will always cherish.

Of course, I wish he could have said these words to me, but overhearing them said to North that first night had to be almost as good. I had a witness that Papa loved me.

Chapter Four

Ray kept an eye on the boys as he slowed the truck. North marched with big strides and planted his feet carefully. The other boy seemed to drift, head tipped to the side, looking anywhere except where his feet might land. There was a tightness about the smaller boy that warned Ray before he rolled down the window and called out to them.

He knew the face, had known the boy's ma a long time ago, and only once. She was his first even though he'd been twenty-four. He'd worked the ranch for his uncle and then for himself; he'd not yet met and fallen in love with Claudie. He had a bit of cash in his pocket, a drink at a bar, first time for that too, and he'd sure been in love with Marie Larkin, who was Muriel Tesmer at the time.

He couldn't help but be curious about her son. He knew the man guessed to sire the boy, a miner given to heavy drink, a real fighter, a loner from his Indian blood. The local men tolerated the man, fearful of his temper, but it was acknowledged that he was one good-looking son of a bitch. That one had to be the boy's pa.

North held the door and Key crawled in first. He could curl his legs around the gearshift, which North couldn't do. With Key in the middle and North hanging out the window, Ray eased the clutch and hoped the leaky old Ford would manage the extra weight. His one glance at the boys told a tough story for certain sure; Muriel's boy and beat up bad. That said why North was involved, but Ray would still have to punish the boy for his reckless act. Claudie was home half out of her mind.

He spoke more to ease his mind than to tell the two passengers anything they didn't already know. "We got worried, boy. I told Claudie you'd come home when you had a mind, what with Neelie bringin' in your books and jacket. I took that to mean you intended a fight. Looks like you won." He indicated Key with his hand, misreading all the signs. Neither boy said a word. Ray winced; Neelie was easy compared to this; she talked back and cried and then tried harder to do it right. North did nothing but stare out the window and count the few trees that slipped by in the dark.

Muriel's boy looked straight ahead and Ray decided he didn't like the set to him, the scent of wildness he gave off, like the stink off a feral dog's trail. The boy's reputation was well know, following in his ma's footsteps. Ray shook his head.

It was Muriel's boy who spoke first; "It was me, Mr. McKendrick. Not North. He thinks he's got to cover my back. I told him you wouldn't like it, him comin' along, but he did fix the problem." The boy laughed, swung his head around and Ray had to see the swollen, blackened eye, the split lip that conveniently leaked one drop of blood. He wondered if the boy deliberately displayed his wounds so Ray would go easy on him.

"I own the full blame, sir." Before Ray could nod his understanding and maybe get past the boy to North that it was all right, Larkin ruined the fine words with bitterness. "Bet you'd debate me my hide's worth your North's savin' it." Ray grimaced, wondered what he'd done to let his feelings show to these wet-eared kids.

Key twisted around the gears, drew himself in from both Ray and North as if desperate to protect himself from something unseen. When he spoke, Ray wished the child had sense enough to shut up. "One a ma's men yelled out your name once, Mr. McKendrick, while he was listin' the men she'd been with, the men she screwed. A long time ago, but it sure was your name." Ugly small words that filled the truck cab and Ray did not try to look at North, could not bear a new wound.

Key didn't let it rest; "Most men with her, they're low as her, dumb and drunk and screwin' cause they got nothin' better to do. You, Mr. McKendrick, you got to hate me for knowin' such about you cause you're a decent man, got a family and a home, got more'n my ma'll ever have. My knowin' you been with her makes me wicked in your eyes, wicked as she is. The devil right before you, ridin' in this truck."

Ray knew his mouth hung open but it was paralyzed like his brain and his hands were froze to the steering wheel and he couldn't take in a deep breath or get rid of the weight on his chest. Damned boy, truly damned for such knowledge. He tried, North's face making him seek an answer. "Why're you tellin' us this when you don't need to, when North was goin' to ask a favor for you." He glanced across Key and read the hurt in North's hunched frame, wondered if it was for him or for Key, or both. He shook his head. "Boy, you're pokin' holes in the only friend you ever had. Why?"

The answer felt like a trick but it was also awful close to a truth. "Mr. McKendrick if I go 'long with what North's askin' and don't let you know what I know about you, then when it comes to light and sure 'nough everythin' comes back on me, you'll hate me more than you do right now. I'm tryin' to be clean and honest and it ain't easy. Tryin' to let you know I got no sense a things don't somebody already know. What you done with my ma is less'n what most men done. You never hit her, I know that. I asked her and she remembered you. She don't remember most a her men. So you hear me, I got no feelin's on this, and I ain't speakin' more about nothin'."

It was a bluntness of truth Ray had not encountered before, not with a child for certain, rarely with an adult. An acceptance of what was done with little anger or remorse. Ray felt like he'd tangled with a bobcat. North was still quiet, still glaring into the darkness. So Ray tried to finish it with the Larkin boy.

"This ain't how a fifteen year old boy talks. You're too smart, someone's fed you, primed you to talkin' this way." He waited, wondering if the bait was taken. "Sir, I am smart, I can talk correctly too, using better English than most of the people around here." Ray listened, knew it was a truth, knew the boy could change color at will then, and vowed to be extra careful dealing with him.

"I ain't a nice kid, Mr. McKendrick but I ain't all bad. North here decides on his own to be my friend, I don't ask for that kind of favor. But I 'preciate what he done back there and that's as close to 'thank-you' as I'll ever get." The drawl was back, the local slang but Ray knew he'd heard the truth.

North, too, heard this truth. His face was cooled by the wind, he did not have to look at his uncle or at Key. He was scared by Key's talking up 'bout Uncle Ray, and admiring at the same time. Finally he glanced at his kin, saw the cool, level eyes, flinched inside and hoped the tug did not show. Ray spoke as if the past five minutes did not exist, as if none of the words had been exposed. "North, you still want to bring this here son home?"

North knew he meant the question. "Yes sir, he's got nowhere to go. Man beat him last night, bad, he can't go there." Ray nodded thoughtfully. "You willin' to take responsibility? He can stay in your room, later we'll clean out the 'dobe, if you want. For now he can have supper and the night with us. That is if Claudie don't throw us all out for bein' late." He added as an afterthought; "And if he don't eat much as you."

Ray saw the wince and knew soon as he spoke the words how cruel they were, felt Claudie's hand on him that first day at the bus stop, pleading with him then to go easy on the boy's size. Here, without her to guide him, he'd stepped in it; "Sorry, North, you can't go on being that prickly. You earn your keep and every mouthful it takes to keep you workin' that way. Go easy son, it's only meant to be foolin'." Ray hated the pleading in his voice but he'd been wrong, spoke up wrong and needed to make amends.

It was quiet then. North eased himself back against the truck seat, conscious of Key and how close and crowded it was in the old Ford, how much room North himself took up, how much Key pushed against anything tried to tie him. He couldn't quite get a feel for his uncle now, Ray could be angry and covering it with rough jokes and that quiet smile he carried most of the time he knew someone was watching. He said it was fine, kept telling North he was family, kin, welcome to the house, maybe even loved North but that word wasn't never said. Still there could be, must be, a hidden side to Ray McKendrick North hadn't glimpsed. Yet. Ah darn, North repeated inside his head where no one could hear him. He'd wind himself into crazy he kept this up. Right now he was tired and hungry and worried more on what Mrs. McKendrick would keep for his meal even though he missed coming home.

The truck's buck and rattle hurt. Chewing on the inside of his mouth helped Key hold down the cry pushing from his throat. Sweat stuck to his belly and between his shoulders, he was too damned tired and relieved no McKendrick was poking or asking more questions. He was real careful not to look straight on at the driver, he didn't want to appear curious or unsure. Ray McKendrick's like or dislike of him was important.

They surprised him, these two McKendrick men. It'd be a lot easier if he could go back to his life of one, only one, him, Key, skimming around his ma's men, landing in school cause it was safe and warm during the winter and he liked reading, liked the questions, standing up and giving a thought-out response and seeing the narrowed gaze and puzzled expression, if only for a moment, on the teacher's pale face. Like maybe Key wasn't just another rough, dirty, throwaway kid.

The truck rolled on, with the separated travelers deep in private thoughts. Until Key burped as the truck bounced over a pothole; immediately he put his hand over his mouth, rolling his eyes in outrageous apology and it was North who giggled first, then laughed and burped and then the two boys bucked and gyrated in adolescent stupidity. Ray grinned to himself, glad for the dark, and kept his eyes on the road.

Claudie listened and recognized the old Ford's transmission whine as Ray downshifted to get over the half-humped ditch just before the house. Then as automatically she frowned, wiped a damp hand on her face to push back any lazy strands of dark auburn hair. There was just enough red in it to know where Neelie got her brighter coloring. Ray better have North with him, and a good explanation.

It was Ray and North, and another body, one she didn't recognize by the walk. It wasn't Neelie, she was upstairs, having had her solitary meal and choosing to study over sitting with her ma. Claudie knew the girl was waiting, just like she was. She tried to guess who the third person was; obviously male and not much on size, so it wasn't kin to Ray and it wouldn't be her family, none of them would come out this time of night, too old and narrow, too hide-bound for a surprise visit.

Under the backlight she saw it was only a boy, hanging suspended between North and Ray as if he would fall without them. They were crossing the flat stones Ray had spread out around the back door. He kept meaning to set them in sand so Claudie wouldn't have so much mud tracked into the kitchen.

She saw the boy's face outlined in the kitchen door, and was shocked, but not by the bruises for she had already guessed at some kind of fight by the way her two men carried him. It was the pure beauty of the child, the smooth skin and fine jaw, the thick hair damp and curled along his neck, and those eyes which finally looked up and straight into her although she figured he couldn't see much right about now. Whoever this was, he was the most beautiful male Claudie ever set eyes on. She shook her head, hoped Neelie wasn't watching too close, didn't see what her ma felt. The girl was too young anyway, hopefully she'd not recognize the chill of such a feeling.

Then the trio reached the narrow back doorway and the boy hopped away from his protectors. His voice rose in battle, commanding the two men; "Leave me be, there ain't room for us three through there." His voice was clear despite his battered condition and both Ray and North nodded in agreement. Ray laughed at something Claudie couldn't hear and the sound soothed her; if Ray could laugh that way then it was all right, this boy being here.

North came in first, then the boy, behind him was Ray, patient and quiet, his usual self with a small difference; his eyes were restless, they failed to meet hers and Claudie got worried all over again.

"Claudie, this here boy needs some stitchin' and maybe a meal." Ray's beginning of an explanation, one Claudie wasn't certain she would believe now, was sheared off by the boy who stepped forward almost tipsy, off balance for sure. He dropped his head in a parody of bowing; "Ma'am, my name is Key Larkin." Claudie winced, knew her reaction was visible to her family, and hoped her eyes didn't underline what she felt, but the boy must have seen for his eyes shifted, he even shook slightly, so small a movement maybe she was seeing things. "North here thinks he's my guardian angel, and Mr. McKendrick, he's been kind enough to invite me into your home. Now ma'am, it's up to you for I won't come in where I ain't wanted."

She knew all about Marie Larkin, the fancified Muriel Tesmer, she heard all the early gossip about that woman and her Ray, this was her child and obviously not Ray's, not with that coloring and puny size. And he sure was a pretty thing, even though he was Marie Larkin's bastard, Muriel Tesmer's wood's colt. Claudie recollected the woman from school, way older than her, thin and always dirty, skirt too short, and the boys crowding around her, the good girls scorning her.

Claudie wanted to hate Muriel's bastard but manners gave her the kindness to invite him in, to ask if he would like to wash up, if North and Ray wanted supper now, dried and cold from sitting too long but good enough for those who come home so late to the table. Or would he rather go home to his own mama so she wouldn't worry like Claudie had.

She knew the answer to that question, and wanted immediately to bite back the cruel words. North's face turned red and Ray's mouth got tight and Claudie wanted to scream out that the bastard could not stay in her house, not her clean, scrubbed, moral house but it wasn't Christian so she let go of a deep breath and started reheating the meat in the skillet, putting some of the cornbread on a platter, fussing, doing ten things to hide her guilt in false charity.

When she turned away from the stove she saw Neelie sitting at the top stair, watching and that made Claudie glad she held her temper, didn't let out what she truly wanted to say. She kept moving, spinning from the stove back around to the men and faced a tableau that startled her.

North stood behind his friend, the smaller boy swaying, his face gone white. Ray sat at the table, chair tilted back that little bit, eyes weary but asking with no words: let him stay, see how bad it is, give him food and shelter this one time.

Later she told Ray that his face and North's eyes meant little to her then, their kindness was evident, their concern touching but it was the defiance and pride in the boy that convinced her. He did not look away as if hiding something, he did not ask for charity, but nodded to her when her gaze got around to him and tried to say 'go home, boy.' He must have read the words inside her mind for she hadn't let them come to her lips yet. "Yes, ma'am, I know it's wrong me showin' up here. Can't blame North though, he always thinks the best of people."

She was caught and with no escape; Ray pushed his chair upright, North put a hand on his friend's back as if he would fall without that support. But it was the gray eyes, one swollen shut, the other deepening in color, yet unafraid to look straight at her. Claudie coughed, saw the eye change, felt the half-smile that no one else could see and knew she was lost. Except up on the top stair, Neelie grabbed at the stair rail and Claudie believed she could hear the girl whimper.

"Of course he can stay." The boy trembled, his hands came together and his mouth thinned. Claudie saw her small victory; "I would never turn away anyone who so obviously needs our help." That would keep him in his place, a charity that began at home. "What are you two fussin' so about, Ray. North, I'm surprised at you, it's clear what happened, you two have been fightin' and he took the worst of it. You should be ashamed, North, he's so much smaller than you are." She was rambling, speaking nonsense and knowing it, offending North who would never hit a body this way. Yet the men couldn't stop her and she didn't know how to hold her own mouth shut so the words kept pouring out; "I'll fix supper and North, you help your friend with whatever he needs to get cleaned up. Ray I need to talk with you, no, not about this but somethin' that Mr. Rushton wants." She would have babbled on and on, but the boy interrupted; "Ma'am, thank you." The voice was sweet and she could not look at him, he was trouble no matter how pretty the package. But in those eyes, or rather the one eye that charmed her and the other eye which looked so painful she saw more trouble yet she couldn't in good conscience throw a child out into the cold looking like this.

She calmed herself by sheer force of will. "North, get the salve from the barn, that black tar's as good as anything for the cuts. Ray, will you haul in a couple of buckets of water, I need to heat some for later." This was a less than tactful way to remind Ray he still had not provided indoor plumbing and she knew it was a cheap way of pricking him but she was angry at the lateness of the hour and the task ahead of her.

When Ray returned with the buckets, she expected a show of anger she would match to batter down her confusion but he smiled and put one bucket down, poured half the other into the black iron pot and lightly ran a finger along her cheek, his signal he was pleased. How could he? Then she relaxed and let that smile of his do its best work, taking away her anger and worry while slipping into the old pattern of affection and trust.

The Tesmer, or Larkin, boy would be fine here for the night, no more trouble than a sick calf or a wire-cut horse, certainly less worry. And most likely he wouldn't kick when being treated or bawl for his ma or shit all over the kitchen floor. At that point, Claudie laughed and everyone else in the room relaxed; if they only knew what image put her in a better humor.

It was fried salt ham curled at the edges and dry so she made quick gravy, boiled potatoes that she covered in gravy too and greens that were steam-heated. The pitcher of lemonade set in the table's center was soon cut in half by the boy, Key, drinking two glasses like he'd never tasted nothing like it. North ate fast, silent, focused on the slabs of ham, the greens, rolling the potatoes some before risking a bite. Then five of the things disappeared one after another.

The Larkin boy chewed slow and Claudie knew more than his eye was hurt. That jaw looked lopsided, the potatoes and ham hard going. And he couldn't seem to sit still or get a hold of his knife and fork to cut proper. Absently she reached out and chopped the meat into small pieces and smiled when the boy had the grace to blush which in turn her feel silly, but he gingerly put the smallest piece in his mouth and made the effort to chew and swallow before whatever it was botherin' him caught up and he clamped a hand to his mouth. She began to wonder would he throw up.

Ray cut right in; "Boy, you goin' to be sick?" Key shook his head. "Well then you tell us." Nothing, no defiant eyes, no pride, just a short gasp of air and a head shake. Ray took charge then and for once Claudie didn't argue with him. "Boil up some of the greens, Claudie, I know you got broth in the ice box. Be easier on the boy. I'll take a look, maybe we better get him tended to before we feed him." The 'we' bothered her, she thought to set her husband straight then remembered Neelie watching from the stairs and decided acceptance was the better choice. But she'd speak to Ray tonight, in bed, and tell him exactly what she thought.

Busy at the stove, it was the hard sound which surprised her. Looking over her shoulder as she picked ham off the bone, throwing in cut carrot ends and a bit of cooked summer squash, she stopped all movement, knife in mid-air, no quick retort or killing comment coming to mind, nothing to say at all.

North had stripped off the boy's shirt, North's shirt by the size of it and Claudie remembered buying that specific one new for him. How could he lend it to a ragamuffin like this child. Then her anger evaporated at the sight of a boy not much older than her Neelie and half North's size carrying a long slice across his ribs, fresh and leaking yellow fluid as well as new blood while Ray scrub with a cloth, picking off the dried scab. Right at the supper table, no more ceremony than cleaning up after a dogie calf come to sleep in the kitchen warmth. But that wasn't the worst of it, that wasn't why she relented in her heart and made peace with the boy's unwanted intrusion.

Layered under the knife cut, which had to be why he walked in that tilted way, were older, paler scars of other beatings, bruises on his chest and shoulders, a puckering of scars high up near his throat. Claudie remembered the stories she'd heard, of what Marie Larkin's men did to her boy. Here it was, proof of the possibilities of human cruelty.

She couldn't look anymore, and wanted to be sure Neelie wasn't seeing this horror; how could a mother let her child be maimed and beaten so, how could anyone maul a youngster as if he had no more value than a pig.

A stirring noise, a boot scraped across the plank floor, brought Claudie back to the bright room with its smells of home cooking and death. North, eyes wide, face pale, shifted his weight from one huge boot to the other as Ray scrubbed and washed and laid black tar salve along the fresh halves of the knife cut. The patient was quiet, head bowed, nothing showed except the movement of his chest and shoulders as he took deep, hurried, gulps of air.

She thought North would faint, then he cried, eyes clamped shut, tears heavy on his face, a big hand reaching blindly to wipe off the shame. Claudie quivered but knew better than to help. She marveled that the boy who had grown up in that Texas cow town had enough heart to cry for a friend.

A small form slid around the kitchen door, a shall hand reached for North's fingers; one tug and North opened his eyes, a second tug and he bent down, lifted up his cousin Neelie and held her. Gently, not giving in to the need to draw tight on something precious in order to push away an ugliness which should not be, Neelie rested against his chest, head cupped under his jaw, giving North comfort from what they both were witnessing.

Neelie saw her mama over North's shoulder and Claudie was going to reach out to pat her when Ray brought them all back to reality. "Claudie, honey, the soup's boilin' over. I'm done, bet this boy's hungry now." The kitchen moved into action. North set Neelie down in a chair and pulled a shirt over Key's naked back; Key reached for the bowl of soup Claudie ladled; Ray picked up the salve tin and the filthy towels; Neelie took the basin of pale pinkish water outside to throw on her ma's flower beds.

It is easy to sit and tell myself that I knew from that first time when North brought Key home that only trouble would result. The whole evening was a nightmare of emotion and feeling and pity as well as anger and misunderstandings.

What I know of that night was frightening to me then and still troubling now; I saw Key's bare flesh and felt an unwilling response in my own body I was only thirteen, often perceived as still a baby by my parents but harboring all those impending changes which plague the school years. It would be impossible to say that Key did not fascinate me that evening, seeing his coppery skin revealed, the well defined muscling, the crossing of old scars and bruises which heightened my hidden female sensibilities and needs. It was a revolution inside me, an intense pleasure at such a beautiful, pain-filled life so completely unlike my own. Not just male and female but love and hate, compassion and cruelty were exposed in Key's bared skin.

What went on that night introduced me to my beckoning puberty. I experienced an emotional lust which had never been part of me before. I felt internally what I had seen only with my father touching my mother's skin or read in a scandalous novel alluding to baser feelings in a highly read book underlined and handed around school.

In other words, much more succinct and true, I was sexually turned on by watching Key being doctored, imagining all sorts of dangerous situations where it would be my hands stroking his scars, my body so close to his, and as I thought of these scenarios I squirmed and felt a strange internal burning. It all sounds silly now, so many years later, when I know more of the truth about love and sex, that the two are not always compatible nor are they mutually exclusive. I wanted Key that night although I really didn't know what I wanted him for.

I wish I knew exactly what Mama and North were feeling during these moments; my father's state I could guess at, tired as he rubbed the old scar above his eye, removed from the chaos by his task, focused on his wife and how he was going to feed another mouth. Always the pragmatist, at that time I didn't know the word but I thought I knew what my father was. What I also didn't know was the connection Papa had to Key's mother, and that my own mama also knew. What a tangled connection which by rights would have driven Key away from us. I believe it shows the inherent character of my parents that despite the interwoven history they accepted Key with so little fuss.

In my child's way, unexpectedly angered by what Key had stirred in me, I spoke out what I expected my mother was feeling. It was cruel and childish but I was a child and trying to protect our family in my own way. Our family bond could absorb a cousin but perhaps I saw we were not strong enough to take in Key Larkin and survive.

Whatever were my motives, when I realized that Key was becoming accepted, I stamped my feet and cried as they talked around me and when no one listened I finally shrieked and got their attention but all my commotion did no good, no one listened to me and eventually I got sent to bed.

I hated Key then, and North, only very briefly. I always hated my mother when she got angry with me and Papa paid me no attention but let Mama finish the discipline. Later they would both come upstairs and into my room and even if I pretended to be asleep, Mama would bend down and kiss my forehead and tell me how much they loved me. I counted on that ritual, to know I was always wanted, always loved despite how badly I behaved.

North started talking. First he wanted to explain about the fight and as he got into the explanation he saw that neither Claudie or Ray knew about any of the doings, so he backtracked and explained something about Key's wounds and the truth North had dragged out of him, but Key kept on eating and Ray made the comment about a fight never solving anything even as he touched the scar over his eye and then went to rubbing at his chest.

Claudie set then all back; she glared at North, wouldn't look at Key and spoke her mind. "You think an excuse will get you out of this. A boy does not go to a saloon to fight with an adult. I don't care what the reason, you do not do such a thing, North." Then her determination vanished. North saw the beginning tears and that they stayed shimmering in her eyes and did not spill over upset him even more.

Ray entered the discussion; "You listen to your aunt, North. What you did was wrong no matter what they did to Key here. That's why we have law and police and all those elected officials. They know to do the thing right and proper, protect Key and protect you, North, from what you done on your own." There was a moment when Key lifted his head from the soup and looked at the three faces surrounding him but he had nothing to add.

"Now, North, tell me what you think happens next?"

North looked to Key for help but his friend was wiping out the last of the soup with a hunk of bread and nothing would distract him. Then he brought a hand halfway to his mouth, saw the napkin folded next to him and used it instead. As if he'd heard none of the talk going around him, he looked at Claudie; "Ma'am, that was good. Thank you. Didn't hurt at all."

Then he dug himself, and North, a deep hole. "Now if I ate like that more often, who knows but I might grow big as North here."

The shriek startled everyone; Claudie jumped right out of her chair, Ray half-turned, half-rose as if ready to fight. North's head flew back, only Key stayed calm, finished wiping his damp mouth with the checkered napkin. "No he can't come live here, he can't have supper with us every night. He can't stay, not even in the barn where he belongs. There's only room for me and North. Me and North. Not him."

Ray spoke before Claudie could comfort Neelie. "Girl, you got no manners talkin' so to a guest. You 'pologize." She stood next to North, a hand gripping the back of a chair. Defiance showed in every muscle until tears burst through. "No, I won't. 'Pologize. He's not a guest, he's hateful." North took a half-step and pushed Neelie with his bulk, then swung around to steady her. Claudie held still, calm and knowing. North's voice was clear and firm; "He's only Key Larkin, kid, not the devil on the hoof."

Ray's face darkened, he rubbed at his chest and frowned. Claudie reached her child, held her lightly. North was mute, unmoving except for his eyes which could find no place to settle. Claudie felt for the boy, caught in a family filled with argument. But even as she grabbed Neelie she knew the child would not quit, knew the child had some right to her screaming. Her small heart pounded, the beating high in her throat and Claudie put a finger there, stroked the pulsing blood, talked gently to her daughter. Then put a hand across her mouth, knowing there were more hateful words waiting to be spilled.

"She's tired, Ray, and upset. I'll put her to bed now, we'll deal with this tomorrow." Neelie turned her back to the men, hand tight within her mother's fist. She marched up the stairs without crying, knowing she had acted like a child, knowing too, a fierce knowledge, that she was right, this stranger had no place in the McKendrick clan.

Key looked down at the table but heard the questions Ray McKendricks asked his nephew. "What's the plan now, you two? After this? What got you to thinkin' there was room here? Boy's got his own family." There was a distinct break around the word 'family' that Key felt; maybe there still was a chance.

It was North who spoke, putting words in Key's mouth as well as spouting them out of his own. "We planned on askin' if Key could work for free, sleep in my room or maybe fix up the 'dobe like you said. But he wasn't comin' back with me till you picked us up. We were arguin' that, him of a mind to go back to his ma." It was the wrong way to put it; North and Key both heard the small accusation and McKendrick picked up on it too.

"Tryin' to blame me for him bein' here just because I came by in the truck? There's always a choice, boy, you got to learn that." Key stayed quiet, admiring North but knowing he was out of the house now. No reason for the McKendricks to be generous and that forgiving, even with North as his champion.

Awkwardly Key pushed the chair back and stood, took measure of his friend again; sitting North's head came almost to Key's chin. Damn he was a big 'un. Key laughed and saw the jump on McKendrick's face. Mrs. McKendrick came back down the stairs and Key took a lesson from North, told the straight, honest truth.

"Your daughter says I don't belong here. She's right, I don't. Thanks, Mrs. McKendrick for the food and doctorin'." He stepped towards the door, wobbling some for real. "Mr. McKendrick, sir, 'preciate the ride." Then he looked to North, "You got a jacket I can borrow, return it come mornin' to school." He took a deep breath. "It's cold out there."

Ray knew when he was out-maneuvered. It was too cold for a kid to walk those miles back to a saloon. "Stay the night, Key. And maybe there's work here on the weekend, we'll see. I'll have to ask Mr. Rushton. Feed and a bed, that's all I can pay. You know much 'bout cattle?" He gave himself away then by looking at his wife but he couldn't help but think of the gossip about Marie Larkin and the rancher up to Pryor, the stories of the boy being involved.

Key saw the exchange and that knot turned in his belly, grabbed him and squeezed but he wouldn't let it win. "Yes sir I know horses." He slowed down, pushed a hand to his gut. "I can learn 'bout cattle but I am good on the broncs." Here he took a risk, another one, and let them know right off the extent of his tough pride. "Wendell Dana up to Pryor, he taught me a lot about horses. Sir."

I learned to smile from my mother, as I learned almost

everything about being a woman except for flirting, which Papa taught me, and sex, which is not to be taught from parent to child. Mama was a very pretty woman in the plains sense where a face told about its owner with no artificial help. Mama's features were regular, her mouth wide and well delineated, her eyes a clear, deep blue the color poets liken to the western summer sky. Her hair was thick, a dark auburn, almost always pulled back and pinned. We rarely got to see that mane freed; now I can imagine Papa's pleasure at night when he ran his callused hand through its luxury. It would be a sensual moment, a privacy between husband and wife.

Her real smile was infrequent and it took me years to see and understand the difference, from when she was truly delighted and the stiff, full smile she produced upon demand to approve of something she did not like. I don't know if this is explanation enough, or clear, for I don't know if all women of her time had this talent. Now the discussion of two smiles becomes a feminist issue and I would guess these differ in degrees of disgust and approval, her support of a husband and family ahead of her own self.

My parents had a good marriage I believe, at least through much of my teen years. I think often of their signals to each other, small gestures I took for granted until I became a married woman and began to experiment with the difficulties of truly communicating with another human being. I can see now the length of my father's hand, I can almost touch the nicks and healed cuts, the knot of crushed knuckles, as he would lay one finger gently on my mother's jaw just below her ear, a delicate place and a tender touching, so unlike my father's physical being.

I have tried hard to keep alive the memories of how it felt to be a child so I could have mercy on my own children. Sometimes I have been successful, sometimes I fail miserably. And as I struggled to keep those memories viable, I struggled equally to see my parents, to understand them now as they were then, young people faced with tragedy, working and keeping on, dealing with a hard life and still having room for laughter. I have tried to imagine their sexuality, for without it they would not be human. Growing up I could not accept my parents as sexual beings; it was too ludicrous to think of my father as the aggressive male, my mother as the receiving female.

Now I have learned a new lesson; as a woman deemed old because of her years I have been relegated to the non-sexual. I don't mind this from the children, it is a natural protection for them, but I know my body and the pleasure I still seek from my husband's touch. In the middle of my parent's marriage this magic disappeared, the gestures remained, perhaps out of reflex, but the deep passion was slowly filtered out of their lives.

My father's death in his late fifties must have devastated my mother yet she went on, as usual, and remarried quite happily when she turned sixty. I wish I could ask her questions of a most private nature but her mode of living would not allow me the closeness necessary for such personal talk. My mother taught me how to smile and ask a man's permission for deeds already committed. It was manipulation pure and simple, a necessary item for the women of her time, her only recourse in moments of desperate wanting. Papa was not tight or controlling like so many men but we had so little it was difficult for him to offer much. And there were few times when Mama truly seduced him by her acts; she was honest, mostly, telling him her truth, accepting what was possible. It was her one major lie, her lone hidden seduction which destroyed Papa and shocked us all, led us to take on another lie to cover up her final betrayal.

I learned that smile from her early and used it sparingly on my family as I came to understand more and more the horrors of what had happened. Being an adult gave me distance from my childhood and the time to puzzle through my own behavior. I think immediately of that night Key came into our house. I was terrified of this new entity who might take more from us than he could give back. North asked me days later why I had screamed and acted like a baby and I could not answer him. Not because of my usual stubbornness but because I did not in truth know or understand myself.

The screaming was all the more terrifying since I thought of myself as an adult, not a baby. I had begun my period that fall, which had been a terrible revelation. We used no disposable napkins then; Mama dutifully folded and pinned old white cotton sheets in my panties, admonishing me to change them often. It was a humiliating example of how close to poverty our family lived. Shamefully I couldn't look at the line of wash without cringing, there the change in my life hung clinically exposed.

None of this explains the screaming: I was supposedly different from the other girls in school, I was bold and out-spoken and read all the assigned books, I could ride a horse as well as the boys. And after Key rode with me in the long summer nights, I began to be in rhythm with the horse and less of a bully. Key taught me that much at least.

About Mama's smile. She wasn't a truly calculating woman on an ordinary level. She'd not been raised to want her own way. But she was, above all, an intelligent woman and wanted to work hard to fulfill her end of any bargain. So she smiled at my father and prodded him to do more than he would chose to in order to keep that smile only for him. He did not understand, none of us did at the time, that the smile had become automatic, a façade behind which Mama withheld her growing, turbulent feelings. We worked hard to be blessed with the lovely vision and she rarely knew how much we gave in to insure that the signal of all being well in our small world would remain constant and safe.

Chapter Five

Ray was difficult and becoming impossible. Of course she knew that when she accepted him as a husband; any man capable of the self-discipline to wait ten years before marrying just so he could own a ranch had to have a strong streak of stubbornness in him. On the other hand, if he hadn't waited, then Claudie never would have been his wife.

She'd have to think some on this. She fiddled with the frayed collar of what had been her dress blouse, it needed darning along the back and was getting too thin in places. She didn't want the extra work of two boys, it was hard enough with only North. That Ray mentioned fixing up the 'dobe to give them all some privacy was no answer to Claudie's complaint.

She tried explaining her distress to Ray, never quite certain he was listening. "It isn't room I'm talkin' about, Ray. It's that boy himself. He seems to take up more'n his share, food, time, energy, you name it, it's always him needin' more and not North never mind he's less than half North's size."

She knew without looking around that Ray heard what she said, so she bowed her head, counted to five and waited. And right on time; "Claudie, he works more'n most grown men and all we do is feed him. Mr. Rushton agreed to keep the boy on, he's been givin' us extra for the groceries. We ain't out of pocket on this deal and the boy keeps North from feeling lonely. North told him, I know for a fact, North laid down the law, he keeps away from Neelie."

She didn't like even the vaguest reference to the boy's reputation. But it was more than Neelie's safety, it was in her heart and unless she spoke it clear to Ray, he would never understand. She tried again, in a normal, patient voice, not wanting to let emotion come between her and her sometimes-blindfolded husband.

"Ray, the boy is wrong." She held her breath, let it out, "I can't explain more than that but you know what they say about him, and you know his ma for sure." She needed to be careful here, not let on that she was playing to his old guilt. But the temptation was strong, to say what she felt, that having the bastard breed son of the immoral Muriel Tesmer in her house, eating her meals, laughing with her husband and teasing her baby daughter was an insult she could hardly bear.

Finally Ray turned and looked straight at her, into her eyes, and she knew she had lost this battle. "I said it, Claudie, the boy works hard, don't cause much trouble and keeps North company. Can't ask for more, ain't goin' to throw him out on account of your 'feeling.'" He'd rarely been that blunt with her, he was usually softer, more gentle, working around her worry stead of standing plumb on his opinion and saying no.

Then her husband spoke a piece deeper to his heart, and Claudie had to listen. "Honey, please, he makes less work for me, I don't get so tired, I got more energy for you." His voice was soft and soothing, Ray's version of sexy and Claudie almost laughed but knew better, never laugh at a man about sex. Not even your own beloved husband. She had two choices, give in and accept the boy or fight back in a guerilla war only she and the boy would know was joined. "You're right, Ray. Darlin'." She played back to him, it wasn't much of the truth but there would be cuddling and kissing and a quick union later, maybe, so it wasn't really a lie.

"Claudie, you got more a that pie? North's got a hole in him this noon, must be all that wood he cut." It was an acknowledgement, if unspoken, that the discussion was ended. Claudie got the last word: she put an empty pie plate scattered with crumbs into Ray's hands and walked away.

Charlie Rushton wanted new fence post in the north horse trap and a new well dug in the eight section west pasture. Ray figured if he got the Larkin kid broke right then the dogged work of those miserable chores would belong to the boys and Ray could make it through another miserable winter working for Charlie Rushton. And at the same time find the bottom to the boys with them digging through froze ground. He knew pretty much about North, the boy would work himself to death given a tough enough chore, now he needed to know the depth of the Larkin kid.

Late October it snowed, and again before Thanksgiving, then twice before Christmas. The holiday came and went; Key was missing both days but showed up later, quiet, lacking his usual wild spirit but ready to get back to work. And as Ray was learning, Key Larkin could do the work, if he said he would. It was a comfort to Ray, and company for North; not a bad bargain despite how Claudie felt.

There was no lack of snow. Drifts piled up to the mesa where cattle stood too long to wait out a blow and froze in their tracks. Key and North rode out each weekend, breaking trails to get the half-starved cattle to home pasture and the coarse hay Ray shoveled off the back of the borrowed flatbed truck, cursing all the time that he didn't have a good team of Belgians and a sledge to do the job right.

Ray and North both noticed that Key got extra out of his horses. The horses seemed to work harder for him, angling their heads into the wind, bucking drifts, plunging again and again to pack down the snow. Key would slip off and stamp out more of a path and lead the horse back and forth so the weakened cattle would find it easy to follow. North got stuck up to his waist, couldn't drive himself through the snow. His bulk held him in the deep snow while Key seemed to float over the treacherous white fluff, barely sinking into the drifts. The broncs knew Key made a good trail, and the cattle lined up behind him, bellowing softly, hungry, waiting for the path to be laid out to home.

Key told North a truth, that it was his size made it easy, for himself and the broncs but North got sullen and then mad before he admitted maybe Key was right. But he also knew, watching his friend, that Key was better with the broncs. Key's hand seemed to know right when to stroke the soaked neck of a struggling bronc and the horse would try harder, he stood in the stirrups, keeping his weight off the bronc's back, letting the horse work under him. North was jealous of his friend, about the horses and Ray's words of praise until he laughed at his own stupidity and wanted to cuff Key on the head and knock him down, then pick him back up and be where they belonged again. He didn't know how to act with the new Key, competent, quick, quiet and polite. School was different, or the same as it used to be; Key smarted off, got in trouble, fooled around in class, more a bother than a student.

But still, watching Key work the stock, North recognized what others hated in the hard competency of the kid, that clean, wide grin, the quick temper, an edge in the pale eye, the copper red of the winter-burned skin. Then North would shake himself, rub a hand through his lank, baby-fine hair and have to grin. Key was the same, taking what he wanted, working just outside North's control. All he was doing was making Uncle Ray want to hire him full-time come summer.

Key took note of the twinges and suspicions in North and nodded, more tuned in to those reactions than to any affection. He had hoped the rare trust between him and North would last through the envy and anger and whatever foolish knot North tied in his gut. On his part, Key wished for North's strength, his reach for a stranded cow, his ease at shouldering the hundredweight of grain, the fifty-pound cattle cake, one in each hand.

Separated by mutual envy, the two strays worked at their chores, neither quitting or complaining, except sometimes to each other. Once Key sputtered about the starvation wages Rushton paid out to McKendrick and flushed when North looked him up and down, his meaning obvious. Key's belly reached to his belt now, his shirts needed tugging to button.

Other than those few moments, they rode hard their two days each weekend, and went on through the school week eager to get back into the freedom of the ranch.

Claudie cooked a lot of stew and biscuits and cobbler or pie, maybe a plate of brownies when she could afford the chocolate, and while she was finally used to what North could put away, and felt a decent sense of accomplishment when he pushed himself from the table full and satisfied, she was awed at what the Larkin boy could finish without adding more'n a few pounds to his skinny frame. Both boys were polite and ate anything she put down, but she still had that edge of mistrust when she stood too close to Key or handed him the salt or pepper or the hot sauce North got to liking in Texas and talked her into buying.

Neelie worked too, sometimes with her mother, sometimes in the barn with her pa, saddling horses, going over the ravaged calves or yearling stock for cuts and sores. In the kitchen she learned from her ma how to act when the half-frozen men bulked inside, stomping and peeling off stiff gloves and hats, moving awkwardly on numbed feet. When Claudie smiled encouragingly at her husband and the boys, Neelie tilted her head in an unconscious mimicry and smiled as well.

That spring calving began, and North and Ray worked around the clock, checking each cow, helping with the difficult births. North missed a lot of school and Key came to help on weekends. Ray refused all pleadings that Marie's boy be allowed to skip school as well; it wasn't his decision, Ray said. As if Key hadn't become family.

Without his bodyguard, Key was fair game again at school. Of course Stevie Plunkett saw his chance for revenge. He and two other boys the same size as Stevie beat Key to a motionless pulp, quickly and efficiently and with complete enjoyment. Key didn't make school the next day, or the day after. And he didn't get to the ranch that weekend.

On Monday Key reappeared at school, both eyes almost open, one ear still crusted with blood. North was there for once, and quick to take charge, feeling remorse and guilt at abandoning his friend. He pushed hard for an answer to his tough question; "Who did this, Key? I'll beat the son worse'n he beat on you." Key only grinned, which had to hurt. "This ain't for you to fix, North. It's done, I ain't dead. How're the cattle comin' without you nursin' them?"

It wasn't enough to satisfy North's private pain; he cornered several of the younger boys and demanded names but they honored Key and refused, as did the girls and even the grade school kids. Neelie was North's last resort and even she refused to tell, declaring he'd heard Key, it was over and done. It was the first time Neelie chose to support something that Key Larkin wanted.

Summer came as a relief. North turned sixteen in May but never found time to get his license. No one asked about Key, how old he was, when he had a birthday, and Key never said. He'd turned sixteen the second week of January and didn't care. North was persistent, wanting that paper which let him drive legal but Key was indifferent to this particular rite of passage.

It slowly became apparent that Key cared more about horses than he did about any truck. Charlie Rushton was the first to recognize it so he brought over some rank stock, for the Larkin boy to ride he told Ray. Said too he would hire both Key and North in a few months at full wages, not just pay them day work through Ray.

Rushton had ridden in rodeos as a boy, and still held a Turtle Association card as a badge of independence, an honor held by only those few willing to take on the established rules of the fledgling sport So now he prided himself on raising good stout horses, and only a few passed his judgment each year. He sold the lesser mounts, or gave them to McKendrick to use on the ranch.

One of these second-hand broncs was a deep-chested

runt no bigger than thirteen hands yet capable of sending any good cowboy skyward. If the dark bay had been bigger, he might have gone on to the rodeo, as it was, Rushton sent him to McKendrick as a prank, to see how good the Larkin kid really was. It was one of the few times he ever spoke direct to Key; "Ride him hard, get some of the bronc off him and maybe we'll pay you rough-string wages." There was no mercy in Rushton; he saw the quick grin on the boy's face and thought on how the bay would mess that pretty face up with high bucks and hard kicks.

It was slack time, branding done, summer pastures cleaned and waiting. Even the summer rains had come early, leaving the dirt tanks filled and overflowing. Ray allowed there was time for Key to play with the broncs, and for North to get his license. He wasn't sure which was more dangerous.

The morning came when Key walked out to the small corral holding the bay, his face relaxed, his walk easy, but Ray knew the signs and wandered out to the corral, a cup of coffee in one hand. This could be interesting, and less dangerous than North getting his driver's license. Far as he could tell, the boy paid no attention to the little horse's reputation; this first morning he saddled up after spending maybe twenty minutes rubbing the bay with his flat hand, drawing up each hoof, holding the leg, pulling the black forelock, all as if he were testing suspicious tires on a third-hand pickup truck. The bay accepted the process, his swiveling ears the only hint of nerve.

Neelie came out to pretend to hang the wash but spent most of the time watching whatever Key did. North caught and saddled his brown and leaned on a corral post, content also. Only Claudie refused to appear for the performance.

Key slipped up on the bay before anyone thought it was time. One moment he was standing near the bay's head, next he was in the saddle and the bay's ears flicked back and forth. A wave of his hand and the bay reared, pawed the air then humped into a series of hard bucks. Key got thrown forward, backwards, sideways; with each pounding it looked like he would fly until the bay stopped, snorted, wagged his head and reached around to bite Key's boot.

North was the first to laugh. Neelie giggled and then Ray let out a whoop which threatened a second outburst of bucking but Key rubbed the horse's neck and the animal stood quiet. Then Key wiped the back of his hand across his mouth and licked those few drops of blood told him he'd bit his tongue. "Mr. McKendrick we got work to do now?"

"Always, kid. Always. North, you know where the fence is broke. Get going, we lost half a day already with the entertainment." But there was no sternness to Ray's voice and Key lifted himself in the saddle and the damned bay pony bucked again, figuring maybe he'd gotten Key off balance and could finish the job. Key laughed and tugged on the reins, put both spurs to the bay and headed to the west gate. Neelie was quick enough to pull the gate wide, and with a wild yell Key and the bay burst into the pasture, the horse half running, half bucking and Key hollering to help him get along.

Barbed wire is ugly, and fixing it a constant chore. North set a new post, tamped it down with flat steps while Key untangled the mess of knotted wire, all they needed to fix a big hole in a boundary fence. Rushton and the neighbor got along reasonably well but a good fence between their main pastures was a necessity.

Today's hole was the biggest North'd ever seen in a

fence not made by a truck or train, three sections stood open and inviting. Already a small herd of curious whiteface had gathered, waiting their chance, watching the boys but not so bold as to get too close. North thought he recognized some of them as the winter's survivors he'd nursed and shoved along the rutted tracks, chousing them closer to the home pasture where Ray stood forking out thick piles of hay.

Key turned to him, hands waist high and tangled in wire; "You know, North, it was that bull went visitin' right through here, chasin' prime tail like what's on this side ain't good enough. If we fence him in over there, Rushton's gonna speak to your Uncle Ray and then we're in it deep."

North used the flat of his palm to check the wiggle of the new post. "And how to you figure to get that bull back in. Not like we can rope and drag him home." North winced, raised his head. "You ain't thinkin' serious about doin' such a thing?" No telling with Key, he could dust off the oddest ideas and make them work.

"Nah, just thought I'd ride through, see if I can spot the randy sum bitch." "And do what? Whistle for him?" "Don't know, North, somethin' might come to me. I ain't much help here, you got two more posts to set and I dug the holes already and this wire's ready to be strung higher'n a hanged man." North looked for these holes but found only a few short mounds of rock and dust pretending to be dug. Heck, no harm in Key riding around the neighbor's pasture, he might find something. Then Key put in his last card; "Be good for the bay, get some more of the buck off him. Rushton sure did your uncle no favors unloadin' this one on him."

When he thought to look up and watch, Key was seated on the bronc, going in half bucks that covered ground but couldn't be much fun for the rider. North laughed, darned if Key didn't figure out the strangest things. He could hear Key's running comment on the bay's performance until all he could see was the tip of Key's hat and occasionally the flicked end of the bay's long, matted tail as they went down-slope off Rushton's property.

Some time later, maybe a half hour or more, North heard a rough pounding coming up the backside of the hill. He rested from the digging in Key's postholes, patted his wet hair and put his hat back on, never good to be caught naked in front of company, like Neelie coming in at noon with sandwiches and pie. But it wasn't company, it wasn't Neelie with something sweet, but Key and the catty bay bellied down and running like the devil was behind them.

North's mouth dropped. He stepped back and planted himself up against a new post. For it was the devil himself bellowing full steam, head low, tail up, great lengths of slobber streaming from the gaping mouth: the biggest bull North'd ever seen. He figured it out then, Key's great plan, and laughed, half-choked on fear. Key and the bay skidded through the open hole, slowed to a lope until the bull took aim and roared on through. North caught the animal's stink, pure male fury, and checked on his own horse. The brown gelding raised its head from the grass in mild curiosity, took a few hobbled steps, then decided the whole venture wasn't worth a fuss.

Key galloped the bull at an angle from the new fence towards the ranch, right through the herd of shy, curious, delectable female whitefaces. The ladies scattered, the bull slowed and forgot about Key; it raised its head in a commanding bellow which had no effect on the cows at all. North found he needed to breath; Key rode up on his left side, the bay blowing hard, white foam thick at its bit. Key was soaked, blond hair darkened, eyes starry. He was gasping for air and grinning at the same time, that same grin got him in trouble most of the time.

"I brought the bull in, North. How come you ain't got the fence done?"

The matter of getting a driver's license came to a head as Ray took his nephew down to the right department in town and sat with him through the lengthy test and then waited, impatient but certain, while North and the examiner headed out in Ray's truck. Neelie and her mother planned a celebration, as much as North would let them. Neelie baked her first cake, for her cousin, a sliding chocolate pile stabilized with enough icing to glue the adobe hut back together. No one wanted to complain. Key was the only guest, if he could be considered such. He lived with them full time now, sharing the adobe he and North had hammered and plastered at until it withstood enough of the few rains to be livable.

Ray began the small celebration with what passed for a speech from him. " Congratulations on passing that test, North. Here, it's your own set a keys to the ranch truck. Mind you, we still got to share and it's hard to start, uses a lot a gas but when you need it, best I can it's yours." This speech was prompted by Charlie Rushton. Ray and Claudie had their own elderly Ford but Rushton indicated that it was proper giving North a set of keys to the Jimmy. "That North boy works hard, Ray, give him this responsibility and he'll live up to it."

Neelie got things off on a different tact: when she asked Key when he was going to turn sixteen. "You got to be close, maybe already past, maybe you don't really know." It was a cruel thing to say, even Neelie saw that and put her hands over her mouth. The family watched Key and left Neelie to her own humiliation. "January;" was all he said. "The last one." Then he dropped his eyes, picked his fork through the small bit of cake left on his plate.

She tried for redemption; "You got a license? I saw you and North driving the Jimmy up to Poplar Wells and you was at the wheel, haulin' pipe it was, this spring I remember sure."

Key looked up, his eyes had brightened and nothing showed of his earlier sadness. "Little girl, you do see everythin'. 'Course I can drive, been drivin' since I could reach the pedals and see over the wheel. 'Bout time you started learnin' yourself." Neelie wouldn't let it go. "Then why don't you get yourself a license?" His voice was soft, and deadly; "Who'd let me drive their truck? 'Round here I ain't worth the bother."

Claudie watched the word play, saw the skip of hurt in the boy's eyes and marveled that he had the compassion not to hit back at Neelie for her unconscious stab. Then as she listened, he turned the asking around, caught Neelie off guard and Claudie liked seeing the child's confusion. Do her good to not always be the brightest star. Claudie laughed, and in unison all heads turned to stare at her; a batch of puppets on the same string.

It was also the McKendricks' nineteen year anniversary and Ray decided, without prompting from his wife or their child, that the boys could keep an eye on Neelie and he would take his wife into town for a special meal at the hotel. The boys promised, at least North said yes and Key nodded, that they would check the stock tank past Powder Wash that had a leak in it, and keep watch on the cow in the back lot with mastitis, and they would leave off deviling Neelie since she'd have no protector with her ma gone. That sounded too final so Ray backtracked, "You boys have the number of the hotel, you can reach us there if there's trouble. We'll be gone no more' n four hours so how much damage can be done." He immediately wished he hadn't said that, as Key's grin widened, and North laughed. Then the boys got solemn as Ray scowled at them for their foolishness.

For all the plans it was useless advice anyway, there was no phone to the ranch, Rushton didn't want to pay the pole fee, and the closest neighbor, two miles back towards Branson was unfriendly, wanting to buy out the ranch from Rushton and put the McKendricks off.

Still, when Ray glanced at the Larkin boy and saw those smiling eyes and the easy set to the head, he figured at least the boy could talk the neighbors into the use of almost anything they owned. Except maybe their eighteen-year-old daughter who was ugly as a post and then Ray stopped himself from any more thinking. "Boys, it's on you for a while, You, North, you 'specially."

The big kid blushed and Ray looked off, not wanting, to make the reaction worse. Even Key glanced to the mesa walls and then down to the corral where the little bay paced restlessly. Anywhere except North's reddening face.

It was tough getting Claudie out of the house; she wasn't wanting to visit a friend the other side of Trinidad and she wouldn't ever gracefully do what her husband asked without knowing why and how-come. Most likely, Ray decided, she guessed a surprise was waiting and she didn't always like that, her being the one not to know.

Finally it was Neelie who pushed her ma into the

old Ford and closed the door quite firmly. She put her head in close to her ma's and whispered something that made Claudie smile; Ray would lay into the child if she'd given the secret away but Claudie turned to him and asked, "Why didn't you just tell me Andy and Ruth have a party planned? I thought they were up to somethin'. Really, Ray, you can be so devious about nothin' at all."

Ray reached across his wife and touched Neelie lightly on the arm. She grinned, said "Have fun at the party, Papa," which made both Ray and Claudie smile as it was well known Ray hated parties.

Then the boys were left with Neelie and the ranch truck, only a few chores, and too much energy. The responsibility lay on North; Key was untouched by Ray's words. Of course Key started it. Later, when all hell had broke loose North never admitted that he'd listened to Key or it was Key's idea. He took the blame and Key let him, after all it was North done the driving.

Two boys sat on the front stoop of an empty house, their bellies full of good beef stew, a hot summer night waiting for them, blank and empty except for what their minds could imagine. Neelie sat separate from them, licking the last of the ice cream. She was already mad at them for a whole lot of reasons. She'd tried to take their picture earlier with the camera her ma gave her but they'd fooled around and teased her so badly she'd snapped one quick shot then gave it up as a bad idea, then they'd pestered her until she'd washed the dishes, 'women's work' they called it and she hated North and his ugly friend.

Key chewed a bit of grass and judged the narrow ranch track which bisected the county dirt road going to Trinchera Plaza and on to Trinidad. The road went over a ridge and out of his sight but he could imagine the flat gravel and the traffic headed the back way into town for a Saturday night.

He and North sat on their butts looking at the world passing by, doing nothing but sucking on some lemonade and staring into the coming night. "Hell, North, we're nothin' but baby-sitters." Key raised his chin at Neelie who wouldn't look up from her task of finishing the ice cream. Key knew better than to get between North and his cousin but he could push to start something; he was restless, anxious, needed to be moving. "The truck's got gas, you got a key. Hell, North, we can go for a ride, test out how good you drive legal. Most folks're in town by now, road'll be empty."

Key focused on the bit of grass in his hands, well chewed, frayed and bitter tasting. He picked a new piece growing between the flat rocks set loose at the steps. Positioning the grass between his thumbs carefully, he blew hard and tight, created a deep melodic note which unraveled into a raucous cheer. Neelie looked up at the startling noise.

North shook his head; "That's crazy." Key agreed with North. "Still it'd be fun, seein' what's left in the old truck engine." The boys looked at the GMC, sagging on worn springs, canted to the left as if a driver already sat behind the wheel. Key tasted bile in his mouth. "We can take the kid with us, won't be no sayin' we left her alone."

His words were settling in North so Key watched the road, fiddled with a new piece of grass, watched North's arms and legs twitch, his foot lift and fall. Living on the ranch was easy for Key, do his chores, keep his temper, do whatever Ray McKendrick said, eat what the missus put in front of him and not tease the girl too much.

Nice and easy and it all got tiring after a while, made

him restless, feeling the urge in his belly yet not ready to go find what he needed. It was wrong, no one had to tell him, what his ma did with her men. Picturing her laying under some bum; hearing what the neighbor ladies told him not with their words but how their hands and eyes spoke differently. He'd look at Neelie, her child's face, and see Mr. Ray touch his wife and he would choke on the damned memories and stuff them back around the edges of his life.

Still, there were times when the recklessness caught up to him, like now, with the old truck sitting there and the McKendricks gone and North holding keys he'd been given as a present. Told when the truck weren't in use and North wanted it, it was his.

The worst that could happen, they'd get stopped by some local law and there'd be hen-clucking and heads shaken and words like 'boys will be boys' and 'it's summer and they're young,' and the worst, that Key knew would follow him; 'what can you expect, it's that Larkin boy.' No matter to Key, words hadn't hurt him, not for a long time.

Ten minutes later they were on the county road, Neelie tucked between them, her legs curled around the high gear shift. Key had his head out the window, he howled, spat into the wind, felt his own spit come back on him; he howled again, shook his head like a wild dog and leaned out farther until North got nervous and yelled at him. "Might take Neelie with you, you durn fool." That sobered Key and for nearly a minute he sat proper on the truck seat, legs together, hands folded neatly until even North saw the dumb bit of acting and both boys laughed. "Come on, North, this ole bucket'll go fast." Fast wasn't much in the rust-bucket truck but even the illusion of speed gave Key a moment's release. Rocks bowled through the undercarriage, the tires spun on loose dirt and North's big hands were strained to hold the wheel in line. The GMC bucked and rolled and skidded on the empty dirt road and the two boys howled together.

Neelie pretended she was safe, wedged between North's huge legs and the vague touch of Key's leanness. She was fascinated while knowing she was terrified, her knee and narrow thigh bounced and ground into Key's hip when the truck spun into a curve. She inhaled deeply, smelled the boys and knew each one; sweat from the day's chores, a deeper scent that was the sinful wrongness of driving the truck this way. Key smelled of sweet grass, his fingers stained a rich green. North smelled like the corral he had mucked out before supper, after Mama and Papa left on their supposed visit to friends. After they left Neelie in the care of two maniacs.

She was almost fourteen, not strong enough for this passion. Key's hand left pinpricks on her, she trembled, shook, was glad when North pried a hand free of the wheel and helped settle her. Without raising her eyes to check, she guessed at the glance between the boys; North glaring a desperate message, Key grinning, always, denying anything except an offer to help.

The truck speedometer hit fifty; Key leaned forward, caught the foolishness of his gesture and grinned, North laughed full out, it felt good to laugh. He was intensely aware of Neelie snugged in beside him, her girl's elbow caught in his ribs, knees drawn up against his thigh. Such a small thing and quiet, too quiet for Neelie. That made North take his eyes off the road to look at her, wondering what scared her, was she all right.

The truck bounced and skidded as North wrestled it. Then it wobbled back to the center of the road.

North was shaking, couldn't bear to look over at Key, or Neelie. Key was right though, speed was a wild freedom. North changed gears, coming down into third with a squeal. The truck slowed too quickly, North lost the gas pedal, stamped down for it and the truck shot ahead, grinding in the reluctant gear. A hill slowed them; the road was washed out on the right so North went straight for the middle. He heard a choking, saw Neelie bounce eye-level, then an arm grabbed her, held her down, protected her.

Topping the hill the truck went briefly airborne then slammed onto the downhill slope; North and Key yelled, Neelie cried out. North let go of the wheel briefly, to pat Neelie for comfort, then the truck slued sideways towards a ditch, North's strength dragged it back on the gravel road, flying across a rise.

A horn blared, the grill of a Dodge one-ton hogged the road. North yanked the wheel, the GMC tipped into the drainage ditch, front tires in too deep, the truck all but helpless. Caught by its fender, the tire skidded along the ditch, cab at an angle. The truck plowed on. The Dodge never stopped, leaving only a long blast of receding horn. The GMC thumped to a halt, quivered, settled. Dust rose over the ditch then drifted away, the right side of the truck lay half buried in the ditch; the left tires spinning off caked red dirt.

Key fell out on the ditch side and crawled up the banking. When he leaned on his left arm, half way out of the ditch, he cried out; "Shit." Eyes closed, he lay motionless, then used his elbow and right arm to keep crawling. Neelie appeared at the truck window when she heard that single oath. She too crawled free, rolled sideways and sat up, her chin and blouse a bloody mess. Seeing Key sprawled on the flattened grass above her, she got up carefully and walked to him, looked down, said his name, but he did not open his eyes.

The truck groaned again. Neelie looked back, on the

driver's side the jammed door was forced open. Neelie wiped her nose, Key rolled over, stopped before resting weight on his left arm. Sure enough it was North, no one else could have forced that door. North appeared, first his head and shoulders and then the rest of him. Key lay back, Neelie sat down beside him.

North jumped the ditch to his companions. Despite Neelie looking up and calling to him, North knelt and when he reached out to her face she saw his big hand trembling, shaking something terrible. "Neelie, I didn't mean this to happen...you're bleeding, is your nose broke?"

"North, quit, you're scaring the birds." A flock of cowbirds was already mid-flight, gone into the pale dusk sky. Neelie rubbed where the blood crusted on her chin. "Sit down or somethin', I can't look up at you this way, it makes my head hurt."

She couldn't have said more troubling words. North sat on the bank next to her and turned her head in his hands, looked hard at her, trying to judge her condition. His eyes were filling, one corner of his mouth spasmed; Neelie was scared.

"Her nose ain't broke. But my wrist is god damn it." Key, of course, lying motionless on his back, staring at the darkening sky, his left arm carefully held across his chest. Neelie started to giggle, then she laughed and North rubbed his jaw, found himself laughing. Even Key got caught, had to roll over and half-sit up as a small laughing cough escaped him.

Then Neelie leaned on North, her body hiccuping occasionally but relaxed, released. Her weight was a feather's touch against North's humming flesh. He stared at the truck corpse. One tire had burst and he could see its innards, wire and black rubber interwoven with metal strings. Neelie touched him, "You're cut." North followed where he felt her hand and saw his wrist opened to his elbow, bleeding but not bad. "Yeah, not like that ole truck though. Axle's broke, tire's blown, heck of a wreck."

"We got to get home, North." She stared at him, then glanced at Key who other than lying back down showed no sign of movement. She pushed a toe into Key's ribs, he grunted. "It was you grabbin' me in there, wasn't it?" Key didn't answer. "You set up, Key Larkin, you ain't hurt that bad." She made as if to kick him harder and all he did was draw his left arm closer to his chest. Neelie rubbed at the mess on her blouse. Her voice was lower, softer, almost with an edge of kindness. "You ain't foolin' me, Key Larkin. You get up." Key didn't respond so Neelie snorted in disgust.

Then she spoke to North as if Key wasn't in listening range. "You were hangin' on to the wheel and I bounced up and down and hit my nose and someone grabbed me, pulled me in close and I quit bouncin'. Think I owe him a thank-you?"

North knew that right behind his cousin's eager, worried face Key was struggling to sit up. "Neelie, sayin' thanks to Key's like tryin' to bribe a grass fed pony with last year's hay. Don't think the words mean much to him, never heard him say them, not never."

His wrist was broke and it hurt but it was North's sermon hung in his mind. Key shut his eyes hard, squeezed till the spots blinded him. When he finally stood up, wavering on funny legs, Neelie was watching but had nothing smart to say. North was nearby, ready to protect her. Key felt a small loss he would not consider. "We best get walkin' you two, less you got some other idea. That truck's done for." He talked to cover the ache in his whole left side. He felt North's stare and didn't return it. North raised his head as if angry words waited inside but Neelie slipped her hand into his fist and he relented, almost patted her on the head but knew better. Key watched the performance and felt the deeper edge of once again being alone.

Dark came in fast, only the light gravel of the road gave them a trail to follow. Neelie flinched every time something rustled or moved in the tall roadside grass but she refused each time North offered a piggyback ride. She was too much a lady, she said, for such an indignity. And too brave, although her voice falter on the final word.

Key followed, slow and unmoved to hurry when North commanded. Just his way, Key said, he hated walking, didn't plan to move faster than he had to. They got maybe two miles when a truck came at them, its headlights bouncing and skipping over the gravel surface. North drew Neelie in close to give the truck room but Key kept walking. On past North straight at the truck as if the glare and engine noise weren't in his world. For a brief moment Key was outlined in the truck lights; North saw the big red lettering told him it was another GMC, a new one this time. And about to run over his friend.

The truck ground to a stop, dust from its wheels covered Key but the boy kept walking till he hit the grill and stood there, between the two headlights, a high, thin, lopsided silhouette.

A head poked out on the driver's side. "That you, North McKendrick?" It was Charlie Rushton. "Yes sir."

"Thought so, had word the ranch's Jimmy was stuck out here, knew your folks were to Trinidad celebratin'. Thought I'd come get you, save your uncle the trip. Figured I'd find Key with you. Didn't count on the little girl. I already called Ray, told him what I was doin'."

North felt Neelie's fury and despite himself started to laugh until she poked him in the ribs. "Neelie's fine, sir. Me too. I don't know about Key." "Can't be nothin' too serious, you all get in. Him, too." Rushton leaned across the seat and opened the door for Neelie; North hesitated but Key walked 'round the back of the truck, crawled in over the tailgate and settled in up against the cab without having to be told.

As North settled himself inside, next to Neelie, Rushton nodded once, his head tilted back towards Key's head showing in the truck cab window; "Boy's got some smarts after all." That was all that was said until they got to the ranch where the lights were on and the old Ford truck waited. North shivered, felt Neelie stir beside him. Ray was waiting for them at the kitchen door; inside, through the window, North saw Mrs. McKendrick busying herself filling pots with water, setting them on the stove. Her face was determinedly down, refusing to look out to where the children stood. She even refused to acknowledge Neelie as the child was pushed by her father to go inside and ask for comfort. North felt that same tension, if he spoke, if he let go at all, the world would crash around him

Slowly, awkward with only one hand, Key climbed over the tailgate and banged hard, once, on the truck door; Rushton started up his new truck and backed out of the yard, the roar of his engine filling space, allowing a bit more time before words had to be said.

North went first; "It was me drivin', my keys, my choice." He could not meet his uncle's eyes. He was aware of Key, standing to one side, still holding that arm, no one paying him much attention. In the kitchen he heard the rattled pans, a few muttered words but nothing erupted, nothing blew. McKendrick spoke and surprised North. "It ain't the blame that's important. You done a fool thing, and you risked Neelie. You'll pay out for a long time. First there's cash for towin' the truck out a that ditch. Then earnin' trust back, that'll be the toughest."

North was dizzy; "I'll work all summer to get it paid off, won't be no trouble to your or the misses, or Rushton." Ray didn't make it any easier; "It's goin' to take more'n hard work, North. You know that. But you might make the money end easier by gettin' your friend here to help you, he's partly to blame." North jumped. "He'll help, Mr. McKendrick. Even if I have to break his other arm."

Ray McKendrick was relentless; "You'll find Mr. Rushton less willin' to trust you again, boys, till you prove yourselves. Don't know how long, but it won't be easy." Then as if North's words about Key finally sank in, he turned and took a long, silent look at the Larkin boy. "Get inside, the missus knew something would be broke. Might as well be you, less of a loss to the rest of us anyway."

The worst of what Ray said came to North; there was no dislike or temper in his casual dismissal of Key, just matter-of-fact and relieved, as he said. Neelie was all right, North looked no worse for the accident; the truck was totaled but it was close to wore out anyway. The only real casualty was Key Larkin. Had it a kind of retribution Ray admired.

Then Ray confounded North. "Be careful, boy, your aunt's on a tear and I ain't too sure I'd go in there 'ceptin' if you don't she'll come lookin' for you. Watch it, boy. She's trouble right now." He was laughing, looking over at Key and shaking his head and laughing, and North had no idea why.

There was no doubt Key had broken his wrist and when Mama set it Key's face went white, the only time I ever saw that happen. But he never cried, never made any noise until it looked as if Mama was torturing him on purpose. Thinking about it now, I would guess she was applying extra pressure as revenge for her spoiled evening. Whether she did this on purpose or not, I don't think even she would have known. Nineteen years of marriage when you're not forty is half of your life. And to have another woman's bastard child spoil the celebration could raise bitter feelings in the kindest of women. Mama was a strong, loving woman, but she was no saint.

I sat on the bottom step of the stairs and could look into the kitchen and observe the proceedings. In a scene which was repeated several times in the next few years, I saw my mother wash and clean and bind the wounds of my beloved cousin, and Key. I heard her scold and mutter and complain to North about the carelessness and lack of feeling while my father sipped at some cold breakfast coffee and then strayed into the office to pretend to sort out more of Rushton's paperwork. She said nothing to Key, not even a question as she bound up his arm and tied it with an extra knot.

I recognize now that during this night things passed between Mama and North and my father that I never was privileged to share, a bond and understanding which would add to my jealousy if it had been spoken out loud. I think it was this night that North found a true family, despite his insistence all evening on calling Papa "Mr." until Papa told him kindly but firmly to shut up and what happened to Uncle Ray or just Ray.

Even worse for me was that I did not comprehend the profound change in Key, which would affect my life in the ensuing years. All I could see of him was once again the injured hero, the silent suffering boy whose mouth tightened in a stoic line until his eyes slowly rolled up in his head and Papa intervened, said they'd best take the boy to the hospital or at least tell his ma that he was injured.

Mama put it all in perspective. "Oh yes, let's take this...child into town where they can rebandage his arm and give him an aspirin and charge us a nice bit of money 'cause this happened while he was here with us and his delightful mother will talk about how badly we treat her boy. Oh yes, certainly, Ray, let's take this...poor child right into town so he can be treated better."

Her outburst startled me, I can still see its effect on Key. His face went whiter, if possible, and his mouth drew into the thinnest of lines. But he managed to keep anything at all from showing in his eyes. I believe it was then that any bond which might have formed between Key and my parents dissolved in the usual excuse of harsh words and envy and irrational anger. Mama wrapped the last bit of cloth around the arm and tugged hard enough that Key finally grunted, deep in his chest, where he could not hold back on the pain.

Papa ended the matter by grabbing up Key, with North following he shoved Key in the truck cab and drove off into the dark. Not a word was spoken on the trip, North told me later, and Mama and I didn't find out what happened even after they returned, Papa's face grim, the boys silent and obviously worn out.

North told me finally that when he and Papa did find Marie Larkin she was drunk and wrapped up with a man in a bar and barely seemed to understand when Papa interrupted and told her that her son had busted his wrist, did she want him to come home so she could take care of him. Papa still believed that there was good in the most base and evil of us.

Marie Larkin laughed in his face and Ray jerked back from the stink of her whiskey breath, then she cursed in such a foul string of words that North hurried out of the bar with his uncle not far behind him. Obviously the woman didn't care, obviously Claudie was right; they took Key back home with them and never mentioned going to the hospital again.

I thought, in the morning, that it was all over with, finished, that the harsh words were forgiven, that the extra fine breakfast of eggs and flapjacks and syrup and thick bacon cooked just right meant that Mama was apologizing and we were all back where we started, a loving, small unit which now included North and Key.

Key's wrist mended quickly. He rode with the stiff bandage for two weeks before he and North cut if off with a castration knife, using the sharp curved blade with skill. So the wrist healed crooked, with a knot at the outside, but it never seemed to bother Key.

His ma never once got in contact with our family or inquired about her son. From North's description it is possible she didn't remember my father and his visit into the bar. And knowing the company she kept, none of her companions would bother to remind her in the morning that her son had been hurt.

It was a busy summer for the two boys; they had a truck to pay off. Key especially put in extra hours and Papa had Rushton pay him direct to give him a sense of responsibility, not because anyone thought it would work. North was religious in his extra chores which was what we all expected. By summer's end the tow bill was paid on the truck and Rushton had brought in a slightly newer Ford truck to be used as the ranch vehicle. North got to slowly pay off and eventually ended up owning the battered GMC

That summer and the following year I became a woman, my figure developed much to my embarrassment, my hips and breasts were too obvious and the boys watched me, whistled at me when they knew North wasn't around and that made me even angrier. Key on the other hand paid me no mind, as if I didn't exist. Perhaps the truck accident and the aftermath of Papa's harsh words stopped him from considering me as any sort of female at all.

I also suspect that Key had so many females waiting for him that my country charms, as well protected as they were by Key's only friend and my papa, kept him from ever thinking about me in a sexual manner. It is amazing how wrong we can be about attempts to understand another human's thoughts. At the center of each male's predations on me, I presumed it was because of me, my charm, my figure, my talent or lack of it that attracted or detracted from my desirability.

Like all children, and at fifteen I was still a child, I presumed that whatever happened among those of my acquaintance, it revolved around me, that I was somehow to blame. North suffered from this disease also, for in him it was a full-blown illness, that he was responsible, how could he not be, for all the sadness and the early death of his mother.

Me, I simply took on the notion that because Key Larkin paid no attention to me, I must be extremely deficient in some sort of sexual, female, feminine attribute which I could not quite understand. So I became more obnoxious, more physical, strong, athletic, yet doing well in school. There would have to be something, or someone, who would seek me out as a desirable woman before I could possibly get over the lack which kept a boy like Key from wanting me. After all, if he would sleep with some of the women who were pointed out to me, why wouldn't he at least look at me or tease me like he used to or maybe he and North would let me ride with them, be with them the way we had been before the truck accident.

I never fully appreciated the pain which North felt upon seeing me afterwards, covered with blood, pale, trembling, trying to make him laugh. He must have been fully convinced that his world had come crashing down again as once again he had not fulfilled his responsibility. He had broken his promise to my father to protect me. It took North a long time to get over that devastation. As for Key, he simply shut me out, knowing that whatever he did, I was closed off to him, poison, unattainable and therefore not worth the risk and trouble. North and my parents meant more to him than an ugly, rough-mouthed country girl

Key turned seventeen just after the next Christmas, which again he did not spend with us. North finally got to met some of our far-flung relatives that year, for an ancient aunt had died just before Christmas and we had a family gathering in town, at Papa's one remaining uncle's large home. North was reserved, and uncomfortable, but then as a family we were all surprised by the numbers of McKendricks and Bachs and Altons who showed up to honor Aunt Roberta.

No one knew where Key disappeared to during the holidays. He came back as usual, thinner, worn, silent, at mid-January, when school had been in session for two weeks, grinning and unwilling to share any stories with North.

That summer, with North also seventeen, my parents' twentieth anniversary came and went and only because I remembered the date of the truck accident did I think to make a card for them and Mama quietly thanked me and put it in the front room where no one ever went and so no one saw the card. She must have been mad at Papa about something terrible for there was no celebration meal, but we never felt it in the day-to-day routine of a ranch summer.

There would be days when our meals consisted of half-boiled macaroni with fried slices of bologna and canned peas which were barely edible. I can't imagine what must have been tormenting Mama to produce such torture, and then a change would come over her, the meals would be brisket and hot beans, fresh corn, even salad made with lettuce instead of marshmallows and flavored gelatin.

During the second year Key lived in the 'dobe, he and North kept up their regime of hard work as if paying for the truck found them a routine they dared not break. It didn't matter to me; I was studying and learning how to flirt, and North and Key and my papa were of no use to me at all.

That summer Key rode full time for Charlie Rushton, living up to the old line camp, while North stayed down at our place and kept laboring for Papa, doing the dirty jobs of trying to fix, one more time, the Dubble Wells pump which Rushton refused to replace, and always, forever, digging post holes and stringing wire.

Key went up into the mountains, tracking down Rushton's half-wild cattle and riding a string of Rushton's broncs. He brought the horses down in the fall cow-broke and quiet. In that matter, Key was a genius. Even Rushton said so.

By the fall of '59, the boys were seniors in high school, kept there mostly by Papa's word that if they quit there were out on their own, no ranch, no pay-check from Charlie Rushton through the winter, no meals cooked by Mama who was back to her true form of stews and roasts and wonderful fruit pies. I can understand North hanging in, he had ambition to go on to college though his grades could be better. Key, as usual, was a complete surprise. He chose also to stay in school. I believe it was on North's account. We never saw a report card, I don't know who signed them even, since it was obvious that his mother didn't care, but one of his teachers slipped and said she couldn't understand how a boy who studied so little could get the grades that Key did.

Consequently, their senior year, it was only North and Key and three other ranch boys and two townies who made up the male side of the graduating class. Several of the absent boys had gone into the army and wrote home sad letters from their station in Germany. But for Key and North, and Papa, life went on at the ranch, endlessly, relentlessly, to the point of exhaustion. Working full time as a cowhand and going to school was hard for one as tough as North; Key added the element of women and often I saw him sneaking in at dawn, and I knew, from all the gossip about town, just where he had been and what he'd been doing.

I wrote in a journal that year, which was a fancy name for a notebook I had left over from the previous year. It was filled with my longings and odd curiosities. Friends and I huddled at school and talked endlessly about our movie star crushes and none of us wanted to relate that ecstasy to the smelly, dumb, foul-mouthed males who were all we had available to us in school. To imagine sex together with these boys was unthinkable.

One special event of that year was Christmas, which Key finally shared with us. Eager as I was to involve Key in my fantasies, I knew instinctively that his presence at our celebration could be disastrous. When Papa suggested he stay, Mama seemed surprisingly indifferent and once again it was I who complained, like the spoiled child I was, that Key was an outsider, always trouble, and why did we have to share our holiday with him. It was in this manner that an invitation was issued to Key, to spend the Christmas holiday at the McKendrick ranch instead of doing the usual disappearing act. When Papa uttered the words, Key was slow to respond, searching each of us in turn, wanting to see just how deliberate and well intentioned the invitation was. I saw him linger at Mama's face; she shrugged and said, "I think it's a fine idea, Key, if you want." Less than cordial, certainly, but she was, for once, not pushing Key away.

North, of course, was pleased, excited even, although I suspect he thought he'd outgrown such excitement by then. I knew enough that when Key in turn came to ask me with those mute eyes, I smiled my most gracious smile learned from my mother and the recent memory of her elbow dug into my ribs, echoed her; "Why yes, I think it's a grand idea."

It was in this way that the invitation was issued and Key Larkin came the last day of school to spend the entire Christmas holiday with us.

Chapter Six

All by themselves his fingers rubbed the bony protrusion on his left wrist until Key grimaced at the now familiar gesture. A poor reminder of his own bad judgment.

He and North were riding out to rope a tree, a whole new experience for Key. They'd drag it back carefully for Neelie and her ma to decorate. It was the first time for Key, a virgin he thought, the first time in years that could be said about him.

His ma thought a potted cactus or a green paper cutout were enough. He knew to feel indifference at her way but a Christmas tree with ornaments and silvery tinsel, a few candles, some songs, these were the images he'd had read to him in school, listened to and wanted without knowing why.

Each January when school was back in session and Key heard the reality of the individual Christmas, the drunken fathers and crying mothers, the burned turkey, the arguing relatives, then he knew he was lucky, he had to suffer none of these tribulations. He also knew that the McKendricks were not like most of those families. And when they had invited him to share

Christmas with them, this time he accepted.

"Come on, Key, step up on that bronc and let's ride." North sat way up on a sorrel's back and looked like for once he and the horse fitted. Key swung up on the outlaw bay who of course spooked and bucked out a few times with Key laughing and fanning the bay's shoulders with his winter cap for a bit of exercise. When the bay quit, horse and rider drifted in beside North on the new sorrel. And North's few words stunned Key; "Daydreamin', huh. Plannin' on what to get Ray and Aunt Claudie and even our little Neelie."

Key leaned back against the old saddle's high cantle and tried to cover his tracks. "Why you guessed it, you got it all figured out, I can't decide what out a all them stores in town I'll pick up for the family." There was a heartbeat when the last word stuck in his mouth until North said something dumb about it being a pretty day and gave Key time to collect himself, get his mouth working again. Then, too, maybe North didn't like Key using the word 'family' about the McKendricks.

North couldn't meet Key's eyes. Gifts cost money, Key never had none. This time most of his summer earnings had gone to paying off the end of North's debt on the old Jimmy. North shook his head, the bay jumped and Key let him. North gave them a head start and then gigged the sorrel into a run. Rushton had delivered the horse two days ago in a snowstorm, said he thought it might be the horse to suit North's size. Made it sound like an offhand gesture, but it was a Christmas present from the old man, and a forgiveness of sort.

The sorrel was fun. North felt it gather muscle to run, and leaned forward to let the big horse go. They had themselves a horse race, first time he rode a horse big enough to maybe catch Key and the stubborn mealy bay.

Even as they raced, way back in North's mind was

the notion that if Ray McKendrick were standing at the door watching, judging as the boys whooped and hollered, he would never let the sorrel go full out, he'd never try to catch Key and the bay. Then too, Key wouldn't be spurring the little horse that way, desperate to keep ahead of the much bigger sorrel. The way they were riding, no self-respecting rancher would treat a good working horse so. Then again, they was only cowboys, ranch hands, not yet full-growed and still allowed some foolishness.

Each boy slowed their mount back to a walk, and felt the labored breathing and knew they'd run off some energy but it was right, it felt good in the cold air, the bright sum, the rock-strewn mesa ahead of them, no school for a week, no one to tell then what to do, except each other and their own conscience. Each boy slapped their horse on its wet shoulder and laughed with the pleasure.

North wouldn't look at Key. "Got to you, didn't it?" Key nodded; "Yeah, I can hear him, he's right too, I guess. But damn it felt good." They rode in silence after that, in no particular direction. It seemed to North as if Key was letting the bay pick and choose until they came to the mouth of a brushy draw, the low scrub oak now all copper with dried leaves, some of the juniper on the north side dusted with snow. A good place to start looking, North thought, until Key jabbed his bay with one spur and the horse made a tight circle, then Key let him out and he spooked, ran a few yards until Key hauled him up snug.

North rode a short trot to catch up. "What'd you buy them, North? Huh?" North thought it over, put some logic and sense to work and came up with the scary notion Key never bought a Christmas present before. "Nothin' fancy, I...well, Uncle Ray helped. I got Neelie a hair thing, and Aunt Claudie a scarf Ray says she admired all fall. That's it, Ray, he told me not to worry 'bout him, he don't need nothin'. But the ladies, can't ever forget them." He chanced a look, saw nothing on his friend's face, about what he would expect. "Goin' to make a few things too. Little stuff, kind of fun." "Like what?" Key's face opened, his eyes got that light. "Little things, Key, nothin' fancy. Like maybe a belt for Uncle Ray or a promise to Aunt Claudie to help her plant trees in the spring like she's been askin' me to do. Little things. "

Key's face went into that blank look again, like the matter were nothing after all. "Guess I need to get to town, huh, buy them each a pretty." North grunted; "Yeah, Key, somethin' pretty."

Then Key's bay bolted again. North held the sorrel back. As if it was the bay taking off, with that spur buried in its hide so North wouldn't guess how bad Key felt not thinking about gifts at Christmas. He watched the bay circle and buck until he felt sorry for it, but not the rider, and let the sorrel out to make it a horse race again. It was good to have a horse strong enough to out-gallop Key and the bay pony.

It took two hours to find the right tree. First North said that one wasn't big enough and Key asked how he knew and what made it the right size and was there a shape too he needed to recognize. Then it was Key who passed on a taller tree, didn't have just the right number of branches, as if he'd know what was right and proper for a Christmas tree. They swapped complaints and small lies and the horses got tired slogging through the fresh snow.

As if by miracle the perfect tree exposed itself, each boy claimed he'd seen it first. A pine maybe six feet tall, set apart from its neighbors so its branches were full on all sides. Key said it was a piñon, and North being from Texas, allowed he had no opinion on its ancestry. They left the horses tied loose to a tree; both seemed content to half-sleep, rest up from the morning's jaunt. When North looked back as they climbed to the tree, he saw steam coming off the broncs and knew for certain they'd ridden too hard. Uncle Ray'd be real mad if he saw those horses right about now.

Key thought to bring an ax so he started to cut the tree but gave up part way, steam rising off him too. North watched over Key's back, keeping an eye on the horses. Occasionally one would lift its head or flick an ear in vague interest but mostly they slept, hind foot cocked, ears loose, eyes partly closed. North found he envied them.

When Key gave him the ax it took only a few hard strikes to bring the tree down. Key stepped back, wiped his wet mouth and shivered in the sudden chill of not working. The tree rolled partway downhill and startled the broncs awake; the sorrel thought on bolting but North must have tied him tight enough so the bronc had to be content with snorting and flattening its ears. The tree caught a rock and held, where North picked it up and dragged it to the flat.

"We ain't tyin' that monster to the bay." Key's voice was mocking, North wasn't sure what was wrong. "It's all yours, North." That was it, Key still was on the outside looking in. North shook his head but kept silent. They both checked their cinches before mounting. Key's bay stood placidly, the sorrel swung its head while North dallied the tree, leaving lots of room so it wouldn't scoot up and tangle the sorrel's hind feet. That tree wasn't much for a horse of this size to pull, he thought as he mounted. Mostly it would just skim over the snow's surface. North was tired and ready to get home.

Three strides was all it took: the sorrel spun around,

stared at the tree following him, then reared, spun back, kicked at the object and when it kept following him bolted against the tightening rope, kicking, half sideways, running, bucking, all at the same time. Key held in the bay, laughing at first but then fearful for North. The sorrel ran, tail flagging, hind legs skittering under its belly in terrified panic.

The bronc hit a cactus, went to its knees, squalling from the prickers. North was jolted from the saddle, the bronc came up running, North holding on under the sorrel's neck till a front leg caught him on the thigh, too close and he let go. The sorrel ran kicking but the devil tree still followed. The rope wove back and forth over its rump until finally, inevitably, the rope got under the sorrel's dock.

Its blond tail clamped down, the horse hit a choppy stride, the tree got stuck in between two rocks and the horse quit. Eyes rolling, mouth white with foam, the sorrel trembled, turning in the deep snow to keep the dangerous tree in clear view while holding its tail firm so the rope could not shift and burn such a tender place.

North wiped off snow, his hands quick to find cactus spines in his arms, his sides, even his back. He made no move towards the snorting bronc, not yet. Key let the bay drift in close before he stepped off, the bay wandered to the sorrel and both horses snuffled at each other and began to settle down. Key pulled the old, half-broke knife from his jacket, picked out the one useful blade, took a deep breath and eased a few of the spines from North's side where the canvas coat hadn't protected him. "Damn," North said. Key kept his own mouth shut. Better North than him.

Snow filled North's collar, melted, ran down inside his long johns and soaked into his britches. Flesh showed through a tear in his jeans, white skin that filled red. "You cut bad, North?" North looked down, flinched, saw the blood. "Just a scrape." Key yanked on another spine, North grimaced at the effort. "Be glad that's all you got, North." They looked each other straight in the eye, knowing how close it had been. Key went on, "Guess we know why Rushton gave you that bronc." North glared at Key who turned away after taking one more spine from North's backside

The sorrel stood for North, too frightened by the rope to move. Allowing no fight, North grabbed the bridle, hauled the bronc's head around and picked up the tail, shifted the rope, which as it slid down the sorrel's haunch threatened to spook the bronc. "No you sum-bitch, no." North's voice was enough to settle the bronc.

As North went to mount, the sorrel lifted a hind hoof in warning. North kicked the sorrel above the hock. "Stand, you miserable-." Then North looked up at Key who had to be ready to burst. "Whoa." North swung up, pulled in the tree by its rope and the sorrel panicked, eyes white, ears flat. But when the big horse tried to rear North's fist punched it alongside the neck and the horse settled to North's command.

It took a while to get home, Key used the time to half-doze on the tired bay. The sorrel progressed in short, timid steps punctuated by half kicks that got nothing but a spur and a curse. The tree arrived at the McKendricks mostly in one piece but left behind it a trail of green needles and broken tips.

They didn't tell the McKendricks much about the accident, except to say that North got scratched by a tree limb jumped in too close. There was an odd look on Ray's face as he put up the tree. "Boys, you brought us a mighty pretty Blackjack Pine. Where'd you find it?" Key refused to look at North and North tried to describe where they'd cut the tree without mentioning any of the sorrel's antics.

Finally the pitch-soaked crown got covered by a

paper angel and glass balls of a different colors and carved animals got hung from the branches. Any obvious holes were filled in with long paper chains that Key remembered being forced to make in grade school. Now he stood on tiptoe and draped a fresh chain from a real bad hole he'd seen made, when that rope tugged the tree through a nest of particular rocks, the sorrel kicking the whole trip.

When everyone stepped back to admire the work, the tree looked pretty enough it needed a song sung in its honor, a glass of something raised in high toast. Mrs. McKendrick wanted to celebrate. She and Neelie had been baking while the boys were gone so long, they'd decorated two dozen gingerbread men, with hats and vest and boots, colored hair and silver candied dots for eyes. Mrs. McKendrick's had an apron and a smile, and there were three with big muscles outlined and pink cheeks meant for North. Ray's had a beard which wasn't right but Neelie said they didn't have a cookie cutter that was so tall and didn't smile. She gave Key one gingerbread man. It had yellow curls for hair and those silver dot eyes. North ate his three likenesses greedily, biting each one in half. Key played with his, uncertain as to what he was meant to feel. North ate until his uncle laughed and snapped the head off his own doubtful likeness. The women went into the kitchen for more cookies and some hot cider and Key put his gingerbread man in his shirt pocket.

It was of all things the ornaments that troubled Key. Those paper chains, a wire star made by Ray to please his newly wed wife, tiny animals carved crudely but meant to be a donkey and a camel, even a lace doily used for serving platters in fancy restaurants had its place on the tree.

Claudie said they put candles on the tree Christmas Eve and lit them but never left the room until they burned out. It was late when they did this, and they would sit in the darkened room to watch the single lights, singing a carol or talking, and sometimes Ray would recite as much of "The Night Before Christmas" as he could remember, with Neelie's prompting of course.

Before supper Key volunteered to help with the chores and had a chance to ask Mr. McKendrick, could he go in town with him some day? He didn't say why but the man guessed, even asked if Key had any money, Key lied and said yes, he'd kept some back all summer. A lie but a kind one, not making McKendrick worry, making believe Key understood and accepted the responsibility of having been invited to share Christmas.

Ray took him to Trinidad the day before Christmas Eve. Very softly, Key said he wanted to see his ma. McKendrick nodded and asked if he preferred to spend the holiday with her. Key felt like he'd been sucker-punched. "No, sir, I don't live there...I just need to see her."

He'd walk into town later, meet up with McKendrick at the hardware store. "Maybe you'll help me, boy. I want to pick up a knife North will like and maybe, well, you know him better'n I do. What he likes and all." Key nodded; "Yes, sir." This way he knew he wouldn't be abandoned at his ma's.

She was drunk, sitting in the small back room she used too often. The room smelled; Key back-stepped when he got a whiff from the partly opened door. He almost turned to leave, had one foot in the air when her voice stopped him; "That you, pretty boy? Come back to take care a me?" Key shuddered, wiped at his suddenly damp face. Now there was no choice but to enter the room, and see his mother.

She wasn't quite visible in the dark. Heavy cloths were pinned over the one small window and there were no lights to turn on. When his eyes got used to the thick air, he could make out her silhouette, then her features became clearer. She was thin, and wrinkled, her hair was streaked gray at the roots, the rest a bright orange he'd never seen before.

Maybe she wasn't drunk; "It's good you've come home. I been missin' you some." Her voice was soft with the husky drawl she used on her men. "We can have our own celebration." She stood up, held out her hand and Key smelled her scent again, that reek of whiskey and sex, and he pulled back instinctively. She must have felt his disgust. "No, ma'am, I come for my things is all. He'll be back soon enough I reckon. Whoever he is." She fell backwards, hit the chair at her knees and slumped into it. "Yeah, he said he'd be back when he got his cigarettes and a fresh pint of whiskey. To celebrate, him and me, we'll have our own Christmas, don't need you hangin' 'round. Take what you want, boy, I been through your junk, sold off what had value, ain't worth much but it helped."

He was froze solid listening to her, so cold he didn't care, so fearful that she sold whatever of value he'd ever owned. It couldn't be much, no more than outgrown clothes, maybe a pair of boots the rancher gave him, a leather jacket, a knit sweater one of the ladies pressed on him, knitted for her own son, a lady trying to use the present as a reason for him to come inside with her. He didn't care, whatever his ma'd sold it couldn't be much, there was so little of value in his life.

Unless it was what he had come for; he doubted she would look at a book as a possible sale, no one in this town would give more'n a quarter or maybe fifty cents for a secondhand book, wasn't even for school, had no sex in it, no steamy paragraphs some folks could heat up over.

"Thanks, Ma, you and him have a good Christmas." She nodded, at least he thought she did, and went back to looking nowhere past his head, not seeing him at all. It didn't matter, most likely she wouldn't remember he'd even come for the brief time.

The book was where he left it, high on a kitchen shelf, back of a dust-covered pitcher no one ever filled up to offer coffee and a biscuit to a neighbor or put syrup in it for a 'pass the syrup please' at breakfast over flapjacks and bacon. He had put the book next to the pitcher, admiring the painted flowers, wondering now as he fingered the book should he take the pitcher and wash it, give it to Mrs. McKendrick instead of what he already thought to offer her.

No. The pitcher belonged to his ma. He shoved it back against the greasy wall. It would be a terrible blasphemy filled with spite to give such a gift to Mrs. McKendrick. But the book really belonged to him. A long time in the past one of Marie's men had left it, actually suggested Key read what it contained, said he might like the words, might take to their song. Only one of the men that Key remembered clearly that he liked.

An anthology of poems it was called, and inside were all sorts of pieces from childish doggerel by Milne to Shakespeare which Key read and didn't take to but could almost see the merit, and the newer poets, like Frost and Spender who he understood, and Eliot and Cummings who annoyed him. And one named Henry Reed who wrote about war and love.

Neelie would like the book. He would clean the cover with a damp towel and rub it shiny with harness oil. And he would write inside the front, like some of the library books, with 'thank you' and 'love' and 'happy birthday' scribed so all could know who gave the book and why.

For Mrs. McKendrick he'd chosen three poems

which he would copy and tie together. Special poems that drove a deep line into how he felt, what he saw and maybe she would begin to understand and like some part of him. But the book went to Neelie. Dividing it was the only way he could give each a gift. For Ray he had composed a promissory note, for a cleaning of the winter pens without complaint and without pay.

For North, he could not decide. He couldn't come near buying anything, besides with Ray getting the boy a new knife, how could Key compete? He'd think of something, he had to, but for now it was time to get out of the stinking house. Key shrugged into his jacket, tucked the book under one arm, stuck a hand in each pocket and walked out the door.

It was a good knife Ray McKendrick set on the truck seat between them. Wrapped in brown paper and tied up with string, it looked no different than the supply of nails in their box or the bucket of roofing tar next to Key's boots. Small things to keep the ranch going, so no one would ask what was in another parcel.

Key envied North, he could already see his eyes when the parcel was given to him, tearing at its wrapping, revealing the engraved bone handle, the stainless blade, the smooth-working mechanism that unlocked the knife so it rested safely in a man's palm, ready for work, weighted just right for any task. A gift good enough for Northern McKendrick.

Supper waited for them, a fine pot roast and potatoes, salted green beans and a cobbler again, Key's favorite. He said little during the meal, just nodding when Ray spoke of Key visiting his ma. He felt the women's eyes touch on him and ducked his head, conscious of not wanting her to see the smallest bit inside.

It took him five hours to hand-copy the three poems for Mrs. McKendrick. Then, exhausted and elated, he got inspired and stole one of North's belts. On its exact middle, across the back, clean and simple, he carved North' name. When it came out looking good enough, he tried carving a cactus on one side, a horse's head on the other. The head looked more like a cow, or a mule, but it made its point and Key was satisfied.

For more than two months, at odd hours, North's fingers had stuttered through the horse-hair hitching, a skill taught him by one of the sprung-handed cowboys helped keep an eye on him for his ma when he was little. He made a brooch for Mrs. McKendrick, using contrasting colors of a white mane and the deep black of the bay's tail and some bright yellow from a horse Ray said was a palomino but it didn't have a white mane and tail. The brooch was in the shape of a butterfly, and North had taken great pains to get the wings as colorful as he could.

For Ray he'd hitched a watch chain to replace the old rawhide one he usually carried. Maybe this one, in degrees of white and black and gray, would become his favorite.

Of course he already had the store-bought gifts but they looked puny to him. Neelie had all that thick red hair so North hitched a long, knotted string she could use to wrap around the ends, make a pony tail with it, keep the hair out of her face when she was riding, though he loved to see her mane free, loved its wild color and the sense of movement.

It was toughest working out a gift for Key. But his name looked real good hitched in black through a square of sorrel hair. Then he used brass rivets to hold the name on the back of a belt Ray gave him, it was sort of worn-out and scarred but the name piece could be put on a nicer belt when Key had one. A good oiling, some hand rubbing and the leather wasn't so bad after all.

North let the belt run through his fingers, enjoying the tiny pricks of horsehair when he got to Key's name. Last year it'd been simple, store things like the years before. Before that it was Texas and his mother and costly new underwear and socks and one year he filled a glass jar with flowers begged from the local pharmacy and she hugged him extra for it.

This year it felt like his first adult Christmas, deciding on his own what to give and making objects for the people who meant the most to him. He physically cocked his head as he thought of the internal statement; there was a loss there, of his mother and her love but a gain, that of the McKendrick family, and Key Larkin. North felt the raised name on the belt again then put the belt down, carefully placed next to the watch chain for Ray, the brooch and the knotted ponytail thing for Neelie. The colors were shiny, the knots pretty even; North decided his gifts were almost good enough to give.

He heard Key moving around in the front room and did not call out to him. He had his preoccupation with gifts, maybe too that was what kept Key in the cold room for such a long time. Finally North wrapped his treasures in an old cotton shirt he'd outgrown and packed them in a drawer only he used. Then he lay back on his bed, unaccountably content, and fell asleep.

The musty book lies in our attic in a small box next to other objects which were once important. That Christmas being given the book startled me; it was my first adult present, the first book to acknowledge my real interests and challenge me to go outside myself and my age. Previously, my parents had given me such choices as the Nancy Drew series and teenage romance or horse books, which bored me since I had a horse and why would I want to read about them. But this anthology by Springstead, Anton, and Parleisi, published in 1940 and in reasonable condition, inducted me into a world of differing ideas.

I was always an avid reader who had gone through the children's library section and moved on without the librarian's approval into the adult section. I brought home only those books my parents would accept; I stayed at the library and read in the stacks, never at a table, consuming some of the more titillating books in our library

Being Trinidad, Colorado, in the late fifties, the list of problem books was small and rather dull compared to what I read later in college. But Key's book, most likely a college level anthology, included women poets and non-rhyming poems and free verse, and it opened a world for me. It did not radically alter my life, although in a way it was the foot in the door to later events, but I was pried from my easy reading and delighted with the new world into which I had been shoved.

Tucked into the book is a sheaf of carefully copied words, poems given to my mother that same year as her Christmas present from Key. It wasn't until many years later that I finally read all three of the poems, copied in his wavering hand, and began to understand the deliberate importance of their choosing.

There is a small footnote to my musings about our Christmas; that year. Mama cooked the best Christmas dinner I believe I have ever had. I don't know the process by which she set out to woo us, but she was successful. Papa and North killed a wild turkey that had been roaming in a flock through an abandoned apple orchard near Johnson Mesa in New Mexico. I know they didn't have any of the right licenses, but the area was so close I guess they decided it was a neighborly situation. In any case, there was no problem with their bringing the turkey home.

Papa told me later he and North had figured that turkeys grazing under and around apple trees would naturally take on a sweetness not always available in Mama's cooked birds. I think they were full of something pressed from apples and allowed to ferment, but I never said a word back then, and of course now it is too late. However it happened, the turkey was delicious. I don't know why Key wasn't included in the hunt, another question I didn't ask.

Fresh, home-made rolls, sweet churned butter, garden runner beans that Mama blanched and froze instead of canned, carrots glazed in honey and butter, mounds of the best mashed potatoes possible, relishes put up over the summer, turnip, which none of us ever liked but this time it was sweet and delicate, sliced thin, baked in a cream sauce instead of mushed and beaten, white onions in a mix of bread crumbs and herbs, again I don't know what allowed our mother to make such an effort. But believe me, it was worth every single morsel and bite, and there were no leftovers, not a speck of food remained at the end of the meal.

However, we all kept room for the pies. This year she tried a recipe from a cookbook she bought for five cents at a rummage sale, a book from England with older recipes. She made mince pie, which sounded terrible to me but it was flavorful, different, sweet and yet tart enough we all had seconds. Even Papa who hated surprises, and was taken back when he found out some of the venison he'd shot in the early fall went into the filling, ate a piece and declared the best deer he'd ever had.

But it was the apple pie that did us in; sweet yes, from apples out of that abandoned orchard where North and Papa found the turkeys. I have no idea what kinds of apples, they had been running wild for a long time, no one had lived in that canyon for over twenty-five years. Ah but the taste, the crisp pastry, the perfect cinnamon and allspice and nutmeg Mama mingled with the sugar and butter coating the slices.

Obviously I could go on and on about that meal, it stands out even now as perfection. What created it, beyond my mother's energy, was a mystery for a long time. Finally I believe I am able to see past our greed of the moment and understand the gift Mama was trying to give us all.

The knife Key helped chose for North was actually Ray McKendrick's gift to him. Along with an apology, "Boy, I've spoken hard of you in the past and now you been with us long enough I know my words ain't always the truth. Been listenin' too long to other folks, I made a mistake, here, this is for you."

The words were of more value than the gift, but Key could not stop his hands from continually smoothing the blade or feeling the intricacies of the carved bone handle.

The missus gave him a warm winter coat. She said that Neelie was partly the giver too. It was wool and canvas, with lined pockets, snaps, a storm flap. The best Key had ever owned and when he tried to say that the words got stuck in his throat and all he got out was 'pretty color ain't it.'

It was a joke when he and North exchanged presents. They all laughed, two belts, one half the size of the other, each bearing a rendition of the other's name. Neelie said it best, without any trace of laughter or surprise. "You two are brothers." Key pushed at her shoulder, North bent down and kissed the top of her head.

Mrs. McKendrick opened the box meant for her and

Ray both. The envelope lay on top, she handed it to Ray. Key offered up his new knife to slit open the glued flap, Ray accepted the gesture, withdrew the bit of paper and read it out loud. 'Good for a clean winter pen upon demand.' He looked sharply at Key, then his jaw relaxed, "Not a bad idea, boy. Thanks."

Then Mrs. McKendrick opened her folded papers and glanced up at Key in bewilderment. "What is it, Mama?" Neelie urged her mother to tell them. "Poems, dear, hand-copied poems." By then Neelie had opened her own book and it looked as if she understood what Key had done. She cradled her book, rubbed its spine, looked at him in a wary manner.

Then Claudie McKendrick read the first of the poems, Robert Frost's "The Road Not Taken." The room sighed in unison, Ray looked out a window, North fiddled with his belt. Ray nodded when Claudie paused and said, "That's nice of you, Key." And that was all. As Key thought, no one cared to hear the other two poems. He ran his fingers over the rough-hitched belt and sighed.

Later on he and North had a mock fight with their different belts over the last slice of the apple pie and Key forgave North and his uncle for not taking him along on the turkey shoot and making him feel like an outsider. He knew better, he belonged here, at least for this time.

If I could see the future, I would have done better with what I thought at the time were passing moments, when in truth they were to be all I would have of that time or place.

This is a foolish, and human, regret, one we realize as we get older, more able to see the patterns which form our lives. As younger adults, we have not gone through enough of the sequences to fully accept the limits and confines of what our lives are and will be. Even a beautiful sunrise or sunset becomes matter of fact after twenty years. But we can convince ourselves to appreciate its endless beauty at sixty as well as fifteen.

Patterns repeat, events sort out, if we allow them enough time. One of the difficult concept for humans to grasp is that despite our choosing to believe we are each unique, humanity is a repeat pattern, eventually all is discovered and the pattern begins its circle again. For a person to remain pleased, they must bring to each day an awe and wonder not manufactured but genuine, a pleasure in small things, a need to laugh and smile and enjoy. Since that Christmas, I read Key's book of poetry and began a search for more writers like these, especially women whose existence I had not known. I became enamored of Emily Dickinson and Edna St. Vincent Milay, Adrienne Rich, Linda Pastan, and Maya Angelou. They were similar only in their sex; their views on life and men, dreams and passions, were divided and yet became part of my mental wanderings.

This slow course of literary enlightenment did not prevent me from succumbing to temptation nor did it honor me with wisdom and compassion or understanding at a time when I needed those three virtues and many others to survive. What I gained from my reading was a scent of imagery, a taste and hope for more than the world I inhabited. I can remember the sound of Mama's anger when I stalled at chores to finish a poem but I was consumed with these other places and wanted to make up my own stories, put them to rhythmic meter and enchant others as I myself was enchanted.

I outgrew this fantasy of necessity; I had no gift for the poetic word. My poor family had to live with me in the interim, and they waded through this phase as they did others such as my wanting to be the first female jockey or, after North's arrival, a football player.

What I am attempting to say, and which shows up my inept handling of words, is the sense of how I was affected by the gift of those poems, and how that dent in my very timid sensibilities opened me to so much more which awaited in a different world.

Two major events occurred in the spring of 1960. The boys were both eighteen now, and eligible for the draft. North got automatic deferment because of his acceptance to college; Key on the other hand was courted and papers followed him around until he showed up for his medical. I know this only because word spread through town, a giggling, 'I told you so' story of his day with the Army board. None of the particulars were ever known but he was deemed unfit for both physical and emotional reasons. The physical quickly became a dose of clap, and no one doubted the emotional lack in Key; even the Army didn't want him.

The second event was much closer to home. In the spring of 1960 I became aware of my father's age. To me he looked the same, from the vantage point of a child to whom all those over twenty are old. His face was as usual lined and drawn, the bottom half darkly tanned, the top white from wearing his inevitable hat. His eyes showed their tiredness, the first place I began to recognize the signs. His hands were spotted and scarred, coarsened from old injuries. I loved him deeply, I still do. I can feel those hands steadying me on my first pony; he was always there, strong and clear, always right; my father. Yet this was the time I began to see him as old.

Chapter Seven

The cake sat at the back of the table, which was outside under a tree. The house wasn't roomy enough for all those who promised to show up for the party. Claudie hadn't decorated that cake with candles. It was Ray's fifty-fifth birthday and she didn't want to upset him. She'd written his name in wavering blue ice against all the white spun sugar, and Neelie drew an outline of the ranch, right down to the dirt track leading from the county road. The girl had put in green for trees, and a few stick horses chased plump plastic cattle. Those who hung around the table and saw the cake before it was cut made lots of noise about Neelie's talents. They were mostly older women, housewives, rancher's wives, tired and worn and frayed.

Ray stayed to the back, near the one elm tree that gave some shade, and tried to grin his appreciation of all the fuss. Claudie read his expression more correctly as a grimace. He hated celebrations, hated even more his age and how it separated him from his wife. The fifteen year difference had been a lot when they courted, not much as they lived through the births and death, yet now those fifteen years seemed to eat up whatever intimacy Claudie and her husband still had left to them.

There was another cake on the table, to one side and in front, loud, bright with store decoration. It was for the graduating boys; North was surrounded by school friends, boys and girls, almost the entire senior class, come all this way out to shake North's hand and laugh as he told stories. Key, naturally, stood to one side, the only person he talked with was old Charlie Rushton, spitting chaw and holding a flask of whiskey, cutting through the pretty girls and awkward boys with his old man's tongue. Key got along with Rushton better than Ray ever did. Claudie had invited the old man mostly on Key's account.

North was off to college in the fall, a two-year institute to be sure but still college, still a mark for the boy. Key was to work full-time for Charlie Rushton. And Ray was turning fifty-five. Claudie, well, she stayed home with Neelie as her company some of the time. Sweet, hardheaded Neelie who'd filled out to where Claudie couldn't make over her old dresses and shirtwaists anymore but had to buy store-bought or a yard more of material. The girl wasn't fat, just tall, a good inch over Claudie's 5'7" and shamed by her own development, hugging herself half bent over most of the time as if the pose was a shield. Claudie felt some sympathy for her child, and anger too at the child's growing figure. Claudie felt she had no man to pay attention to her any longer; Ray was too tired always, the boys had moved on, gone even though they remained physically for another month or so.

She was glad Key hadn't noticed her Neelie yet; his reputation still awed the town and Claudie knew he was a danger. In her heart, and no secret to Ray, she was glad the boy would soon be gone. But she would miss North, hulking even as a boy, massive in size, sweet in temper; with him around there was a male presence in the house, she felt him as he entered a room or even just opened a door. A good boy, always polite, offering a plate of cornbread to her first or asking permission when no one else was taking that last piece of pie.

"Ma'am, I wanted to thank you, for includin' me in the party...for these past years. Been the best time in my life." Key watched the woman, she held her face still. It was obviously not what she expected, him speaking those words. Every woman at the party seemed to stare; mother, wife, schoolmate, they would all want to see what Claudie McKendrick did next.

She was polite to him, like always; "Thank you, Key. Those two...", she indicated Ray and North with a hand. "Those two don't like all the fussin' yet they're having a good time. Look at them." She wanted his eyes off her, her words were intended to get their gray intensity focused somewhere else.

Key leaned in. and she felt him close the distance until she was uncomfortable. Then she looked straight into his pretty face and his eyes laughed, his mouth wrinkled in its familiar grin. He was teasing her. "I can't do nothin' here, ma'am, not with that crowd. You're safe, if you want to be." Why damn him he was flirting. "You take that mouth and your ideas to your lady friends, Mr. Larkin. Don't fool with me now. You've stayed decent while you lived here, leave it right for once."

The strength of her anger was a shock; Key stepped back as if she'd hit him hard, and a flash dimmed his eyes, their pain a clear sign of his surprising fragility. She was ashamed. "Yes, ma'am. I don't know much how to say what I feel, ain't had much cause to...you, ma'am, you and your mister, and North, acceptin' me, like you done. First time for me. I kinda like it." He coughed; "Best I can do in return is to get away from your home soon as I can."

He was offering himself as bait for her anger. "Key, I'm the sorry one. For hurtin' you right now. But you can't play with us like you mock the rest of the world, we're your family, we've been so for these three years. You got no right to fool with me. Not like this." He cocked his head as if not fully understanding; she herself wasn't sure of what she said. Trying to be polite, trying to tell the truth without more hurt. "Boy, you have a reputation of lovin' women, and I want to be sure you keep Neelie and me out of your gossip, away from those old biddies' tongues." There, that was plain truth enough for anyone.

"Ma'am, I've done nothin' ever to hurt you and your girl." His eyes closed, Claudie wondered if he was ill. "Not unless you ladies want me to, I won't never come to you. Each of you. I promise." An odd promise, she thought, given how he had been living, speaking to something which would never happen. She had to hope her Neelie was strong enough on her own to see through the likes of Key.

Neelie broke into their sparring and Claudie silently thanked her. "Mama, we're out of ice cream and Papa is mad at me and hello, Key, I didn't see you there." In those few words the child's voice went from girl to woman and Claudie guessed Key knew something about her daughter she herself didn't, that Neelie was more woman now than child, and Key was an attractive man. Thank God and Charlie Rushton Key was about to be removed from their life.

"Neelie, you go get the ice cream and don't fret about your pa. He's feelin' old is all. Nothin' you can do to change that fact, and nothin' you ever done can hurt him. He's just your pa gettin' old." Key stepped in, mock bowing again; "I'll help Neelie with the ice cream, ma'am." Claudie shot a hard look at him, he smiled sweetly in return. Her Neelie took more direct action, she kicked Key, lightly, in the shins just above his boot shank. "He won't play any games ;with me, Mama, I know him too well, let it be his hands freezing with the cold, it'll help keep them where they belong while I drive the truck."

Claudie smiled, relieved that her daughter understood. Soon enough she would meet a decent man, marry, and give her parents grandchildren, which might be what would bring the smile back into Ray's eyes. In the meantime, there was North to fret over. Going to Pueblo to college, a job already his working in the grounds department. He'd have to study hard, he wasn't stupid but learning took him a long time. Too bad, she thought, that Key didn't try for a scholarship. Despite himself he'd finished almost at the top of the class which none of the teachers wanted to admit since it certainly wasn't from their teaching.

Claudie stopped, rubbed both hands on her face. Enough worrying about the boys, they were graduated, at least they would be in two weeks. It was her husband and daughter deserved her fretting, not them. That's where her fussing was needed, over her child and her husband, both of them perched on the edge of new revelations.

I was sixteen that summer, just after North turned eighteen. We laughed a lot about memories, not too surprisingly we had many shared moments. The old truck and the midnight ride with its after effects. North kept the truck running for a year but now it spent most of its time sitting out in back of the lean-to where we used to keep the milch cow. Now we could laugh at that one ridiculous night among the many we shared through the long summers. It was the first time I directly survived a moment which was terrible, could have become a tragedy, and then later was a fond memory, a place where laughter was appropriate, where I could say blithely that I had wet my pants and the boys laughed even harder. That time when Neelie and Key and North went joy riding in the ranch GMC and rolled it over, the night of Ray and Claudie's nineteenth anniversary dinner in town. Even Charlie Rushton's part in the farce became fodder for our jokes.

It doesn't sound funny but North could make the incident silly with his shy manner of speech, and Key put in a few choice words of mocking deprecation, and the story came out a winner.

I was sixteen that summer and my mama told me to be extra careful at school the coming fall and my papa told me I was beautiful and to bring home any boy interested in me so he and Mama could decide if I could go out with him. It never occurred to me until he said those words that I was old enough now to date, that I could be 'interested' in a boy and vice versa. How incredibly young and innocent I was. At the beginning of that summer.

The main ranch for Rushton's holdings was set ten miles down a long rough track. For that reason Rushton now lived in town and appeared at the ranch only on weekends; he was seventy and beginning to let the younger men do the hard work. He liked to sit in the Chrysler he drove, a rich deep burgundy-colored car that had to be washed constantly to allow the color to show through the dust, his hands gripped on the steering wheel, and order the boys about, watch them ride the large, well-bred horses Rushton kept. He didn't ride anymore but he chose carefully each year which horses would stay to the ranch and proudly wear his mark on their branded hide.

Key got to ride a lot of the broncs, got thrown a lot too in the beginning, but he finally learned to stick and most horses didn't fight him so hard as some of the other men, didn't buck so high and wide when he set his saddle on them. After a while Rushton had just Key work the broncs in a pen and the old man would go inside for coffee with a good dollop of whiskey added, and drive back into town late in the afternoon, drunk, but then everyone who drove the same roads knew to watch out for the burgundy-colored Chrysler. The foreman, Ben Willard, would sometimes call the local cop when Charlie was particularly drunk, who would tail Charlie into town, seeing the old man to his front door.

Ben Willard was married and lived in a small house on the ranch with his wife. He left her alone most evenings to play poker in the bunkhouse, chawing and spitting and betting more than he had in his hand. Key didn't like poker, never had any money to begin with and hated betting off what he did have, didn't like to sit that long in the company of nothing but the men he'd worked with all day. He'd wander about, pick up a harness or bridle part needed fixing, go outside and fiddle with the leather until it was too dark to see what he was doing.

The wife's name was Brenda. She was thin, withdrawn from her lonely life, went barefoot most of the time in good weather, and rarely smiled at the collection of men who worked for her husband. As if none of them existed in her world. They had no children; she blamed this on herself and would watch her Ben with a shy hungering eye as he walked out right after supper to play a few hands with the boys.

Key watched, noted the sadness and got himself in a whole lot of trouble, this time without North to back him up, to get him out of the inevitable fight, the beating which would follow. Ben Willard was a thick, balding man with large hands and a small mouth, who despite what his wife thought was careful with his money and often made twice his salary in a night's gambling. This was no man for a randy kid to be fooling around with his wife. It was easy to underestimate Ben Willard, and doing just that got Key in a lot of trouble.

North came home from college the first weekend they would let him go. He was hungry for air and food and a good run on the sorrel, if Ray hadn't got rid of the horse since North wasn't around to ride.

Neelie started the trouble with a few words. "You hear about Key up to that school of yours, North? You hear he's been chasing Ben Willard's wife." She snorted at the look in North's eyes. "Whole town knows it 'cept Ben himself. Or maybe he don't care that Key's playin' 'round where he shouldn't be."

The coarse words shocked Claudie, even Ray's jaw dropped and North could barely swallow. Finally Neelie had the grace to blush a deep crimson when she heard the bland ugliness of the tale she'd repeated with no thought to consequences. "Oh dear," was all she could manage. Those around the table were silent. North pushed a last bit of pot roast around his plate. "Neelie, you ask forgiveness for what you just said. Child, there's a meanness in you, repeatin' a tale when you don't know the truth." Claudie wasn't use to reprimanding Neelie anymore; she'd grown to a steady, quiet, mostly responsible young woman. Maybe it was North and the expectation he carried with him that Key was outside, waiting to be invited in.

"Apologize to who, Mama? North doesn't care, he doesn't live here now, and Key, he never cared about any of us and I don't know Mrs. Willard or her husband and I can't apologize to them without–" She stood up, folded her napkin carefully before laying it on the table, began to stammer; "I'm sorry," and then burst into tears. North and Ray were open-mouthed, Claudie waded right in; "Well, child, you can go upstairs, I'll clean the dishes. And we'll forget this ever got said."

It was quiet for a moment after Neelie's outburst. The sounds of her running up the stairs had time to settle, and then North spoke. "Gosh it's good to be...home." There was always that hesitation, that bit of doubt. Ray responded as he often did; "Boy, it's your home till you don't want it no more. Me, I'm bettin' you want to ride so I brought up the sorrel, put him in a pen. With that bay Key rode. Rushton wants that one up to his place now, with Key there to ride him. It's Saturday, most of the boys will be in town. You can take the horse up tomorrow, you want to do some visitin'."

Ray's voice dragged but North heard him, thanked him silently as he often did. Without his uncle, without Neelie and Mrs. McKendrick..., he never finished the thought, just left it hanging, waiting to remind himself how fortunate he was. "Ma'am, I'll do the dishes, ain't had my hands in dish water since I got to school. I miss it, though I wouldn't want you to be tellin' folks that truth, no ma'am."

It was all right now; Claudie could hear that Neelie's crying had stopped. She guessed that North figured Neelie would come down to help him once her parents were out of the way; no apology, no attempt to explain, just him and her and the dishes, soap and rinse water and playing around with the wet towels and letting her know how much he missed her, how much she was his family.

It wasn't that she was pretty, or young. Key didn't need a woman's looks to entice him. She was female in a crowd of men, she was lonesome and willing, and vulnerable. The way he liked his women, even her age, older than him by some years, he liked older women, willing for his touch, so quick to know just where the bedroom was and how it was meant to be used.

He put up a clothesline for her that Ben didn't want to bother with, in doing so he had to ask where she wanted it, was it the right length, could she reach up to show him what height was best for her? A glass of lemonade was her response, she worried as he sweated, marked and nailed up the two lines of cotton rope, maybe she was asking too much of the good-looking kid her husband hired on to ride the rank horses.

A single touch of his hand on her arm, a soft 'thank-you' for the crisp sweet drink, brushing against her as she stretched for the clothespin bag, a rub along her arm while he replaced the fallen bag; easy, quick, already unsettled by the attention she turned on her bare feet and he was waiting, mouth parted, hands raised to waist height, willing to reach just for her.

She was sweet as the lemonade in bed, flowing motion, moist mouth parted, hips raised, thighs opened, waiting, she was an eager married woman, wedded for five years, older than Key by at least ten years and wanting back her fair share of the unused marriage bed.

They'd come together maybe ten times in the past three weeks, which wasn't easy with Ben riding Key's butt, sending him to the farthest canyon, setting him to ride drag when they moved the mother cows. But

Key was clever, and persistent, and Brenda found a whole lot of chores she wanted Ben to do for her, and with a great show would allow her husband to offer up Key in his place. A smart woman who never finished high school, she knew now what she wanted and would do anything to get it.

The boys knew, they recognized the signs, they saw Key walk too close to her, knew better'n their boss the boy's reputation, two of them had been in school with Key, three years ahead and never graduating, but they remembered the Larkin boy. With the ranch fifteen miles out of Branson, and the town itself consisting of not quite fifty souls, there wasn't much for the ranch boys to do evenings but spit and play poker and gossip.

Finally it was Eldon Plunkett, older brother to Stevie, who said the wrong thing to Ben and gave the secret away. Maybe Eldon didn't mean to betray Key, after all he did more'n his share, rode the hard broncs, kept the boss's wife from harping and complaining and having the boys do house chores for her like fixing windows and putting up a low fence around the shack to make it look like they had a yard.

Maybe it was that Eldon lost his savings to Ben the night Key was pumping over Brenda in Ben's own bed, taking risks that heightened their pleasure. Key liked the thrill of knowing the boss could come in, anytime and throw a fit.

Still, when it happened, when Ben stormed into the bedroom, the rest of the boys hanging back but wanting to watch, Key hadn't figured on the force of such a beating. From what he remembered, it wasn't that much fun. And when Willard took the fight outdoors 'cause his wife objected to them breaking up her rooms, he relearned what he'd forgot in the past three years, that North McKendrick had saved him from a lot of pain. Ben's boot swept across Key's face and rolled him and he couldn't stop the groan, couldn't hold in the damnable weak sound. He struggled to crawl and find his balance, on his knees first and then pushing both hands into the rocky dirt, rose halfway before Ben decided he didn't want the boy corning for him and doubled his fists, slammed them on the boy's neck, dropping him with the only sound a gasp from his excited wife.

North held the bay's lead in his right fist, let himself relax and enjoy the day. Not a bad chore, riding the sorrel over to Willard's to deliver the bay and visit some with Key. He missed Key, it surprised him how he could hear Key's voice in class some times. Mocking the teacher, making North laugh.

He rode into the yard seconds after Key's fall. He knew his friend instantly, even covered in dust, sprawled in front of one angry man and a curious bunch of cowboys. North directed the sorrel carefully; he stopped in front of Mr. Willard and North tipped his hat. "Mornin', I got this bay for you." Then he handed over the rein, settled in the saddle, continued on in his best conversational tone. "You best leave off beatin' on my friend. Sure 'nough he's wrong, whatever he done, but you hit him enough for now!"

He was careful stepping off the sorrel, watching out for Key who had regained some of his senses and his voice and rolled over, said what North thought was his name, in relief, like there was never a question North would come to his rescue.

North picked him up, steadied Key on his bare feet and never noticed that his friend was naked from the waist down. "One of you show me his bunk. I'll pack and get him out of here in maybe ten minutes or so. Mr. Willard, you leave us alone till then." Ben Willard, ever willing to take an opportunity, stood with feet wide apart, hands raised in fists, showing he was willing to let the fight continue. He wasn't fooling anyone, they all knew Willard was a coward, had beat down the Larkin kid 'cause of his puny size and being caught hunched over Willard's woman, hard at the work Willard didn't want to bother doing. Willard's wife had been clawing and moaning, holding on tight to her lover, enjoying the ride. Neither of them had known when Ben came into the bedroom until he'd jerked Key off the bucking woman by yanking on his mane of tangled blond hair.

Now it would be a good idea to get some clothes on Key, a man's nakedness wasn't much to look at, and Key didn't help by not trying to cover himself. Head hanging, blood from his broke nose dripping red and bright into the settling dust, eyes bright and shining as if he enjoyed being a spectacle, he stood beside North's bulk, swaying, unsteady, his mouth pulled wide in a bloody grin. Eldon Plunkett showed North where to go, the rest of the men trailed behind as North took no notice of than but walked with purpose, pushing Key ahead of him as if he were nothing more than ten pounds of wheat flour for the kitchen, A half hour later the two boys were on the sorrel and headed back to the McKendrick place. Key rode behind North, arms wrapped purposefully around North's comforting middle. North tried talking and when he got no response decided Key was unconscious again and thought it better that way; he could ride and think and not be bothered with Key's excuses.

Claudie had no qualms when North brought Key into the kitchen. She'd done this before, years in the past for Ray on a few occasions, and for North and Key both when they rolled the truck. But the most heart-piercing of those times was the first one, when there was no explanation of the wounds and the whole family fought around the boy in short-hand, trying to understand who he was and what had happened, with Neelie crying and North explaining, and Ray too quiet, Claudie all upset and refusing to show it.

Now it was time again to treat the boy's wounds, maybe even do some stitching for she knew Key would not go to the local hospital. Can't afford it, he'd say, face ain't important enough that I need to pay for prettyin' it up.

He didn't know, maybe he did and didn't want to care, that his face endeared him to a lot of folks, not just the women he slept with but even those men too wise to give in to his charm but still could be enchanted with his smile and his presence, the wild, throwback life he chose to live.

And she knew she was talking to herself as she washed and stitched, thoughts she didn't want to share with the men. Key's damage was bad this time, not in broken bones or smashed ribs but in his beauty, now torn and pitted by Ben Willard's boots. A gory line was drawn across his forehead, a dent crushed his left cheekbone. The broken nose was nothing much, it would heal easy. She couldn't mend the cheekbone, it would have to heal itself, but a clever woman could sew the open flesh on his brow with neat quilting stitches.

Key was quiet under her hand; she tilted his face by the jaw and felt him grimace, she moved his head sideways to be sure she got the edges straight and felt him withdraw from her fingers. She knew the pain he was enduring, but he made no sound, gave her no opening for sympathy.

Later Claudie lay in their bed with Ray and found

herself touching him the exact way she had caressed the boy's wounded face, fingers stroking, pleading, smoothing flaws and worried flesh until it was pliable in her hand. Ray groaned, she knew it wasn't herself making the noise; he rolled to her briefly, his arm weighed on her shoulder, his belly and hips pressed to her thighs. But there was nothing for her, no rise of flesh, no parting of her own body to receive her husband. Only a soft pat on her arm, far away from her breast. "I'm sorry, Claudie, God knows I'm sorry."

It was over a year since they had joined together. Claude put her fingers to her husband's mouth, a practiced move she had done too many nights. "It's all right, hold me." She hated the words but they were needed. She did not know what happened to Ray. He wouldn't let her know, he was afraid to talk. He loved her, she knew that; he wasn't tomcatting around with the likes of Marie Larkin. But he wasn't coming to her, stiff, eager, and in need of what only she could give him. For all his words, his promises, his loving hugs and lights kisses, she could not feel she was of value to her husband.

In the morning North was a surprise, and an unpleasant one. "Mrs. Claudie, Key's got a fever, he's real dumb about it too. Goin' to ride back to Rushton's, says he's got to go to work. I can't get him to listen." She didn't want to help anymore, she didn't want to take time from her own problem to tend to a silly feverish boy who couldn't stay within decent human boundaries.

She moved away from the table, left her coffee on the wood stove hoping it would keep warm. North walked sideways ahead of her, trying to talk and hurry her at the same time. She had to counsel him; "He's goin' to be fine, North. Key's tough no matter what happens. Nothing on his hide yet will kill a man." But she did worry, she could have missed a vital clue last night.

North hovered in the doorway, barely fitting in the narrow opening. Key's eyes were swollen shut and he couldn't breathe through his nose, the line across his forehead seemed to visibly pulse. North put his hand to his own heart, felt odd tremors there, seeing Mrs. Claudie bend over Key, laid out in the bed like he was dying, her hands roaming light and cool on his skin; North was jealous, mad clean through that a skirt-chasing hound like Key Larkin could get a clean and decent woman to care this much for him.

As she continued her work, stroking Key's face, turning his skull to each side, her voice asking if that hurt, was that spot particularly sore, could he get himself to the outhouse, North tasted a sour, rancid stink as rage roared in his brain.

With some coaxing, Key stood. For once North did not reach out to help him. Instead it was Mrs. Claudie who put her shoulder under Key's arm, placed his hand on her own shoulder and leaned with him to become his crutch. North read confusion in his friend's eyes, awareness of the woman so close to him and pain at the effort each move took. North grinned, outwardly to encourage Key, inwardly to mask his surprisingly stupid anger.

Ah hell, he thought, I'm killing myself this way. "Boy, you look like, well, you look like just what you are...beat to a pulp and plain dumb for gettin' that way." Mrs. Claudie looked at him sharply; "North, you're doin' no good standin' there. Here, you take him, I can't be his guide to the outhouse or nothin'. Bring him to the kitchen when you're done. Best he sit up while I work on him. Now get."

By the time the boys got into her sanctuary, her kitchen, Claudie was composed and settled. Leaning over the boy, raw, almost naked in that bed, had unnerved her, reminded her of the contact last night with Ray, the disappointment when he wasn't there, when he slept instead of reaching out for her; she had to give up all those thoughts and needs. At least the two boys gave her something to do, someone else to worry over other than her Ray.

Neelie was home, watching as North and Key hopped in the door and filled the kitchen. North always was his own crowd in the small room, the one part of the house built before the century, from downed pine and adobe mud. The rest of the house was rock, carefully, artfully shaped and held together by a stone mason up from Mexico, but the kitchen retained its original dimensions of mean poverty and quaint building techniques; the ceiling brushed North's head, he leaned slightly to make enough room for himself.

She put Neelie to work boiling water and then critically inspected her handwork from last night's surgery. As she suspected, the stitches were inflamed. "Have to give that cut a good scrubbin', boy. It's gonna hurt. Guess Ben had manure on those boots of his." Key pulled away from her cradling hands. She grabbed for his shoulder. "That won't do you no good, I won't let you get off that easy. You'll have enough of a scar without infection. Neelie, get me that bottle of whiskey your pa thinks he hides from me. And the iodine out to the barn, North you get that." She hadn't planned this well, alone with the boy while her two soldiers were getting supplies. She kept a hand on Key's back for support, but did not look at him, or speak to him in the short time they were alone.

There was a clean pleasure in the work; the fine skin

of the boy flushed red as she washed and picked clean and washed again, first with Neelie's hot water and then with the iodine North brought in. There was a deep sigh at the end and Key slid halfway off the chair before North caught him. "Guess I done enough, that all looks better. North, you put him back and then come in for breakfast. Neelie, you help me get this mess cleaned up so's I can cook."

It took the boys a while to get moving, North had to half-carry Key, who tried to raise his head and thank Claudie but she dismissed the hoarse words; "You go to bed, boy, sleep off the hurt." She barely glanced at her daughter, not wanting to see the tears or the shaking hands, the mouth new grown to a shape wavering under some deep feeling. Teenage girls had their own set of emotions, Claudie already knew that. She could barely remember, but those trembles and quakes weren't going to stop her or her Neelie, together they would stay tough on the Larkin boy and not allow pity to shake them.

Ray appeared, just his head stuck inside the door. "Got any more coffee?" He winked, like he remembered last night or maybe because he'd already forgot. Claudie stared at him, a tough man getting old. She hated the years now, the difference between them, first time since they'd decided to marry that she thought much on the enormity of fifteen years. "Sure there's more. There's always coffee. Neelie's makin' a new pot now." "Boys up yet?" As if he didn't see the iodine bottle sitting square in the table's center or tile bucket of soiled rags waiting its turn to be washed. "North'll be back shortly, he's puttin' Key back to bed, some a those cuts're infected."

Neelie looked at her ma kind of funny and Claudie refused the accusing stare. None of the girl's business how Claudie spoke about Key, she'd heard the distaste in her voice, no one's business how Claudie felt; she'd done her job, now it was time for the rest of the day.

North took the late bus back to Pueblo on Sunday night. Neelie went in with her pa to say good-bye, though they never said any of those words but teased and told stories and got Ray laughing, then the small truck cab felt warm and safe and for a brief moment the family was united.

Claudie was left with Key, who was up and moving around, slowly, but had no place to go.

Chapter Eight

The spring of her junior year, Neelie got a job after school in the local five and dime store known as Lockwood's. North gave her the old GMC to get her into town. He was never home now, with a full-time job in Pueblo and going to school. He had come back at Christmas, which was a lonely holiday with no Key Larkin to help drag in a tree and stir up laughter and silly stories. It was a nice holiday though, with store-bought gifts from North and a good report on his grades, mostly B's, and he said he was beginning to understand what he was learning.

Neelie's second week in the store, a drummer stopped at the counter and offered a pretty lipstick to her if she would smile. She had a quick retort; "Mister, that's the poorest line I've heard yet. You think I'm just a country fool?" She snapped hard, immediately knowing the man didn't deserve such judgment. Before she could apologize, he had already stammered out his own version; "No, miss. I meant nothing to be a line. It's just that you're such a lovely girl I would like to see you smile. You don't give that away just for talk, I've watched you now for several days. I've been trying this last hour to get you smiling."

She was sixteen looking close at seventeen and she drove her truck to school and worked every afternoon. No drummer could make a fool of her, not ever. Then she took time to study the man; he was dark, older than at first glance, with the clipped moustache and white teeth of a professional charmer. Still, there was a kindness in his face that slowed down her warning system. He seemed to sense her curiosity; "Ma'am, I won't be a drummer for long. I'm taking night courses in accounting and business. I'll be my own man in a few years." He was listing his worth, and he had known her doubts; now she was intrigued. She was being openly courted for the first time.

Still she couldn't be a pushover; "Mister, I told you I am not a fool. What's your name?" He smiled, and she liked the ease with which his face relaxed. "Miss, I told you my name last week and yesterday too and now I'll try again. But if you forget this time, well then, I know when I'm licked." She had to smile he was so fierce in his statements. "My name is Miguel Herrera, Mickey Herrera. Mickey."

The way in which Mickey and I met is so silly that it embarrasses me still, more than thirty years later. He was a cosmetics salesman, I worked on the cosmetics counter of the local store. Nothing a romance writer would be excited about, but that day, when I finally allowed myself the time to really look at Mickey, I saw a man I would come to love as well as desire, a man equal to North in his decency and faithful nature.

I did not fall in love with him immediately. He was obviously of Spanish, now called Hispanic, heritage and I lived in a small town where lines such as race and religion were not easily crossed. Trinidad had a tradition of widely varying ethnic backgrounds because of the imported miners. We each lived within this mining history and drew our separate lines. For whatever reason, although the Greek and the Welsh, the Slavs and Asians mixed comfortably within the context of the mines, the Anglos and Spanish held on to an enmity which had divided them for more than three hundred years. It was our heritage and a bad habit, one I had not yet learned to conquer.

I was a victim of my world, and would do no more than smile and nod at Mickey for the first several months after our initial sparring. I am guessing he came into the store more often that his sales figures warranted, but after a while I noticed his routine and was a bit saddened if he did not appear at least once a week.

In the meantime, I put myself deeper and deeper into a trouble which I knew to avoid but I believed, in my still confident, inexperienced youth, that I could venture into hell and still hold myself as cleanly as if I had done nothing more than walked to the corner store.

Key moved very carefully, conscious that his boot soles folded over every rock and pebble on the dirt shoulder and he hated walking, hated being reduced to sticking out his thumb and asking, pleading, for some stranger to give him a ride. The problem with living in one place, every person knew you, no one was a stranger.

He didn't know where he was going, just that he was getting out of Trinidad and thirty days in the county jail never mind his age and that his crime had been fighting when attacked.

He clenched and unclenched his hands, felt the ridge of calluses and smiled at one good thing, the stone mason who'd come to this country to fit rich men's houses together with great skill and artistry. Fighting was his crime also, and he made it his penance to teach Key the art of fitting those stone slabs together until they became a visual puzzle finished by a master. It didn't matter to Key what the hard work did to him; this man had decided to teach him. Barely able to speak the language, the man had given Key a place where he could hide from the prison brutality. He was a 'pretty boy' to the inmates and paid the consequences, except when he worked for the Italian. Even the local miners and derelict cowhands were in awe of the stubby man's immense strength, shown in the size of his hands, the enormous muscling of his arms and shoulders.

The scar on Key's forehead had faded nicely, only a few marks showed where some stitches had parted. He was dirty, and he could feel the prison filth caked in his face, could taste the ugly fire of bad food and no chance to stay clean, and when his boot turned under him and he went to his knees, he remembered that too from the work farm and the long violent nights.

Somewhere close a truck slowed, stopped, but he would not turn and see pity on the driver's face and suffer the humiliation of recognition and the truck rumbling away, covering Key with dust to hide the driver's escape. Instead there was a door opening and a gasp, and a voice speaking his name until he opened his eyes to see two legs so close to him that he could lean forward and rest his face on them. Female legs, from the white cuffed socks and tied shoes he'd guess a schoolgirl.

No, he thought, shook his head, not her, not this one girl out of all those who lived around here. "Key, is that you?" Neelie McKendrick, scrawny and too young, bright, sharp-tongued Neelie. Key stood, felt his ankle throb, knew his breath smelled, that he was greasy and worn and too ugly for any decent female.

He looked at her and was stunned and said so, flat out with no careful choosing of words, no implied tone meant to seduce. This was Neelie McKendrick, kin to Key's faithful North. "You turned out beautiful, Neelie, like your ma knew you would. North too, he believed, but me, I was a skeptic until now. I can see the truth, though, you are plumb beautiful."

If he talked on enough she'd close her gaping mouth and wipe her eyes shut of the shocked tears and maybe then she'd just say 'Hi, Key' and let it go, get back in her truck, that same truck damn it, and drive on out of his life.

"Key." Well, he thought, part way there. Her mouth seemed to stutter around that single syllable. "I'm taking you home." Clever girl, trapping him with words, drawing him in, forcing him to do what she told him. Instead of walking off like he planned, or standing his ground and talking until she gave up, he climbed in the familiar truck, put his head back on the worn seat and closed his eyes. Something he knew, someone who wouldn't take a bite out of him for at least the next few moments.

Or so he thought: "What got you in such a mess? Oh, I remember...oh." He guessed at school or in that damp, low-ceilinged barn they called a store, she'd heard he had been sent to the work farm, knew he'd finally got caught for his deeds. She more'n likely told Ray and Claudie, it would feel good to relay such a juicy story. Then he hated himself for suspecting Neelie would take to gossip like any old city child, spiking other folks with her tongue, enjoying their misdeeds and misfortunes.

It wasn't much, what he had done. Punched out a man who thought his girl friend didn't belong in Key's bed. She wasn't his wife, or his intended, just a girl he dated on occasion. The son of a bitch attacked Key, hitting him with a bottle first and then coming on with a knife. Key was defending himself, and winning, when the law showed up and put him in jail instead of the other guy. Nothing Key said in the courtroom would change any of that, maybe because Key'd slept with the jailer's wife, and fooled around some with the judge's daughter.

All circumstances he couldn't tell Neelie, not in his own defense, they sounded as weak as they were. Key yawned, coughed, wiped his mouth and tried to apologize in general. She would have none of it; "I'm going to take you home and feed you, good heavens Key, you're as skinny as a tick in winter." He grinned at her in true amusement. "I thought you'd quit the country life, Neelie, I almost believed you were a sophisticated city girl till that last remark."

His teasing hit a tender place, she blanched and stared at him while struggling to keep the truck going. "You may not have dreams, Key, but I do, and I'm working on them. I'll graduate early next year, a semester ahead of my class, and I've applied to different colleges too." She was her mama's child for a moment, not a young woman, but she was right and Key acknowledged it.

"Another apology, Neelie. Don't bite me, you know I ain't worth the effort or the risk of infection. You're right, my dreams are only chasin' girls, havin' fun like. But what you're doin' is great, real fine." He didn't have the words he needed, to applaud her efforts enough without sounding like the despised schoolteaching voices in their past.

"Well, thank you I guess. Now I'm taking you home. Mama'll be upset to see you this way and Papa too but I can't leave you walking along here. No one else comes this way." As if it just occurred to her; "Key, were you going to the house?"

He couldn't answer, there was no truth he could tell. He was scared, and looking for help and the McKendricks, even just their name, was the only safety he'd known. Here was a time for pure truth. "I had thought I might take the gamble, see if you or North was home. You folks sure do take to schoolin', guess that's good cause the world seems to want those who think with their brains." He hadn't meant to say that, hated himself for giving in, playing the fool he knew he was. He wanted to say something more, about fitting a mold, forced into obedience but the words were angry and would drive the girl away. More than anything he was tired and hungry, and wanted to sleep where he could trust those still awake.

"You know North's not there, he hasn't been home since Christmas." She chewed her lower lip, and wouldn't meet Key's gaze. "Papa's not quite right so it was a quiet day, which is why we didn't ask you." She stopped, he could see her making a decision; "Where were you, was it where you used to go, and come back looking...like this?" Her hand made a vague circle, to draw attention away from a lie. The McKendricks had not wanted Key in their home for those celebrations early on; he knew it, so did Neelie.

"I can't let your folks see me like this." He used words to divert her from the insulting non-invitation and to focus her on what he needed right now. He wouldn't beg, hated the thought, but if she didn't get the message he would have to be specific, tell her to take him where he wanted.

Obliging him, she spoke up, careful not to offend; "Well, there's a pond now before the turn-off. We've had enough rain there's even frogs and mosquitoes which I don't like but there it is. Water. You could clean up, it's almost dark. Ma'll worry some but I think the time's better spent gettin' you clean." She said this last bit after looking at Key again and her nose wrinkled involuntarily as his rank scent filled the warmed truck cab. Key sighed. She was his Neelie, taking charge, thinking it was her idea, pleased with herself for rescuing him. He coughed, spat out the open window. She was watching; good. He liked that bit of worry.

"Okay, Neelie. It's a good idea I scrub off some of this filth 'fore I shock your ma and make your pa mad at me all over again."

She didn't mean to watch but the so-called pond had a track leading to the edge and there were no cattle to bother him so she remained in the truck to give him some privacy but she could see him anyway. It was dark enough he had the illusion of being alone as he stripped down and began to wash. Neelie held her breath while she tried not to stare.

Ducks swimming at the pond's far edge floated in a tight circle when Key stepped into their territory. When he drew his shirt over his head it was too much and the ducks flew up in quick, fluttering formation. Key stood a moment, watched their departing, then waited a moment longer as the night air chilled his skin, the stars slowly appeared. Then he tended to the improbable task of making himself decent.

Neelie watched; she couldn't stop herself. Filthy, battered by whatever he'd endured at the work farm, he was still beautiful. Bent over, denim cupping his lean buttocks, he washed great scoops of water over his arms and chest but it wouldn't be enough, even she knew that. He quickly shucked off the jeans, stood for a moment in the thin cotton briefs and nothing else, and Neelie's ears burned, her mouth was too dry.

Mercifully he walked into the water, deep enough the surface scum broke over his arms and he waved them in a circle to clear space. The shadowed water bubbled and broke around him, a rich glassy surface colored by the thickness of weeds. Suddenly he ducked under the water, played both hands through his hair and came bursting up, spewing water, having the nerve to wave a hand at Neelie, holding up a long dangling line of torn water plant. Embarrassed even though he couldn't really see her, Neelie blushed, waved back, pretended she didn't recognize his grin.

When he finally came out of the water she tried to avert her eyes but couldn't. Water slid off his chest and the cotton briefs were dragged down until the white cloth no longer rode at his waist but clung to his thighs, then slipped down as he high-stepped through tall weeds to his clothes. Neelie was no innocent; she knew birth and death and the instinctive act which created one before the other, but she had never seen a naked man other than poorly reproduced photos of statues in a school text.

Now she knew, he was like the statue only real, with thick curls at the groin made darker by the night air and water, real hair and flesh instead of white marble carved into whorls and patterns. The important parts were shriveled, made tiny by the cold she guessed. Nothing much, not like a bull when it sniffed out a receptive cow. But still it was difficult to breathe and even with her eyes closed she could see him clearly, could almost put a hand on his chilled flesh and feel his life. She knew too well the stories behind the scars, now she knew more; that he was like all males only more beautiful for his flaws. Lean and sculpted, cold and clean, forever she would envision him just this way.

When Key climbed back into the truck, Neelie did not immediately start up the engine. With the truck door closed, they sat in the dark. She could smell him, the deep chill, the fresh clean texture; almost too close, too much. Then Key looked at her and for a moment he was the boy in the school yard she hated more than three years ago, the boy North brought home and made his new family accept to please him.

"Thanks, Neelie, for takin' the time. Guess I needed a good bath 'bout now." She wasn't sure, he was so quick to read a mood, but she tried, she looked into his face and saw the eyes droop and glance away. "I mean what I'm saying now, no fooling, no joke." His voice was clear, without hesitation or teasing, a simple apology with no hidden meaning.

As always, he was hard for her to read; quick with the familiar charm, yet quiet, beaten down to the bottom where thoughts and emotions were carefully hid.

Key pressed her; "I mean this." He sank deeper into the battered truck seat, his head turned from her. "I can't blame you for not believing me, can't blame any woman for not trusting what I say, now can I?"

He impaled her, offering the truth and part of his myth together, the two opposing forces colliding to create another Key Larkin. "Hush, Key, it don't matter." She surprised herself by a reversion to the old speech pattern. "Mama's bound to have supper by now and Papa'll be certain glad to see you. He might need help, I don't think Charlie Rushton'll mind if you work down here for him."

The chance was lost, the childish words and tone a brush-off. He gave it back to her; "That's my Neelie, now I know I'm goin'-." He almost said the word but recovered, still she heard it echo inside. "I'll sit right quiet and you can show me how you learned to drive this here truck." He too sought refuge in their shared dialect. Neelie gulped, felt all she wanted to say and lost the words; "Well you sure 'nuff smell some better." Then she put a hand over her mouth, mocking them both, and Key's face lit up.

No matter where they started with their words, it came back to Key and his past. He was silent as she turned over the motor, then once they were on the long narrow road to the ranch he broke the silence with an explosive "Huh!" It made her swerve, he laughed; "Come on girl, don't you put us back in a ditch." She struggled with the truck, glanced at him and saw he was truly smiling, a wide broken grin right up to his eyes. No lying, no ducking, Key Larkin was relaxed and enjoying the drive. With her, with Neelie McKendrick at the wheel.

Neelie went in first to prepare her folks. Key didn't want to hear the sharp words laid against him before she got her way. Without sound, but looking through the window, he could see the downturn of Mrs. Claudie's mouth, the high set shoulders and stiff back Ray turned to the outside as Neelie spoke.

Of course they let him come in. Ray met Key at the door, stuck out his hand; "Evenin' to you, boy. Been a long time." Key couldn't read this, couldn't tell if maybe there was feeling to the words and not just an attempt at polite kindness. But he knew with the woman; Mrs. Claudie McKendrick was mad. Even the back of her neck was white, tense, her eyes skipped from him as she parroted her polite greeting. "Set, make yourself to home." That hurt, and she well knew it, was deliberate about her choice of words. "Neelie'll get the table ready, I'm sure you're hungry." That hurt too.

He wasn't convinced he could sit down and eat, not with this degree of anger rolling around him, but when he smelled the salt sweetness of the ham, the hot steam from snap peas and creamed corn, biscuits with honey from the Swede running bees in Trinchera Plaza, he changed his mind. No man could walk away from a meal like this.

"Yes, ma'am. I can manage. And I'll be gone right after supper. You can be sure of that." At least that much was true, he wasn't going to be given a repeat invite to spend the night. He was too much Marie's hound dog son and not enough of a stranger for them to share more'n they had to.

Right then Key didn't care; all that was important was getting as much of the good food into his mouth without totally disgracing himself. It'd been a long time since he'd had Mrs. Claudie's food or known her kindness, been a long time since he'd enjoyed anything with the McKendricks. And he found with each sweet morsel in his mouth how much he missed them.

"I'll do the dishes of course." He looked up about five minutes after beginning to eat but saw it was more like twenty and there were faces watching him, mouths dropped, eyes watering, and there wasn't a speck of food left on the table. His belly hurt right up to the button on his jeans and he sighed; God it felt good not to be hungry. "I'll do the dishes ma'am."

Mrs. Claudie shook her head. Key pressed the matter; "You taught me how to wash up a couple a years back and I ain't liable to forget such a valuable lesson." He tried to smile, and mean it this time, as her wild eyes blazed around him. Ray spoke then without opening his own eyes; "Now Claudie, the boy means well. You let him do what he needs to and come outside, look at the stars with me. It's goin' to be a beautiful night."

Husband and wife left, Ray's hand resting lightly on Claudie's waist; Key remained seated until they left. Neelie didn't offer to help but let her eyes roam over him; he could feel her stare and managed to attempt a graceful turn at one point strictly for her benefit and he bet to himself that if he looked at her right at that moment she would be red-faced with mixed delight and shame.

He knew she liked to watch him, had enjoyed the suggestion of her eyes on him even as he recognized a threat to his promise with North. She was a child, he needed to remember that never mind she had her license and the clear beginnings of a beautiful woman's body.

Truth now, hard truth inside him; he liked knowing that Neelie McKendrick looked at his naked flesh. Neelie coughed; he looked at the black pot he held, saw scum. and food, scrubbed it harder and kept his back turned to her. With the pot done to his satisfaction, he spun around, the item held high overhead, and discovered that Neelie had disappeared.

I knew he was a bad boy; all my friends, my parents, even Mr. Kopeski who ran the five and dime store said he wished I wouldn't let that Key Larkin sit at the counter and sip one cup of coffee for a half hour. He frightened off the good women of the town, and the other kind, well, Mr. Kopeski didn't want those ladies coming into his establishment.

I knew all of this and yet I would find him walking the road, going nowhere, and I would give him a ride, ending at our house where Mama would grudgingly feed him, he would wash the supper dishes, and disappear.

We didn't know where he slept or who he was working for, if he was working. He managed to keep decent clothes on his back and boots on his feet, even if they were all worn and shabby. Someone cut his hair to help him look almost respectable. He was too young and too smart to be living this life but I never saw a moment's regret or any attempt to do better. He did come in one time to the store to visit, and drink that single cup of coffee which so irritated Mr. Kopeski, and he met Mickey, which in itself provoked an odd and flattering revelation in me.

Life drifted in this routine until school ended and I worked full time at the store, and then North came home from college. He found Key sitting at the end of the lane, under what had once been a fine twisted and gnarled juniper. The boys came to the house together, North carrying a huge canvas bag full of his stuff, handling it as if it were a paper sack filled with leaf lettuce, and Key carried North's jacket, a dented baseball cap, and a big grin all on his own.

What is it that attracts male and female? That makes a mockery of all common sense and good intentions. I don't want an answer, I know all the fine explanations of chemicals and sexuality and forbidden desire, but between Key and me it was so much more than all those romance magazines ever dared promise.

Some days Neelie was so bored with work that she fretted internally, worried that the rest of her life would be cornered this way, inside, listening to shoes and boots rattle the hard wood floor, watching spiders cross the tin ceiling, landing down in front of her when she least expected them. She screamed once, her hands over her eyes, when approached so by a black and very large spider, and one of the customers, a man of course, laughed at her misery and said, "Now don't worry, missy, that little ole thing can't hurt you" in the broadest accent, words slaughtered and humiliating in her ears. She was furious, wanting to tell him about growing up on a ranch and jumping at the spider's sudden materialization only because it startled her, but she knew two indelible things: explanations sounded like excuses, and never argue with a customer. So she half-curtsied in mocking humility and said right back, "Why yes sir, thank you so much for saving me." The man, potbellied and old, probably forty, had no idea she was poking fun at him while relieving her temper, but the boss heard and knew, and lectured her before she could leave that evening.

Such backtalk, he said, wasn't good for the store's profits. In turn, she mentioned that the man never knew she had sassed him. Kopeski's response was predictable, "Yes, well, you have admitted you sassed him. Don't do it again." She was dismissed, supposedly cowed by the lecture.

However there were moments of delight in the store, such as when Mickey came in, at least twice a week now, and she considered that one of those trips was only to see her. Sometimes he came at the right moment and they could slip outside, turn left to the small café which put out a cheap and almost tasty lunch. Soup, lemonade, a cookie. She and Mickey would set and he would tell stories of his travels, she would listen and marvel at the way his eyes crinkled when he spoke, the pleasing cadence of his voice, the hint of a mystery in the complete difference of their family backgrounds.

One day Mickey was leaning on the counter, explaining the uses of a new face cream and she was pretending to listen carefully, professionally, all the while enjoying the texture of his hands as they fondled the small jar, pressing the back of her own hand to smooth on the lotion as he extolled its virtues. A man had never touched her quite this way before, a combination of her mama applying soothing balm to a sunburn or rash, her father's strength while he withdrew a tick or cactus spine, and the clean sculpted line of Key's hands doing the dishes as she watched. This man was a stranger, in whose life she as yet had no vested interest. She had not gone to school with his younger brother or sister, did not know where his parents lived, had no idea if he went to church and liked horses or stayed indoors on a fine day and read without ever looking to the sun or walking in the clear moon light.

A figure approached in back of Mickey and she glanced up knowing that if it were the owner he would be pleased to see her so attentive to the sales pitch. More profit for the fragile business. Instead it was the one person she thought would never re-enter the establishment and especially not come to the cosmetics and lotion counter where only tired women and restless children came, their mamas in search of fleeting new self-visions.

He stopped a respectful distance from the counter, tipped his hat off and let the brim roll through his fingers. "Ma'am, Neelie, I thought it was you. I come in to say hello." Mickey looked up then, his eyes widened, he looked between Key and Neelie and his mouth tightened. Then Key stuck out his hand in a rare exhibition of manners; " Name's Larkin, good to meet you. Sir."

Neelie threw her head back and laughed; trust Key. Mickey entered in, accepting Key's grip, smiling that broad white smile as he spoke. "I'm Mickey Herrera, it is a pleasure."

The two were polite with each other and careful with Neelie, as if she would decide right then and there. Neelie stepped back to study their differing images: Key too thin, tanned to a dark copper, his forehead white, untouched by sun. He had a scruffy beard, his shirt was badly soiled and torn under one arm. She could smell him above all the perfume counter scents. Mickey was all clean and pressed for his work, in a blue suit and tie, a white shirt, hands manicured, dark on their backs, soft, the hands of a salesman.

Mickey smoothed his tie, "Mr. Larkin, It is time for coffee and a moment out of the day. Will you perhaps join us, that is..." He turned to Neelie; "If it is all right with you?" Then Mickey made a statement that endeared him to Neelie even if his other virtues had not already captured her. "It's obvious you are a special friend to Neelie." The sincere graciousness of those words prompted Neelie. "Yes, Key, join us. It looks like coffee and a donut would agree with you." She kept most of the worry from her voice and laid on the teasing maybe too thick; it was easy to see the bad days were still with him.

"Both of you, that's mighty nice, guess I can set a while and visit." Key spoke very cautiously. Despite himself he liked the Mex, no fuss or preening never mind he was dressed right out of a catalog. The man was straightforward and polite, and obviously Neelie liked him so Key would try. He would listen and pay attention, North's words in his mind, that they needed to protect Neelie, shield her from any possible harm.

In a daring gesture the coffee shop had put two glass and metal tables outside, with chairs and an umbrella. Key plopped himself at a table, knowing the owner wouldn't want him inside, near the owner's wife. Ah well, he could save himself and still get coffee outside. Neelie wasn't slow to pick up on his reluctance; she looked at him sideways, grinned at him; "I'll bring an extra big cup, Key, so you won't need to go get a refill. And two donuts, how's that for service?"

Once again Key felt the pain that closeness to a beloved person brought. No bluff of his would work; she always knew. He nodded, shifted until he sat with his back to the window where he could watch across the street and count the few people in a hurry, thinking too much and pushing that thinking out of his mind. The Mex went with Neelie, leaving Key safe and alone.

A familiar shape drifted across his line of sight, a thin woman bent over, eyes stuck to the sidewalk; she bumped into two people and still didn't lift her head. His ma. First time he'd seen her in the time since that Christmas. He lowered his head and looked away, his face was hot, his hands gripped each other. He focused on one fingernail digging into the palm, tearing skin, letting the small pain distract him.

Neelie put a plate with two huge sweet gooey pastries down in front of him. "The best they could do, no donuts, and no toast or muffins. Here, eat up." The cup and saucer appeared attached to the Mex's hand; smooth skin, Key thought, soft yet scarred so he'd done work in the past, living a different life now. He barely looked up; "Smells good," was all he could manage.

Neelie sat and poked at her own sugary confection, then laid a powdery finger on Mickey's wrist. "This is nice, Mickey. Thank you." Key ate quickly. He liked listening to Neelie speak and the two of them seemed to prefer talk to eating. He wanted to eat, needed something in his gut, and as he ate and listened, he decided he liked the Mex; Mickey he corrected himself. Key added nothing to the conversation and without looking at him Neelie pushed the remains of her sweet over so Key was able to finish it to the last crumb.

No one better mistreat Neelie. Key ate, listened, was curious about Mickey's easy talk and obvious attraction to Neelie. He'd have to fight Key if there was damage done. Neelie, North, they were all the good things Key counted on, those two were the only people he could trust.

"Neelie, Mickey, nice sittin' with you. I got to go." No more than that and Key was gone. Neelie sat a moment longer with Mickey and then announced she needed to get back in the store, but it didn't seem that important. Mickey diverted her with what she really wanted to talk about. "I like your friend but he seems disturbed, perhaps something is wrong. His eyes give him away, they don't have the laughter he tries to provoke."

Neelie tried to explain; "He and my cousin went to school together. North's in college, I've told you that. But Key's the brighter one. Now he does day work on ranches, I think. I don't see him often, he rarely comes to the house any more. My parents aren't terribly fond of him without North around to steady him...well, he is aware of how they feel." She knew she was saying too much, that her interest in explaining Key showed Mickey too much of how she felt. "Papa likes him more than Mama, he's always been polite with me."

Mickey moved away from the small table. "It's time I take you back, Neelie."

North never questioned Key's appearance at the end of the road, he never asked where Key lived or mentioned the work farm or Ben Willard and his wife. All he said to Key the first night when they bunked down in the adobe was; "Neelie's grown this year while I was gone. She's beautiful. You sure stay away from her now, she's still my responsibility." Key nodded in the dark and knew that North heard the bedclothes rustle. There was nothing more to be said, what North stated was the truth.

Charlie Rushton came by the next morning, hauling two big horses in a fancy new trailer. He spoke directly to Ray and included North when it came to specifics. "Got these two broncs, threw my best two men, broke three ribs, an arm and a leg between them. Don't want to can 'em, got good breedin'. So ride them hard till they quit their evil ways. Figured North's size'll hold 'em down." He stopped, bit off a fresh plug of chaw and cast his eyes everywhere except on Key. "That one there, he can ride, put him on the buckskin, pitches worsen all the others together. Want 'em done by fall." From all this Ray gathered that Key was getting paid through the McKendrick account and working for Rushton again.

Just this easily, Key slipped back into the adobe and the McKendricks' lives, bringing in a small canvas bag one day after going to town with Ray to pick up grain and salt for the stock. He set the bag inside the doorway and no one mentioned it but he was expected for supper and to be there early morning when the horses were fed and breakfast cooked before the day's work.

Neelie worked on weekends so she had Tuesday for herself. Her ma let her be, said the girl worked hard enough and was saving up for college, she didn't need to work much, 'cept for meals. Otherwise she could read and sleep when she wanted and ride her old pony. North teased her, delighted to have the chance. "Look how your legs hang, you can play hop scotch with the pony, if he slips you'll stab your toe." Neelie gave back what she got; "See Key up there on the buckskin, why he looks like a jockey, riding that sixteen hand monster while you prance around on the puny roan. That horse was made for you, North, you can step off without doing nothin' but puttin' your feet down and the horse'll walk out from underneath."

They were having fun and besides, Key rode the buckskin 'cause he was the better rider, no question there. Rushton wanted the horses back going well, and if they behaved then maybe Key would have a winter job. Rumor had it Mrs. Willard was pregnant and her husband strutted around puffed-up but the second rumor said he wasn't the papa. North didn't mention that part to Neelie, he didn't lie, he just didn't say those who knew how to count had different bets on the kid's paternity.

Neelie often rode down to get the mail which got delivered on Tuesday and Friday, an improvement from when they had to drive all the way into town once a week for mail. She had a tendency to let the pony gallop back to the house, sitting relaxed on him, holding the mail, the little horse churning under her, covering ground fast with his short, choppy strides. North, when he first saw them, had flashbacks to the terrible spill Neelie took his first summer. Now she only wrapped, her long legs around the pony's barrel and floated above his stride, hair whipped by the wind, eyes bright with pleasure. She might say she was a city girl working in town, driving her own vehicle, but when North saw that look, he knew her better, he saw the freedom she craved and knew again how much alike they could be.

Towards the end of summer, maybe two weeks before North had to get back up to school, Neelie came trotting up the long track, eyes bent to what she held in her hand. Without slowing much she laid most of the mail on the stones piled by the kitchen and rode back to the corrals, still carrying a long white envelope. Her pale legs were barely covered at the top by denim shorts, her jersey revealed too much for North. He was over-conscious of Key working in back of him, the steady sweep of stacking wood broke, changed, interrupted then returned to its rhythm. North shook his head, caught in the middle, annoyed at Neelie, angry at Key for noticing her.

The pony's head pushed at North; Neelie handed him the envelope. "It's for you, it's a letter." North snorted. She kept at him. "From a girl, the handwriting is so sweet." She drawled the last word, giving it far too much emphasis. North blushed as his unsteady fingers felt the paper. Behind him the sound of wood on wood did not change and for that he was grateful. But Neelie wouldn't let him be.

"You've gone and got yourself a girlfriend without tellin' us? Why that ain't right, North, we're family, you got to tell us everythin'." North countered; "Like you tell your ma and pa. I seen you sittin' over coffee with that colored fella, you tell your ma 'bout him yet?"

He wasn't ready for her outraged anger. "Northern McKendrick that is the cruelest thing I've heard you say. His name is Mickey Herrera and he comes in and we visit, that's all. Why does it bother you where his folks come from and what about his dark color? You got friends darker'n Mickey." She drew an almost visible line under the last words; Key had to hear them and North felt the source of her anger. He was dumb, and she'd gotten smarter while he was the one in college.

He turned the unopened letter in his hand. "I'm sorry, Key...I didn't mean-." He stopped talking and looked back; Key's pale eyes were directed at him. Key spoke, in that low easy drawl meant he was hurt and wouldn't admit it. "Heard worse, been called all the bad names. Me, I sat with Mickey, had a cup a coffee with him. Nice fella no doubt. Real direct. Can't blame Neelie for wantin' to talk with someone civilized."

There was another word underlined. Civil: not appropriate for Northern McKendrick. Neelie deserved nice and more. North dropped the letter, looked at it blankly.

"Open it, dummy, tell us it ain't from a pretty girl who wants you back on campus." Neelie gave him room. North picked up the letter and tore it open, pulled out the single fold of paper and without lifting his eyes to meet those of Key and Neelie, spoke into the stirred air. "I didn't know it was in me, I 'pologize, to both a you."

"Well, is it a girl? Has to be with that pretty writing." North let her babble over the rough spot. Key was grinning when North got enough courage to look his way; he'd put the ax down and was wiping his hands on his pants. "Yeah, North, what's that letter say. Though if she ain't comin' here to help, and soon, I guess I don't rightly care."

North read quickly, refolded the paper twice then

stuck it in a hip pocket. "It's back to work for us, Key. Neelie, it's from a girl but not my girl if you know the difference. Just about school, that's all." Neelie sat on the pony, her legs swinging in long independent circles. Key deliberately turned his back to her and picked up the ax, then looked to the sky where a hawk circled. North rubbed his unshaven jaw.

"You two are hopeless. Ah damn." She spun the pony and trotted back to the corral. North let out a strong curse, wanting to rant and scream but it was back to stacking wood alongside Key, who did not look up when North returned to the task but worked silently, sweating in the August heat but making no complaint.

That night North thought about the incident, over and over while his mouth and gut soured and a rage boiled in him; he couldn't sleep, couldn't be in the same room as Key so he went outside and sat a moment, then got up and paced, chewed his lip and looked for a moon or a new star or anything to take his attention and relieve him of his guilt.

Ray McKendrick appeared at the kitchen door, shirtless, barefoot, gray hair sticking up like a rooster's tail. "Boy, what's got you so heated we can hear you inside. Claudie sent me, said to pick out what ails you and let us all sleep." He drew a hand through his hair, patting down the errant tufts. "Must look a fool, standing here like this." Echoes of Mrs. Claudie's voice got into North's conscience. .

"I'm sorry, sir. I can't sleep, can't set, can't do nothin'." Ray leaned on the piled stone. "You findin' out the rest of the world ain't so fine, that it's special folks make life bearable? Or you decidin' that we're all fools back here and you can't wait to get goin' on your own? Heck of a mess, ain't it, all these decisions."

"No sir, it ain't you or the ranch, or even town. I know my place here, I know it's what I want. It's that...well, I insulted Key this afternoon, and Neelie too, said words I never knew I thought and it shamed me." Ray cocked his head, "Somethin' about his color, or his pa maybe?" North stiffened; "How'd you know? Neelie tell you?" Ray raised a hand, "No, the girl don't tell tales. North, son, no matter how free we think we are, we grow up in a place, it gives us certain sets to our mind. Most folks around here take no notice of Key's color till he does somethin' wrong or they get angry and the filth spews out, what they really feel. Course Key don't help by bein' who he is but that's no excuse. Me I work 'longside colored men all the time, mostly Mexicans but some Japs, some Chinks. See what I mean, even those words're ugly but they're what I know. I learned them here.

"You made your apology to Key yet? You talk 'bout this with him?" North hesitated; "No sir, that takes more courage than I got." Ray shook his head violently, even in the dark North could see him. "Son, you got it backwards 'bout yourself. More'n likely you're wrong 'bout Key. He knows you, trusts you, and he ain't bad never mind what he does off this place. You talk to him, I bet you'll find the same fear and ugly thinkin' hides in him too. You can't head off to school with this over you, it'll be a bad time studyin' with this eatin' your gut."

Words going in circles; North studied his uncle, saw a deep tiredness in the fading eyes and knew he'd taken too much with his nighttime ramblings. "Yes, sir, I'll go talk with Key now. Thank you ...ah...good night." He tried, but Ray caught him by the elbow and held tight. "Son, don't go hide like you're plannin', you talk to him, wake him if you have to but I bet he's wide-eyed and listenin'. For all I don't approve of Key or his mama, he's your friend, by your choice, and you can't put that aside without wrecking somethin' good. Do it now, no fibbin', no lies."

Ray let go, walked to the door, stopped, looked back

and motioned with his hand that North get moving. "Do what I said boy, talk it out, don't leave things to rot inside. Good night."

The events of that afternoon and evening stick with me; I can feel North's pain with mine, that he would question Mickey just on his color, that Key would stand up for Mickey and me based on that one visit; that North would attack in such a vicious unexpected manner. Dear North, sweet, kind, needing to take care of the world and he slanders a man he does not know based on the slightest of misinformation. It was my introduction to a world I would eventually enter knowing full well I would live precariously because of my choice in husbands.

Other choices were made that night; by North who finally asked Key for forgiveness, which put their friendship in a different, deeper place. It always had been North as the pillar of tolerance, the steadying influence, now it was Key's turn and he became noble, sensitive, exhibiting a side of his heart we had not ever imagined could exist. I expect it was the only time Key held a role where others looked up to him and asked forgiveness. I also believe, from the distance of all these years, that Key possessed a goodness none of us allowed for since he rarely showed it to the world but did, in his own peculiar way, try to maintain a pride of mind, a philosophy of soul that did not compromise him in the way outsiders assumed was his constant choice.

All this sounds romantic and benevolent in connection with a man who later betrayed so many people and divided a family irrevocably. But I cannot believe all bad of Key, I know I saw the hint of goodness which kept leading me to him. North went in the adobe and said words which scored his heart, hearing himself ask forgiveness for thoughts he did not know he owned. And Key, having the chance to punish a companion whose constant superiority to his own existence was always thrown back at him, was the soul of generosity and forgiveness. I know, I heard a great deal of what went on in that small adobe but that night. I crept downstairs and stood at the door and held myself quiet, barely breathing so I would not miss a single word.

The rubbed and smoothed wood of the doorway comforted North, he waited a moment, his hand gripping the frame, his bare feet firm on the packed earthen floor. He and Key had planned to put down great red squares of tile but never got to it and now most likely they never would. He pulled up his toes, felt the powder-soft dust roll in between them as he moved both feet carefully, hand on the door, still tying to see what waited for him.

"North, I can't sleep neither. Heard you and Ray outside, didn't want to get in the way." Key called Uncle Ray by his first name so easily, a sign of his moving into an adult world of hard work and small wage. Key was almost nineteen now, North would be there in the spring. And Uncle Ray was no more than a hired man, working for the same boss as Key. Foolish, a dumb thing to be thinking while a best friend waited for some kind of apology.

"I don't know, Key, what got me goin'. I never thought on it before, you, your color...your pa. Ah." He hated it, the word color with bastard hiding behind it. "Guess it was more than I could hold on to...Neelie and all wearin' those shorts...ah hell, Key, I am sorry. You won't ever know how sorry I am. And not just that I said the words but that I could ever think them."

There it was, the core of his shame. "I didn't know I could feel this way." He spoke into the dark, glad he could not see Key's expression. Key's voice was soft, almost gentle, like he was speaking to a spooked bronc; "You didn't know you could hate and love the same time, did you North?" There was a long pause, a moment of reconnection. "Me, too. It ain't only you thinkin' this way. First time I saw Mickey talkin' to Neelie, well I had the chance to sit and talk to him and he wasn't so bad, for being a Mex. You just ain't had that chance yet."

North could see Key now, lying on top of the bedclothes, hands locked behind his head. It made North more uncomfortable to see Key that way, body exposed, no defense, no protection against North's unexpected and cruel words.

"North, let's leave this alone now? There's shame for both of us. I've had enough, learned too much too, learned what I don't want to know. What do you say...apology accepted?" A slow easy dismissal of North's pain, an acknowledgement of Key's instinctive hate existing on a level without conscious feeling.

"All right, Key. Thanks."

Tension existed between North and me almost until he went back to school, and I stayed really angry when I knew he and Key were stronger friends now, easier with each other after this ugly incident. I guess that what kept me so mad was that North and Key could talk and explain and admit their failings and then still like and trust each other. All this makes little sense but so many things we do as humans make no sense even as we buy into them and keep holding to them for our own destruction.

I almost stopped liking North, until Mama pulled me aside two days before he was to leave and told me to stop being a silly fool and make it up, whatever 'it' was, between North and me.

Mama was an expert at cutting to the heart, and this once I took her advice. My apology to North more than likely didn't make much sense to him as I tried to explain my own convoluted feelings and got garbled and confused until he pulled my hair, tickling me and laughing, giving me a brief, fierce hug and that was the end of our feud.

Mama was right; I am more than glad I did not let the words fester while he was away. So much happened in the next six months that my boiling anger would have been submerged and then would resurface at an inopportune time, out of proportion and inappropriate and highly inflammable. As it was, we had a magical supper the night before North was to leave. Key was with us, a part of our family for that time, and Papa didn't seem to mind, Mama even gave him a brief, almost affectionate hug, and we were ourselves again.

Chapter Nine

"Ray, Wait." Claudie checked again; her purse, the list, then glanced at Neelie, thought without purpose how the child had grown up this summer. Long legs and a tiny waist, too pretty and far too fashionable for a country girl. She spoke carefully to her daughter, letting her hear the love so the words wouldn't hurt. "Makin' you a dress ain't so easy now, none of the lengths I put aside will do."

Then she stopped in mid flight. "You've got choices today, girl. There's school knockin', and the ironin' won't do itself. Me, I'd skip both and think of somethin' else. There aren't many more days of freedom." Claudie shook her head at her own foolishness, Neelie mimicked her. "Well, Mama, Papa won't wait forever. Be careful. Think on what you choose to do."

Neelie never knew with her ma; advice and chores and lists of what to do and a day with the family gone to take North to the bus. Then along comes a suggestion of rebellion.

Ray closed the truck door carefully as his wife settled in the seat. It felt like they were courting again. Claudie had a light to her eyes inside from nothing Ray had done. North, like the first day they got him, was huddled up to the truck cab in back. Ray wasn't sure about Claudie; she'd woke hugging him last night and he rolled over, pulled her to him and felt the tears but no sound, no demand, only the need to be held without words. He relaxed enough to lick the tears from her face and under his tongue he knew her face crinkled into a smile. It had to be enough for both of them. It was all Ray had left.

This morning she was young and fussy, smoothing her skirt with both hands while watching Ray in quick sideways glances. He leaned over and kissed her. She pulled back, then nuzzled up to his ear. "Boo." The unexpected silliness drew then apart and each hoped the kids hadn't seen or heard.

As the truck bucked and rumbled, North saw the ranch as it grew too small and disappeared. His mind jumped from the dissolving house, the matchstick corral, the stick figure Neelie made still waving, to where Key was now, what he would do for the winter. Then his heart leaped almost through his mouth; Key was at the ranch, alone, with Neelie. He groaned and was glad the McKendricks could not hear him.

North still had that promise from a long time in the past, that Key would not pursue Neelie. Said he didn't need to, that even he knew better, that he would not want to break up a family over a moment's fun. North had to content himself with those long-said words and keep faith that Key would not betray them.

The house was gone now, a trail of settling dust remained to show him where he spent the summer. Now it was classes and professors and the girl whose face he could not quite picture, writing to say she couldn't wait for him to come back and take her out for the promised supper and a movie.

He had planned to hitch a ride with North and the McKendricks out of here, and get off at the JO Bar gate to see about work. Gus Olin said late spring there might be room for him. But in the fall most ranches laid off instead of hiring. Still it was a place to start.

Instead Key stayed behind to finish laying the flagstones at the back door for Mrs. Claudie and Neelie. Key's fingers seemed to find the right shape and weight for each stone fitted in its place, what he was taught by the Italian who drank too much and fought and spent two months working for the county.

Part of his plan had rested on Neelie going with them. She complicated everything now, coming by while he worked, offering coffee, wanting to talk, restless and trying to bring him into her orbit of domestic playtime. A future story for her, a jail cell for Key who knew he would never settle for what she day-dreamed.

She was beautiful now, not perfect of course, but those watchful eyes, the clean line of her hip, the long leg, the sweet throat running to her bosom, they could tempt a saint. Key wiped his mouth clean, thought of North and Mrs. Claudie, of Ray and his powerful hands, his tired eyes. Deliberately he dropped a stone, nicked his hand, swore, licked the blood clean. A tinge of pain to remind him. Neelie approached him again, he dismissed her. "Go do all those female things your ma taught you, girl. I got work to do."

It was easy imagining the anger and fury on her face as Key knelt over the stones, tapped and searched for that right piece like the Eyetie taught him; feel the rough edge, smooth, tease, wait until the stones slid into their right place. Good, she was gone, no gifts left to tempt him, no hot coffee and fresh bread or his favorite, a cold slice of yesterday's peach pie.

Doing the ironing slowly pleased Neelie until she guessed it was what her ma counted on so she quit and sat down hard on the bed. It was hot in the close room, heated more by the iron, the steaming cloth. Two shirts and a whole bunch of table clothes and napkins, for Papa wouldn't have paper ones, and Mama thought a table looked pretty set with flowered patterns and clean white dishes. None of North's clothes left to do of course, they were finished yesterday; it was Papa's dress shirt and a blouse of Mama's waited, and more tablecloths.

Her fingers twisted her hair into a long tube, then caught the ends in an elastic band and she ran both hands down her thighs, bare after the shorts ended, freckled like the rest of her, ugly to her thinking, pale no matter how much she worked outside. Through the window she saw North's big sorrel chase the little dun pony. Once she left for school, and had a full-time job, the pony was meant for the neighbor's daughter.

She pushed up from the bed, made sure the iron was off, slipped into loose tennis shoes and headed to the corral. This was her day, her choice was a ride on the dun, going nowhere but to please her heart.

As she swing a leg over the rounded back, the hair tickling her skin, she saw Charlie Rushton's Chrysler slow at the bottom of the lane. She glanced at Key kneeling, at ease in the dirt, paying no attention except to the breaking and fitting of those darned stones.

She grabbed mane, set her knees; "Yihaa!" and the pony bolted forward, she hung on, guessing she'd startled Key and glad, wanting the pony to run forever. When she got to the mailbox Rushton was waiting. Between her legs, Neelie felt the pony's heart pumped wildly, the clean smell of sweat covered her. She inhaled, then became conscious of Rushton watching her.

"Missy you run that pony like your pa ain't to home." Gradually the pony's breathing slowed, Rushton waited, then began to talk, his voice rough and nervous. "I brought North's last paycheck, meant to get it here yesterday." Neelie answered quickly, curious as to what was going on. "North's already gone, Mr. Rushton, but Mama will send it on to him." "Yes, gal, I know. It's not why I come. Got a check here for Larkin too." Rushton waved his hand, stuck between its middle two fingers was a dark, stinking cigar. Neelie deliberately coughed and covered her mouth with her hand. "Real lady, ain't you," was all Rushton said.

Again he waved his hand, this time the pony shied and Neelie had to grab mane as her knees slipped on the wet hide. "I come for more'n this jawin' with you." He went on but his eyes wavered, slipped away from Neelie and looked to those ever-present mountains. "Don't care much 'bout his morals, though I admire him some for his stickin' to things, hell of a rider too." She wasn't sure but it sounded like he was talking about Key.

"You can tell him, missy. Ain't what no man wants to tell 'nother." He waited, Neelie laid a hand on either side of the pony's neck. "What are you saying, Mr. Rushton? I don't understand." He interrupted and for all of his roughness, when Rushton turned gentle, Neelie knew to listen.

"You tell that boy his ma died last night. Beat to death by one a the drunks at Cooley's Tavern. Good thing he weren't to home, doc says it was a mess."

Rushton was watching and that made her keep her feelings from reaching her face. Behind her eyes she felt the strain, her skin tightened even to her hair but she would not cry in front of this crude, knowing, leering man over the death of a woman she hardly knew. It wasn't her dying, it was the ugly chore of telling Key.

"I know, girl, it's a hard one to lay on you but he ain't friendly to me, I don't take much to him neither and Ben Willard ain't been the same since that summer. You tell him, girl, you and North're the family he got. 'Sides, I got a notion the boy won't care."

With that and a wave of the cigar, he let the Chrysler roll away and Neelie clung to the skittering pony. Then the car stopped, a hand waved out the window holding two white envelopes. Neelie kicked the pony up to the window, swiped the envelopes and didn't look at Rushton or care when the Chrysler started up again and sent dust all over her. Good riddance she thought, and added a string of curse words she wasn't supposed to know. The pony laid back its ears and turned towards home.

There was nothing to do but tell him right out; "Your ma died last night, Key. Mr. Rushton come by to tell us. I'm sorry. Key?" She wondered how he could lose his only kin and feel that nothing, show only a weak pull at the corners of his mouth as if she'd brought gossip he didn't care to hear. He folded a bit of broken stone through his fingers. "Did he say how?" Good, she sighed, at last he had a question. "I guess a man...hurt her." Key nodded absently. He was standing in the McKendrick's doorway, his eyes wandering, his face showing neither pain nor sadness. Then simply; "Thanks for tellin' me. The town'll bury her. I can't." Those last words had only the tiniest crack in his assertion the death didn't matter.

He knelt back down in the dirt, fixed two edges of stone, reached for a hammer to tap them in place. Neelie watched for more sign but he showed only a bowed back, hands seeking contact with stone, eyes blind in the dust and fragments. "Key, won't you go to town...don't you want to know more?" He rocked back on his heels, head raised to just miss seeing her. The eyes were pale, the mouth steady, not even the hands shook in the smallest tremble. "Neelie, it's none of your business. You so curious, you go ask."

"That's awful. Your mama died, and you don't care." He moved slowly, pushing himself up from the stones, wiping his hands on his pants leg, scrubbing his face until a hint of copper skin showed through the gray, sticky dust. "It's not for you to tell me how I feel. Why do you care anyway, you never met her, she wasn't much and I ain't seen her in more than a year." The sobriety of his voice, the utter logical response to her emotion angered her more. "She's flesh and blood, Key, all you have." She coughed, wiped her mouth; "Had."

He raised a hand; "She birthed me someplace, I don't even know where. Don't put me and her into your ideas, your life. We won't fit." His voice turned savage and he was frightening her; "I could have slipped out of her in a bar or in a lover's bed, ruined the sheets, annoyed some man she was fucking 'cause her belly was too big and he couldn't get to her. You shut up about my ma – . She's dead. That's all."

Again his eyes slipped from her but Neelie felt them draw a new heat, the color gone to pale fire, the face blanched and ugly. She had never been afraid of Key until now.

"Oh." Silly, dumb, foolish sound, Neelie didn't know how to escape. Key pushed at her with one hand, she slipped, caught herself and he backed away. She thought he shuddered, thought he wiped at his eyes but when she looked closely he was standing, casual, tense but in control. "You finished now? I need to get back to work. Don't want to be here when your folks return." As if nothing had passed between them.

"Sure, Key, I'll get to my chores." She wavered a minute, pulled at her loosened ponytail. "Just thought you might want to know." Then she walked away, conscious of his eyes, not watching her, more than likely looking inward, seeing something she could not imagine. By the time she had the pony unbridled and in the corral happily chewing hay, Key was back in his dirt, surrounded by stone fragments and oblivious to her presence.

Mid-day passed and there was no sign of her parents, and no mention from Key that he expected or wanted a noon meal. Neelie was restless, thought about taking one of her pa's horses, maybe the old brown, but that was crossing a line she knew was sacred. These mounts worked hard, they were not for play. So she finished the ironing, thought of her mama then and was suddenly conscious of the heat, sweat stinging her eyes, a small burn on the back of her hand from trying to point a collar. Her mind jumped: he had to be hungry, she herself was starved.

Mama had a sweet-cured ham from a pig fed scraps and special food 'til it was enormous then Papa slaughtered it right, so today it was ham sandwiches on thick sliced bread with a hot mustard North taught them all to like and pickles Neelie put up on her own with only a little help from Mama. Iced water with a slice of lemon and some sugar; Papa drank it with whiskey sometimes, and he kept the bottle in his office.

When she came outside to offer these delicacies to Key, he acted as if no words had gone between them earlier. Key sat back on his heels and drank all the lemonade, head thrown back, throat working rhythmic swallows, while Neelie watched, still holding the sandwich. "More, Key?" "Yes, ma'am."

Then he spoke again; "Guess I was hungry after all." His voice broke, then steadied. "Hadn't thought you'd be here today. Won't your folks be back soon?" He sounded hopeful, she answered him in kind, distant and ordinary; "Mama had lots of errands. I saw the list." She handed him the sandwich, he was slow in accepting it. "Let me make some more lemonade." When she came back outside Key was where she left him, the half-eaten sandwich fallen from his hand. Tears poured down his cheeks, tracking through the stone dust; his eyes did not blink, there was no other life or movement in his face.

She did what was right; she put down the glass and sat next to him on the ground and stroked his back, rested fingers on his arm, spoke soft, cajoling words and sounds like 'shhhh' and 'that's right' and 'you'll feel better now' until he jerked away from her, pushing her until she sprawled backwards. His voice was harsh; "God damn it – it won't be better. Don't you get it, she's dead and I don't care."

That was it; "You sorry son of a..." She stopped, the next word too obvious and painful. "Whatever she was, and did, she was your mother and you need to cry for her."

When he stood, she got up beside him. He drew back a fist, she put her hands to her hips and thrust out her jaw. Then as more tears blurred his eyes she leaned in and put two fingers to just beside his mouth. "Please, Key, don't."

Instinct guided her. She took that last step to comfort him, close in, taking his breath through her opened lips, feeling the push and rise of his chest as he fought a silent battle. Obediently her arms went around his back, drawing him in, holding him as if he might shatter.

His head twisted from the embrace but she held him,

felt the struggle; when he fought harder, she found his mouth again and kissed him until he quieted, then his lips softened and opened and moved on hers. With her lips parted she could take in his breath and release her own.

His hands rose to her ribs, squeezed and contracted, came between their close bodies and pushed her away but she would not leave and spoke into his mouth. "No. Hold me. Keep me here." He leaned sideways, she went with him still connected to his mouth, her hands crossed on his back, resting in the dent of his spine.

Then what she had witnessed with the breeding animals happened; at her belly a pole pressed into her. Before she caught her breath and truly understood, Key pulled away with his hips, taking that hardness so it did not touch her and she cried softly as she moved with him.

"Neelie, you can't do this. Not with me. I'm Key, the son of a bitch your whole family warns you about. Neelie. Your folks." He went quiet. "I made them a promise." Then he breathed; "Oh God." Through his parted mouth into her own. She found his mouth, nibbled his upper lip, let her hand slip to the waist of his jeans and the smooth long muscles of his back naked, sleek under the light tee. His hands traced hers; they searched under her blouse then found the clasp of her bra and there they froze, scalding her flesh. He breathed in again; "Oh God." She pushed the words back into his mouth.

*F*aces, thoughts, shocked him, stopped him briefly. North, Mrs. Claudie, especially Ray McKendrick. His own ma. Women: with parted legs, mouths wide, arms reaching, hands cupping. Their force guiding him where he needed to be. North again: eyes storm black, thick hands raised to kill.

The intense reality of Neelie evaporated the images; she was a child wide eyed and asking, hands pressed to him, belly teasing against his, rubbing, bringing him to almost spilling over.

"Neelie get away." He couldn't believe the words; he backed up and fought a new war against her fingers which instinctively went across his stomach to touch bare skin and tightly curled hair. "Neelie, no."

Space separated them; they stared, new strangers. Then she cried and took all the heart from Key. She was ashamed, rejected by her first man, not good enough, not for his loving. Key shook all over; "I can't. You know that. Not you, not in this family." His voice rose on the last words, those damning, hungry needs he hated and cursed in his sleep.

He'd do anything for her; now he couldn't look at her swollen mouth, her breasts half exposed, asking him to break his vow. "You leave me be, Neelie McKendrick. It ain't your ma beat to death." That stopped it all. Neelie covered her eyes and cried for real, gasping, drawing air in deep, sudden tears flooding her open mouth, expelling from her as she collapsed against him. From a teasing, mature would-be lover she became a child, a girl untouched by so many things newly discovered, undone by lust and slapped by death. Key almost relented, aching to hold and comfort her, be comforted by what he knew so well. The ghost weight of North's hand rested lightly on his shoulder and he straightened up, shook his head, hated himself even more.

"Pull it together, Neelie. Your folks'll be back and I need to be gone then. Your pa paid me for the job already. 'Sides, ole Rushton himself offered me a job." He waved the opened envelope. "The line camp, a good place for me." He was grinning like all the fools in the world and she was crying but he kept rattling on figuring he was bound to find something would make her laugh instead of bawling like a dogie calf.

He kept going; "Who knows, maybe I'll take up stone-laying for a hobby, 'stead of women. I know, I'll pave the front yard of Rushton's camp, keep it swept clean, a cowboy showplace, wouldn't the ole man like that." Some place in the stupidity she had stopped her mewling, opened her eyes and blew her nose and saw into him as he prattled and spewed. "Thank you, Key." She was a mess, eyes red and swollen, face shiny with tears, mouth hanging, nose running like any two-year-old brat.

Without any planning, he drew out a kerchief and held her chin in one hand, wiped and scoured and had to spit on the kerchief to get some of the dried mucus off her face. It was foolish and unbearably sweet.

Even now I remember the scattered and terrifying feelings Key generated in me but I cannot describe or name them, nor do I want to dwell on them for they almost destroyed me. Despite the talk and the films and the discussions in our school and then outside with friends, giggling and guessing, embarrassed while we made bad jokes and considered the available boys, none of us had any idea as to the force and power of the sexual feelings which until that first moment are denied us. And I guess, having talked with women over the years, who dread the nights their husbands want intimacy, that some women never experience the shattering power of their own newly aroused sexuality.

Secret wants, needs I did not understand, were freed in me by hands touching so gently on my face to wash away my crying. The desire to be close, the intensity of the ache which had tantalized me before was now real, burning, opening me to another human in that manner I had laughed about and secretly thought was silly, overrated, even ugly.

The usual teenage and virginal thoughts rattled me: how could my own parents engage in this wanting act, they were old, they could not see the beauty of Key Larkin behind his face and eyes, they could not feel magic in his hands, smell the sweet raw need in his body. I was being focused to a single world.

The worst, the most destructive element of this initial encounter is what it did to Key. He pulled away from me several times, denying the force between us. I was aware of his promise, his vow, I felt the physical retreat and knowing what I did about him, his need for a family, his close trust with North, I still reached for him at a weak moment and used that weakness to take what I had not known existed. For this single act I still carry shame; later in the farce everyone naturally blamed Key; when I tried to speak up, to make them understand, no one listened, no one wanted to, and Key himself diverted their ability to hear me by bragging about what he had done and the rage was redirected towards him. As a family we still were shattered, his grand gesture for nothing.

This is understandable now; I have to remind myself, looking at the pretty child who is my granddaughter, waiting impatiently for the rest of the story; someday too she will discover the power and fury of a sexual love, or need, and will deny that her parents, and especially her aged, tired, wrinkled grandmother, could ever have known what passion she now ached to experience. Sexual delight reinvents itself for each participant. I am careful to edit and redirect certain aspects of my story but between my grandchild and me there races a current which obliquely, silently, fills in all the missing and important elements which make the story complete.

She was motionless as he wiped her face clean, except in her belly where a deep energy flowed, opened wider, spread down her legs and up into her breasts and she could not imagine how he could touch her so and not feel the heat he'd generated. Her eyes were shuttered, she looked out through soaked lashes to the dusty earth, the remnants of broken stone, the finished pathway to the door. Its pattern was beautiful, each space fitted neatly against its neighbor, smoothed, swept, soft enough to stroke and imagine velvet between the fingers.

When she felt fingertips stay a beat longer on her face she took those fingers and held them to her mouth, kissed them and he withdrew the hand gently, not a pull but a slow departing dance of resignation. "No, Key, it is all right." She looked at him. "Come with me. I know, I do." It was like leading a bottle-fed calf; if she promised what he wanted, he would go where he didn't want to on the strength of the blind promise, the prompting of reward overriding any worry about risk.

The front room in the adobe was filled with tossed blankets, soiled clothing, a bedroll shoved into a corner, the banco molded from cured adobe along one wall was where North told her Key sometimes slept or lay awake when he was restless. Wads of blankets and clothes would make the banco suitable, keeping two bodies on its narrow shelf would be a balancing act. Way back in her mind were the voices of ministers and teachers and doctors and warnings about pregnancy and reputation and none of them filled her like the promise of Key.

"Key?" He had stopped at the doorway, would not look at her or step inside. His nose wrinkled as if offended by a smell; Neelie inhaled, tasted sweat and dreams, manure and raw male energy. "Key." He had to look at her. "Key, let's use the other room." He shook his head no. And she did not listen. Her hand swept across his chest; "Yes, I do know. And with you, no one else."

How could a child like Neelie be certain; Key shook his head again, tried for the grin that always worked but it was wrong, deceived no one, made him angry at himself and forced Neelie to lift her hand to his lips and stroke them until the grin was fading and she kissed him and he knew it was all but done.

North's bed was ready, smooth, neat corners, pillows tucked under the homemade quilt. Key swung her around until the back of her knees met the iron bed frame and he could put a hand to each side of her waist and kiss her, bring her lightly to him and then with a practiced shove tried to place her on the bed. But she would not go, she did not know the game; she clung to him drawing her lips hard against his and wrapping her arms across his back, bunching his shirt until he felt her palms against his skin. He smelled her heat and fear.

"Key." She breathed into his mouth. "I don't know what to do now." He directed her and each word impaled him. "Lie down, girl. Wait, let me...take this off." His expert hands found and unclasped the bra, slid it with the jersey over her head with no protest and she was bare from the waist up. She surprised him by not becoming modest, covering her breasts with two hands, simpering, coy, pretending this was all an innocent mistake.

She was close enough to him her nipples rose in anticipation and he could feel then touch his chest. Fierce dark red hair curled slightly around her shoulders and down her back and Key lifted several strands and laid them across her breasts. Her chest was freckled and his index finger on his right hand tapped the reddish dots in small circles until she quivered and he saw the nipple rise and harden even more and he relished the confusion on her face as the new, unusual, erotic feel swept through.

"This is what it is. Touch and stroke and play until you can't stand it and then a man inside you, poking and pushing until you feel torn apart. Inside, do you get me?" Her last chance, words he'd never spoken to a woman, disgust deep in his voice, anger at the act's crudeness, at the need in him that kept him bending over a woman's form, shoving himself repeatedly into her until she cried and he came apart.

His shirt was gone, his jeans unbuttoned; he didn't know when. As his pants slid down his hips, his hardened penis pushed out the folds of his shorts. Neelie looked down and her smile wiped out Key's fury. "I know, Key, I've seen you before. But not like this." She reached and stroked him through the light fabric and the sensation was overwhelming. Fighting for one more chance, he yanked down his shorts, exposed his erection which butted and prodded Neelie's belly. She laughed, he flushed and started to speak but she placed her hand on the erection's tip and he rubbed against her touch and knew that if she moved he would climax and it would all be over without any damage to Neelie.

She was frozen, her hand an icicle on his penis. Key felt himself slowly wilt but his hands would not leave her breasts and she looked at him with glazed, unfocused submission and he stepped back, her hand fell and he sighed. He was able to unbutton her shorts, push them down, and roll the white panties along her thighs until she was hobbled at the knees. The width of her hips astounded him, the cleft was visible through a matting of red curls. He inhaled that sweet odor and she smiled and he knew there could be no stopping.

His fingers touched the soft lips in reverence and she moved slightly from the strange intimacy. His erection wilted again; "This is a contact sport, girl, not a game of cards." Crude, her last chance, he held his breath, ached in time to his beating heart. Neelie lay back on the bed, one leg raised in an instinctive pose of invitation and Key stood above, eager and shamed. She nearly finished him by reaching up to touch his penis, which bobbed and jumped in her hand and he felt a deep beginning spasm.

"No, girl, quiet. Lie there, let me come to you." She took him literally sliding over next to the wall and simply waiting. Key positioned himself alongside her, on his left hip, one hand supporting his head, the other reaching for her soft belly. Her muscles rippled, she giggled. "Tickles, does it? You wait, it won't for long." He tried to keep his voice light-hearted, tried not to say what he felt, that he was courting a goddess, too pure in her heart, in her conscience and he had no right reaching above his place to take her. It was wrong and beautiful; he could not stop now. Hate and rage warred inside him as he mounted over Neelie and pressed the tip of his penis between her legs, feeling the light curling hair touch and tease him until he began to push, lightly. When she groaned in resistance, he sucked his fingers and moved them between her dry lips and wet more spittle on his own shaft until he was able, by leaning, an elbow on either side of her head, his mouth pressed to her throat and then to a breast and back to the throat, to the mouth, a soft kiss, thrusting from his hips, a deeper kiss, a groan as he moved until he felt the responding wetness.

A hard push, her body stiffened; a kiss, a touch back to the breast, a hand between their hips to rub the small knob which brought women to their pleasure. Neelie's eyes flew open, she stared up at him until he thought to stop. The glow of her eyes, their light and pleasure broke the rage driving him and he sucked in his belly, began to draw away but she arched her back and captured his hand between them.

It was Neelie then who raised her hips and helped him enter. He felt the resistance and then the give as he moved into the slippery deep. He knew to watch her face, her eyes; they widened, her skin flushed, then the eyes shuttered and closed and a tear slid from beneath each lid. He kissed them individually, licked close to her ear while slowly he moved his hips, offering to bring her along with his own pleasure.

Then any pretence at discipline left him; he pumped hard, rose above her, felt her virginal tightness close around him, an involuntary squeezing brought him to his climax and he cursed as he groaned in his release. She did not stop with him, she did not lie quietly but kept lifting, pushing, seeming to ask for more.

Then her eyes opened, wide, her breath came hard and short and she cried gently, then again, with need, suddenly all muscles went slack, all energy left her body. "Oh." She rested her face at the junction of his neck. "Key. "

They dozed for a half hour, wound together in the narrow bunk, their flesh bonded with sticky fluids, a mutual scent rising between them; when Neelie opened her eyes and took in a deep breath it was a strange new smell that told her what she'd done. Key's head lay on her shoulder. She gently touched the new scar on his forehead, and saw the other marks of his life and began to cry. It was nothing she had not know about, nothing hidden from her but now his terrible past was there beneath her fingers, ridged and puckered and shiny. That he could be so gentle, kind, tender, and still bear these marks enchanted her.

"My God, Key, it's my parents. I can hear the truck."

She jumped clear of him to find her scattered clothing and get dressed, but Key caught her by the elbow. "Biggest mistake you can make, flying out of here lookin' half undone. Slow down, brush your hair, don't bother with shoes." She hesitated, looked at him, frowned, then nodded. "Yeah, I know this from experience. I never said different, did I? You're not goin' to turn into a virgin queen on me now, are you. Thinkin' you're the first and we're now sweethearts or somethin'?"

Harsh words she hated, and hated him for speaking them. His hands pulled through her tangled hair, she fought him, kicked her shoes outside and slipped into panties and her shorts, pulled on the jersey wrong side to until Key grinned and she hated him even more. Then he leaned forward, only half-dressed himself, pants still unbuttoned, that blond line of woven hair disappearing along his belly and she remembered what they had done and how she felt. He kissed her lightly.

"Now girl, we ain't doin' this again, least not with each other. Believe me." She did, almost, but concentrated on how beautiful he was, color back in his face, that copper glow of skin, a wild scent mixed of male and Key and new sex, tantalizing her with his closeness, as she was terrorized by the impending arrival of her disapproving parents. He was right, they couldn't do this again. " But Lord knows you are the most beautiful woman I've ever been with."

The words stopped her, she isolated that thought, inspected its merits, saw the possible error and looked to Key one more time, for guidance, trust, or scorn, and saw only the slightest trembling along his mouth, a passage of hurt in his eyes, and remembered what had brought them to this point; the death of his mother, denial, a fight within him to keep an oath, and the unbelievable luxury of being in bed with him. What a mess they made of his sadness, how she wanted to jump on him right now, again, one more time. She wondered about that, how soon could he be readied, when could he perform. Her mind raced with possibilities and needs she'd never considered before.

"Key-." His finger on her mouth smelled of them both. She licked and tasted salt and that other taste. Removing his hand, he pushed her away. "Get dressed, girl. It's your Ma and Pa comin', truck's about to that last curve before the house, they got to slow down and then they're home. Let's get movin'."

I went crazy for a while and Key went with me. From the perspective of forty years in experiencing tragedy and love, I can say the words with some humor and the remains of compassion. But for the six months after our first encounter, I was out of control, truly insane, a child of any family's worst nightmare.

That it was Key Larkin who became my obsession only proves that what we hate we can embrace and love. That in itself is funny, for I would embrace Key anywhere, love him on the steps on the town library if that was all available for us.

I can't imagine how my parents did not see my condition. For all of my initial response to Key, when I was just thirteen, that he was trouble, my crying and having a tantrum when told he would live with us, I now wanted him day and night and he was not always within my reach. In truth, as I know it now, my mother simply could not believe that I would do something so terribly stupid, something as destructive as chasing Key to demand we make love wherever I caught up to him, with no thought to the future, no protection, no concern for my reputation or what might happen to Key.

Through all this frantic pursuit of sex, I could never, no matter how much I talked to myself, and even with the knowledge that I had been produced by these two people in such a union, I could not see them ever coupled in the act. Of course when Key and I were together, we did not see ourselves as pounding each other's bodies but as one individual consumed by the sensations of the other. That flesh, a wet hand and mouth run over a rounded shoulder or a taut, scarred belly; to envision my father doing this with my mother was unimaginable.

Such thoughts are not new nor are they a revelation, but to each child who discovers the act of sex, there is a time when they go through this process until they allow their parents a certain humanness beyond mama and papa and the hands who tuck them into bed at night, the eyes and voice which reassure, the lap which awaits the despairing child in need of comfort.

We each must let go of a need for graphic pictures in the case of our parents' life and accept the overlay of love and desire as higher needs belonging to the older generations, so we proceed with our own affairs freed of the terror of picturing our ancestors in such postures as we ourselves take our own immediate satisfaction.

It occurs to me, belatedly, the horror of what Key learned to imagine about his own mother, and now I think I know why he allowed me to be seduced by him on the day he learned about his mother's death.

I sit here, the photo laid carefully beside me as I rest on the steamer trunk a grandparent used to make the voyage to this country, and my granddaughter stares at me, wanting the rest of the intriguing story. Soon enough she will discover the haunting, need-filled world of sex and love and desire, and will someday look at me with a gaze I hope I do not miss, that sense of bewilderment; "Did Gramma ever do something like this? She couldn't have, she just couldn't. Not her."

Chapter Ten

She saw the change in Neelie, the difference in the way she walked, a glint to her eyes and a sharpness to her tongue that Claudie didn't like but thought she recognized. There was a man, it had to be a man. She blamed that Mickey Herrera at the store, the salesman who Neelie talked about sometimes, deliberately placing a heavy bite to his last name, mentioning his handsome dark looks, the fact that his father was a migrant laborer, that he had ten brothers and sisters. Words and fact used to anger Claudie and get Ray pushing Neelie, telling her she was meant for better things.

Behind the confrontations Claudie wondered what put the edge to her Neelie that disrupted her disposition and turned her to a miserable, willful young woman. She would suspect something more than coffee and chats with Herrera but there wasn't time in their days for any of the critical behavior that would start talk. Herrera traveled, and the word from town came that he never stayed in one of the boarding houses which catered to traveling men or the new motel where names and reasons were less obvious.

Neelie went willingly enough to school and her grades were good enough the principal spoke of a scholarship, and once at church Claudie was told her daughter was a fine example of the kind of young women who weren't affected by the rock and roll music and it would do Claudie to be proud of her child. Claudie resisted being told what do think, she always had, and it was hard to connect her willful child with the paragon of virtue being spoken of around town. So whatever it was had to be a secret between Claudie and her daughter, unspoken by either of them but acknowledged as they looked across a table or stood close to do the dishes. A hint in Neelie's stance, a defiance barely let loose, a taste of some dark freedom which Claudie did not choose to acknowledge.

The cabin was set back in a clearing, part way up the mesa and it suited Key. Rushton left him a truck, three saddle horse, two of which were barely broke to ride, a stout corral, several months worth of provisions and hay, and more than two hundred mama cows with their babies in his care. The land was impossible to fence or regulate. Backed up to the mesa and climbing its side, there were small canyons thick with scrub oak and juniper hiding high thin grass that enticed the cows to graze. There were hints of mountain cats and coyote scat everywhere, so Key rode with a saddle gun and Rushton approved enough to let Key charge the shells at Sperando's Hardware the few times he got into town.

The cabin had its own small clearing surrounded on three sides by low-rising hills and overshadowed by the mesa top. A stream trickled year-round down hill to the left of the front door and the corrals lay behind to the right. Key could haul water or lead the horses to drink. The water ran clean and Key followed it a half-mile back to learn it came out of a break in the rock, a small dribble of water whose constant force had dug a bowl in the rock below. Key sat at the bowl and stared, tracking a single drop of water squeezed from the fissure into the bowl until it ran out over the edge and was flushed downstream to the distant sandy river.

The cabin was tightly made, each timber notched and fitted into its neighbors to leave few cracks. Mud filled the empty spaces, a puncheon floor was laid through the two room. The main living room-kitchen had both a wood stove and a fireplace, and the smaller room held a wide bed, two chairs, an actual closet and a bureau for extra clothing. Key guessed it was a hunting camp from the thirties or before.

Rushton ended any speculation when he said the cabin was built for a son who was to be married but never lived there. The look to the old man's eyes told Key to shut up. And this time he did as he was told. For Key it was the first place he called home, not a borrowed room or shared with no one but himself. No lock, no neighbors, he couldn't even drive the truck up to the house but had to drag supplies on a wooden sledge the last hundred feet.

There was nothing but time for work, time to ride from dawn till after dark, to put together a rough meal, eat, repair broken leather, pound out dents and bends in a shovel, sharpen a saw blade. Even when the sun came down late, he could work on teaching the ringy paint mare Rushton left him with some manners other than kicking whatever came too close to her hindquarters. Protecting her virginity he figured, and wished he had a stallion up here to teach her manners an easier way.

There wasn't any way he could get himself in trouble, not with the truck hard in the gears and the closest town that of Branson which had fifty inhabitants and none of them too inviting. Rushton was betting here that Key would stay free of rumor and fights, and maybe get a lot of miles on the young stock, keep good records on the cows and be safe up on the mountain. Safe as he could ever be.

Behind the cabin was a stand of Ponderosa pine, at the door stood a mix of young juniper and a few cholla over six feet which was evidence of their great age. Woven around the cabin were narrow trails, the daily routes of prairie voles and deer mice, with coyote tracks trailing them as an interesting snack. Key didn't know the birds that chirped and warbled about him but he did listen and came to appreciate their song.

Rushton was his only visitor; on several occasion the old man parked at the base of the trail and called out before he made the hike and Key put on fresh coffee and dug out the whiskey the old man, or someone, had left years ago. Rushton took the libation as his due and spoke no words against the liquor's use.

The first visit, Rushton took a long time to speak. Then it was common words with a note to them Key couldn't figure. "You goin' all right, son?" And without giving him a chance to respond, the old man went on to more question about the cattle, the state of the water tanks Rushton had bulldozed in a vain attempt to control the mountain rains. Key had answers for those questions, and Rushton listened to him. The second trip was only questions about the cattle, and how much rain Key figured they'd gotten in the intervening weeks.

The third trip was different; when Rushton got through his initial labored breathing, he seemed to find comfort in the diminished level of the whiskey bottle and ran his fingers over the label, mouthing something Key couldn't hear. Finally the old man raised his head and spoke; "You know where they buried your ma?" They were sitting outside, Key on the top step, Rushton in the only chair. Key looked out to the trees and then down to where a crowned lizard made a dangerous crossing on a busy trail and finally he had to sit through the same words again before he could begin to answer.

"Do you know, I do. Buried her to the old cemetery up past the Lutheran Church. Seems her pa was buried there, had a place left for her. No room left for you, boy. Just your ma. No sign of her own mother neither. You know anythin' 'bout that?"

Key held his breath, let it out in short spurts, rubbed the back of his hand where the paint mare bit him three days past. "Mr. Rushton, I guess thanks for tellin' me, comin' all this way but it don't matter. She's bone and bits of flesh, that's all now." He gestured to the left where a long bone lay close to a torn-up cholla. Belonged once to a cow, Key had determined when he brought it home. Held it in his hands, rolled it, stroked it to feel the rough grainy texture, then threw it to remain where it landed. "She's no more'n bones."

The dream returned, twisted around itself until Key woke sweaty and guessed he'd cried too; his pillow was wet, his hands and gut pained, an erection pushed to his belly and he lay on his back, seeing the gray sheet rise across his loins. Naked and preceded by the erection he walked out to the porch, looked down the small valley to where the thread of a road could be seen by the lighter tan of its meandering path. His body plain hurt, his mind fought the pictures, Neelie lying under him, grinning up through white bone, his ma flayed alive, grinning too at a man who stood behind Key, out of reach however hard Key tried to find him. Key hated dreams.

Before Neelie, women came to him easily; he was already wanted by them even as a youth, as he grew older he actively sought them out and they laughed to see him, and held him to their willing bodies whatever their age and he loved every minute of it, the foreplay, the seduction; until Neelie came to him, she who was a tender, forbidden virgin, she who wanted only him.

"I tried, North, I tried." Key called out to the woods, and heard more than saw a flickering as he scared a nocturnal scavenger. "I tried." He had not seen the McKendricks since that day and it was the longest he had ever gone without female companionship since he turned thirteen: a month. Early October and soon enough there would be snow on the hill, the mesa track would be impassable and it would take a good horse to ride him out to anywhere at all.

"Neelie you burned the collar, now the shirt's a ruin." Mama was mad. Neelie frowned. "It's a work shirt, Mama, he won't mind." "Well, girl, I mind, I hate havin' my work done wrong." Neelie shrugged and folded the smoothed undershirts. Her mama wouldn't let her fold Papa's undershorts, or North's when he came home. Like there was a sacred, secretive element to these blank cotton garments which might corrupt Neelie before her wedding night.

Mama was hateful lately, ready to pounce on the smallest error as Neelie tried to help. Papa moved slowly and Neelie worried about him, so when she could she rode out to check fence or help pull the bad pump at Dubble Wells. Twice she came close to quitting her job but two things stopped her, the thought of not seeing Mickey and the highly valued wages she brought home. Here Mama was decent enough; she accepted a small portion of the money to help with the house and such but urged Neelie to put most of it in a savings account. “A woman should have some small bit of her own, child, so she ain’t never at the full mercy of men. Now your pa, he tries to give me everything he thinks I want but there’s times when...well, it’s best, child, you keep some for yourself. For school and such.”

Papa worried her, watching him at breakfast he could break her heart; his face pale, eyes tight, mouth pulled. His hands trembled and that had to be bad. But Mama snapped when Neelie tried to say how she felt about her own pa. “Ray’s fine, girl, don’t take on what you can’t handle, you’re still a child, remember that. Your pa’s fine.”

She told Mickey and he listened, took her hand and patted her wrist but that was all Mickey dared to do. Even out of sight of the townsfolk he did not presume to step past the line drawn around a ‘good’ girl. Frustrated wherever she turned in her regimented days, Neelie began to plan a time she could drive up to the line camp for Key. She’d been there once, on horseback, it shouldn’t take too long in the truck.

How much she had changed because of Key came to her three days later when she lied to her boss and took Saturday off and never told her parents. She packed sandwiches and a big jar of lemonade spiked with whiskey, and headed on the county road past Branson to the rock promontory she vaguely remembered. The truck ground over ruts and scattered rubble, until its nose tilted impossibly uphill and it quit, and nothing Neelie could do would get it going. Forward, reverse, rocking side to side and it went deeper and deeper into the soft earth and angered Neelie so much she began to cry.

First it was the head of a horse, half white and brown with a long, shaggy black forelock which hid its eyes that poked through the brush and gave her such a start she cried out and the horse side-stepped abruptly. "Hey, lady, it's only a pretty mare, kinda like you." Key, with one of his dumb comments. "You stop that nonsense, Key, or I'll turn this truck around and go on home."

"Well, girl," he drawled, and she knew he'd already bested her. "You've been diggin' a deeper hole for this ole truck for some time now. Paint and I, we been watchin'. She ain't strong enough to pull you out, I'll be needin' to get to the corral for Bucky, son of a...he's big enough to pull a whole town apart."

Mocking her, keeping her away. Distance. Neelie recognized a familiar tactic. "Key Larkin, you ride up and say hello, you're better taught than this." He'd won, she was already angry, standing on the slippery ground, hands on her hips, her belly tightened as if for war. He walked from the brush, she could hear the mare's inpatient snort. And her anger disappeared, a new, deeper, more intimate emotion rode her. He had lost weight and was tanned to a smooth, rich copper which brightened his gray eyes and gave extra shine and light to the streaked blond hair.

He walked towards her, no hurry, and no hesitation. He came so close his entire body touched all of her, he kissed her, soft at first and then more demanding. His ribs where her hands fitted, his hips which cupped his hollow belly and made room for her, this was where she belonged.

She did not protest or deny or play any game. His mouth opened to her, his arms held her. he drew her closer and there was no shyness in what he asked with his body or how she responded. This was why she lied and brought the truck to ruin and fretted and cried at night when she couldn't sleep.

"Key, how far is the cabin?" "Too far, Neelie...here, now, this time right now." She nodded agreement while he unbuttoned her skirt and slid it free, raised her high enough to remove her panties and rested her on the cooled fender of the truck while he freed his pants, let them drop around his boots, slid his shorts down, his shirttail sometimes covering his erection, enticing her to touch its smooth, silky length but she remained passive, still shy, allowing him to lead.

"Ain't we a sight, both of us." She kissed him to agree and leaned back until he slid into her with little more than strokes of her breast, a kiss to her neck, her hand brought to hold his penis. Then he shoved, she shoved back, arched her hips, met him higher, felt his entry change, felt a gasp of pleasure from her mouth not his.

She opened one eye, saw his face, those wild eyes shut, that mouth pulled back, throat taut, chest beating wildly; she could touch his heart and he would not notice.

Then he shifted, pushed deeper, thrust upward, circled and she cried, cried again, ached to have him deeper until he jerked, quivered, and she knew he was done. He stayed in her although she felt the slow disappearance of the hardness. "Wait, Neelie, wait, don't move, ah, not yet, now...feel that, yes." He shoved into her, hard again, a finger reached down touching his own belly then rubbing her on that spot. Ah, more...oh. "Yes. please oh Key yes. What-." As she rattle gibberish he pushed and circled, not as deep, softer now but that finger rubbed and she felt as if her insides opened, as if that wave of tentative pleasure would spill over and drown them both.

When he came out of her she protested and he laughed. "Neelie, this ain't the most comfortable place for our contact sport. Look, girl, we're both half dressed an gettin' bit by everythin' that flies." He pulled up his jeans, stuffed his shirttail in. The button fly was left undone, tempting Neelie. "We can make the house now, better if you put on that skirt and maybe bring the food. Come on."

As she slid off the truck she left a long, shiny liquid trail. Her face went scalding hot but she put a finger to the stain, then Key stopped her. "That's both of us, nature lettin' us do what we do best." Then, to take the sting from the coarse words, he kissed her sweetly, with kind and tender gentleness she did not think he could be capable of. "Neelie." He spun her around, she held her skirt and panties, legs naked, feeling that wetness run down her thighs. "Neelie, what we done ain't bad, it ain't wrong. You are...I never known a woman touch me like you do. Everythin's wrong with this but it can't be wrong, not feelin' like I do."

She had come all this way up the mesa for what they had just done, and for his words to make it easy; she wanted him inside her, all over her, kissing and exploring, rutting until they were exhausted. It made no difference how she had been taught, it mattered not at all that she knew Mickey was about to ask her to marry; she wanted Key, she wanted to fuck him until they couldn't move, couldn't lift a hand, until the tip of his thumb placed on that spot meant no more to her than a patch on a worn-out truck tire.

To test these thoughts she dropped her skirt and panties, let her hand roam over Key's belly as he tried to speak intelligently and then her hand went down past the loose buttons, into the wiry hair not contained in the silly shorts men wore and found the sticky penis, half-curled, resting against his balls. Testicles. Key's breathing changed, his belly tightened but he did not pull away nor did he complain but she could wrap her hand on the limp flesh and rub gently and then there wasn't room for her hand and his erection inside the tight jeans. When she pulled her hand out and smelled it, Key watched with an expression she did not like or understand.

"That's a whore's trick, Neelie, when she wants a

bigger price. Don't do me like that." The flat words against the reactions from his body shocked her. "Key, I didn't know, I did what I wanted to, just to see...I don't know about men...you that is. This is...I, well, tell me, show me, don't make me feel...help me."

The excitement which had begun in her belly and extended down to where her damp skin quivered had died instantly at his words. His eyes were ugly but she waited, held out a hand, empty and innocent, palm up, fingers curled, willing to be taught. "Key, I didn't know. I don't know. Please."

He carried the picnic things up the rocky trail to the cabin and Neelie followed, distracted by having to watch each footstep so she wouldn't fall. So when Key stopped and she bumped into him, she lifted her head and finally saw where he lived. "Key, it's so perfect."

Key held open the door, she felt him pull back when their arms brushed and again when he had to pass her to get into the kitchen. Neelie held her breath. Then made a decision; "Hey, have I done the wrong thing?" She stopped, uncertain and suddenly afraid. "Mama tells me not to chase a man but then she means Mickey." Here she clamped a hand over her mouth, a childish gesture but as Key's eyes took on a peculiar slant, a flat distant look, she recognized that Mickey's name and the mention of her mother had been a mistake.

There could be no contact between them; Key stood far away, holding the picnic basket in defense of something she did not understand. Neelie felt a sudden urge to pee, or be sick; whatever prompted her to risk so much in this silly venture into Key's world had been lost. "The outhouse's to the back, like it always is. You look like you need it." Cold, flat, like his eyes, far away from the loving man she had used to seduce herself.

In passing she touched Key on the arm and he flinched; Neelie wiped at a sudden tear, angry now, and humiliated. This stupid man was no better than his reputation, no more a romantic figure than a wall-eyed drunk coming from a bar at five in the morning, stinking, unsteady, all talk spewed from a bottle, all heart and soul lost at its bottom.

When she came back, having vomited and needing to sit and cry in the stench, the worn slat walls and spider's nest hinting of more dangerous beasts lurking around her, she walked up to Key and grabbed him when he would turn away.

"Mama's right, you're nothin' but junk." Attack; the only way she knew to get ahead of fear. Key pulled back of course, those dramatic eyes blinking then flat again, the thick hair twisting around an ear where she wanted to pick up the strand and run it through her fingers. "You fooled me but then I wasn't much of a challenge for you, being you're the first and I knew about you from all the talk but I thought I saw some of what North saw in you only different 'cause I'm a girl. Damn you for turnin' on me."

She came apart, crying and choking and hating herself for losing control in front of the enemy and wanting him so badly that when he tried to touch her she kicked him hard. "Don't you touch me, don't come near me, I hate you." All in one breath, leaving her to gasp and need to sit down, exhausted by the tantrum.

He let her outbursts roll over him, the agony in her face punishment enough for his sins. "North." The single word spoken in dry tones broke into her fitful crying. Key's voice was relentless; "North made me promise to protect you, to care for you like you were my sister. Like he was a brother." He sat across from her, hands loose between his knees, eyes turned away from having to look at her.

Her voice was shaky but it entered deep into his conscience; "I broke that promise for you, Key. Me, not you." His head came up too quickly at her words and she ducked back instinctively. Shaking his head slowly, he spoke, the words very soft; "I fucked you." She tried to make the ugly words less potent; "But I came to you, Key, I asked and I knew what I wanted even if I was a virgin. I'm no ignorant country girl, I read, I can see."

Carefully Key opened the basket and laid out the food, sandwiches in one piles, the packet of deviled eggs by themselves, the cake, flattened and with frosting leaked out of its container, was set on a painted dish he pulled from a cupboard and wiped clean on a towel. In his silence he attempted to stop her pleading. Neelie would have none of it.

"Key, what we did by the truck, did you hate me then?" She spoke to his back and witnessed a brief shrug, a shudder that went into his shoulders and she thought she could literally see the hair rise on the back of his neck.

He never turned around. "That was-." He mumbled and she had to wait him out. "Need." He seemed to be shaking, his back hunched up, head bowed.

She barely heard the word but recognized it, had used it in her dreams, only now she began to understand the complexities of that simple word. Her voice was tiny, fragile; "Need. Me...that's what I am for you. So many women and you need me?" She bit down on the word, chewed it; need.

Here it was, she'd been warned. She'd grown up these past years knowing but had to find out for herself. "Key Larkin, you are the son of a bitch I was told you were." The commonplace curse recalled his mother. "One miserable son of a bitch." There, maybe the words would strike him dead.

It was his smile that beat her; she wasn't strong enough to guess what was behind it, she couldn't possibly know how to read its charm. He looked at her and drew one hand through his unruly hair, then lifted his head and seemed to open. Then he smiled; "Neelie, you couldn't know what I said. Words I ain't use to sayin'." He looked away, unaccountably shy and almost nervous. "I need you." Sweat covered his forehead and his fingers suddenly wrapped around themselves. He rested his butt on the rough table edge. "Only you."

Key didn't trust the weight of that word but it came from him and felt right, pushing until he had to say it. "Need." Damnable word binding him to a specific and separate person.

He taught her to play. They were safe in the cabin, no one could approach silently, no one would interrupt them. She learned that food had more pleasures than inside the belly; egg salad smeared on her breasts, around her nipples, became an exquisite torture as Key licked and scrubbed with his mouth until she thought she would cry with need.

In turn she pasted frosting at the wiry hair in his groin and rubbed some of it, with his guidance, around the root of his penis and when she had all of it cleaned he was ready for her, she was waiting for him, poised above him, grinning in lewd anticipation.

Rolling him over that first time, she discovered with her fingers and then with her mouth a deep gouge, a perfect triangle close to the high cleft of his buttocks, a scar now red and smooth, more of an old tattoo than a recent wound.

As she asked she knew it was a mistake. "What happened, were you born with this?" Her finger touched the redness and Neelie saw the phenomenon; Key's buttocks tightened, drew so close together the dimple on either side was more pronounced and she knew she could not push a finger in between the clamped flesh. She knew to wait, hoping his trust was strong enough to redeem her.

His voice came slow and awkward, despairing of any detachment as he spoke and she learned a new horror. "Amazin', ain't it Neelie, what a son of a bitch with a paring knife can do to a kid only wants his supper?"

I went crazy. I became two people, one holding Mickey's hand as we walked down the street to the café in town, the other moaning and crying, kicking and rubbing and taking more and more of Key's body, and never did those two meet fully. I wasn't interested in Mickey in this carnal way, but I also did not wish to lose him. We often sat and had hot chocolate or an ice cream cone and the town grew to accept us as a pair. It was likely that this public persona of the meek and spoken-for young woman who worked at the store and had a scholarship to college kept me from being a suspect in any wrongdoing.

During this period my mother was more difficult to understand than usual. She argued with my father and often snapped at me. Once she came at me with a flat wooden spoon, breaking its handle on the table before she actually hit me. She apologized immediately. I still can remember the flood of tears and the despair in her ruined face but then I was not ready to forgive. In fact I used this display as an excuse to run from the house and drive off in the truck. From her perspective it was to get away from the ranch and her anger, for me it was an extra opportunity to be with Key.

We played with sex anytime I could get to him. Wherever he was working when I appeared at the cabin, he showed up within a few minutes. He must have been able to hear the truck engine and came looking for me, almost always ready to bed me. No more serious discussions, no intimate thoughts or questions that might lead to a future. I had learned this much; if I chose to be with him I could not venture past a certain point and he always let me know when I came too close. Mostly it would be his mother or non-existent father, the future in any shape, even to how long Rushton would let Key stay in the cabin. During the winter we knew the cabin was empty; Rushton didn't hold cattle this far up much past Thanksgiving so there would be no need for Key to stay on. I became frantic whenever I thought about losing the cabin, it meant no easy access to Key and I could not bear facing the winter without him.

I couldn't imagine even a week without him, or a day, right down to an hour when we were in bed, satiated, exhausted, yet still wanting each other. Now I can't remember what so possessed me. Sex is a drug which can consume but it wasn't that I lusted after all men or that Key was a god-like lover. Oddly enough in the years of my marriage to Mickey, the sex was so different between us as husband and wife, fulfilling for me as well as Mickey, that for months at a time I could barely remember what it was that Key and I did those times that made me dare to risk my future.

The lightest touch from him, a whisper of his mouth along the edge of my shoulder blade and my body went into spasms; if I wet my finger, one finger only, and let it drift through the soft pale hair above the cleft of his buttocks, his body tightened and I didn't need to reach in front to know the bulge which stiffened and rose up to push against the mattress before finding me, a willing combatant as he rolled over and arched up in mutual, demanding need.

We were insatiable, intolerant of all others, desiring any part of the other's body we could reach. Thankfully Key did not come into town, and the one time my father asked where he was, I could truthfully say he was staying up to Rushton's line camp and Papa sighed, said it was a good place for him. We were in the kitchen, waiting for supper, and when Papa had his answer, Mama slammed a plate down so hard it broke and Papa forgot whatever it was prompted him to mention Key in the first place.

So Key and I drove each other to the edge of physical insanity and then the inevitable happened. At the first snow, I knew the frenzy was done.

Big white heavy flakes drifted past his window and North wished he was anywhere except inside studying for a science exam. This year was more difficult than the first; his teachers were less forgiving and he suffered from all the distractions possible to a second year college student.

Sylvia called frequently now that they had been lab partners, and he finally got up the nerve to ask her on a date. His first date. Him, Northern McKendrick, clumsy and more so around this girl who was as tall as he but thinner, so pretty, with soft brown hair and blue eyes that looked intently at him when he spoke. She actually listened to him, eager to share, willing to understand.

He wasn't a virgin anymore. They had found a private spot on campus, in the basement of the English building where movies had once been shown but the budget was cut and the projector quit and the screen pulled down from its rollers unraveled and no one could fix the equipment.

There was a couch in a smaller office, dusty and stained but Sylvia shyly suggested he bring a clean blanket so they could sit and talk and not get themselves dirty.

North knew he had taken advantage of her but she didn't mind and she still let him play with her breasts, only through her blouse though, and kiss her neck while they sat together but she wouldn't let him do 'that' again. She was too afraid of getting pregnant and there was nowhere in Pueblo that North could buy rubbers even if he could ever find the nerve to ask. But there was an understanding between them, they were a couple and when he graduated, marriage would be their final commitment.

All this appealed to North. He was safe, stable, willing to study much harder since he had a reason to do the best he could, kind of like when his ma was alive and she smiled and said how wonderful he was when he could read a story to her out of the local newspaper. For the first time since then, North knew where he was going and couldn't wait to get there. Heading to the ranch over Thanksgiving was a prize he held out in front of the dreary days, knowing he needed to do well on the mid-term exam. Sylvia was coming with him, the whole family would get to meet her.

He needed to write and ask Uncle Ray to find Key and invite him too, if Mrs. McKendrick didn't mind.

A dark head pushed through the half-closed door; "You comin' to work, or you studyin' too much again." It was Henry, the first Negro North had ever met; he'd seen some in Texas but his ma didn't serve them at the diner. There was no need for a 'white only' sign, it was known through town the Negroes went to the place 'round the corner fed out chittlins and ribs. But Henry went to the college and worked the same job North did, keeping up the grounds, which were pitiful North decided. They had three hand-pushed mowers and a few hoses, a lot of small dull saws meant to keep the trees and bushes pruned. And him and Henry, both on scholarship, to do most of the miserable work.

"Okay, I'm comin'. Just tryin' to figure out...heck I never will get some of this stuff." Henry grinned and North was as usual amazed at the difference in his face when he smiled. No longer harsh and different but a kid from the country who was trying best he could to get an education out of the sorry two-year college they both could barely afford to attend.

The paint mare was a flutter-headed bitch and Charlie Rushton would hear that the next time he brought supplies to the end of the track. She shied at squirrels climbing a jack pine, blew sideways when a lizard crossed her path, thought a hawk had designs on her fine mane for its next nesting. Whatever the excuse, the sweet, fine-stepping mare took it to bolt, buck, half-rear, jig or plain outright run. She wasn't the kind of horse Key liked to ride but he got paid extra so most of the time he let go and rode and Charlie paid him the bonus for any horse quit bucking.

A clump of grass ahead reminded him of Neelie, it was tall, slender blades bending gently from the middle, tender tipped, not easily broken, and when the mare shied this time and pitched sideways on a ridge, Key was dumped off the mare and immediately grabbed for the trailing reins, cursing and yelling and wishing once again he had a pistol so he could shoot the bitch and take the cut in pay.

Then she came to a digging stop, eased forward from the pull on her mouth and looked down at Key as if he were a monster about to rise up and chew on her tender hide. Lying flat, one hand holding the reins, he glared at the mare and had to grin she looked so damned apologetic and sorry for her impolite behavior. He rolled over and let the reins slip, grunted, came to his knees and then stood and knew without looking that he'd busted that wrist again. Same one, same spot; damn.

No worse this time so he figured he didn't need a doc telling him to pay out five bucks of his own money that he needed a cast to keep the wrist steady and keep off the broncs for a few weeks. It would be that long before Rushton came back up. And about then the old man would announce it was time the cattle came down from the mesa to the flats. Let them winter under the rocks and trees, not on the high, windy, snow-driven top where they could freeze to death during a one-night storm.

Since Key's reputation didn't include being a drinker, Rushton had had the foresight to replace the bottle of cheap whiskey, 'in case a snake bite, son' was how he put it. A broke wrist wasn't a bite but Key knew he would need a few slugs of the liquor to dull what he had to do. It wasn't pretty, looking at the hand bent to a strange angle. At least the bone didn't poke through. Then he'd have to drive one-handed in the battered truck into town, to the hospital where they would boss him around and try to make him whole.

He took kindling from the wood box and two lengths of bandage Rushton stored in a drawer, and drank half the bottle of whiskey to get the contraption around his wrist snug enough to dull the hurt. It throbbed like hell but it couldn't be as bad as showing up in town and maybe running in to one of the McKendricks. Neelie hadn't been up to see him in two weeks, maybe she figured out he was no good for her. But he was horny and lonesome and sorry as that paint mare the girl'd come to her senses.

Neelie found him two days later laid out on the porch. The stock was fed and watered and when all Key did was raise his head when she called to him, she got worried. He could hear it in her voice, that edge of fear. He made the effort then, to ease her into the truth.

"Hey, girl, it's nothin'. That paint mare sent me

flyin', I got me a broke arm but it's set and healin' fine, least from where I see it." She stomped up the stairs then, making a whole lot more noise than was necessary and Key felt the steps bounce in his head, likely from all the whiskey he'd been sipping to keep the pain from taking over.

She was beautiful as she knelt down and really studied him but he didn't care much for her expression. Like pitying a kitten got run over. And he couldn't do nothing about the echo of need rising in him, he was weaker than that kitten and hungry, from eating cold canned soup and crackers and not getting a decent cup of coffee in the two days.

"How come Rushton hasn't brought down the cattle yet, and you with them?" She was tough all right. Key had an answer, one he'd spent a lot a time figurin' on since he couldn't do much else. "It's too warm still and he's bettin' they can graze a week more. Grass'll stay good enough to fill them until a hard freeze." Neelie licked the corners of her mouth and Key wanted to do that particular job for her. "So he doesn't care about this." She swept her fingers over his arm, near up by the elbow where it wouldn't hurt and he grimaced even from that feathery touch. "Hell, Neelie, he was here four days ago. Can't expect the ole coot to keep watch over me like a mother hen. That's for you women." She snorted, sat back on her heels like her cousin and pa did when they was stirring up a branding fire, waiting for the coals to heat. "Key, you're hopeless. I came up 'cause Mama asked me." Here she stopped, hesitated, still puzzled by the expression on her mother's face when the invitation was issued. "North's coming home for the holiday and we want you to join us."

He couldn't do much, feeling like he did, lightheaded and half-drunk, but her lips were parted and he could smell her, almost taste it on the back of his mouth. His fingers ached, he couldn't quite reach her with the one good hand. She'd have to come to him. "You are beautiful, Neelie." She smiled, she was growing up. Two months past she would have blushed and he could kid her for it but this time she leaned to kiss him the way he liked, with mouth and tongue while her hands roved his body until he moved instinctively and the pain from his wrist came so hard and fast he didn't have time to complain just fell back and was out like a dumb rabbit hit by a thrown rock.

When he came to she was watching, in the rocking chair, high above him. "You know, Key, there are times you're not too smart. Injured like this, you still want to fuck." The word stopped him. "What's the matter, Key, you say that word to me when you want to hurt me, need me to back off. Now it's me telling you. Probably for the same reason."

She was a cat-eyed wonder, bright hair and beautiful face, gaze steady on him as he watched her. No doubt about Neelie, she spoke her mind and he could love her for it and forget the perfect body, the great eagerness as she rolled under him, leaned her head back and howled and grabbed and pulsed, taking him to higher and higher passion until he... "Neelie, you best go home, I ain't no good to you about now."

"On that you're right, Key Larkin. But do you remember, I'm here about the invitation from Mama. I need an answer." His hands were cold and he wanted a jacket or sweater or to pull a blanket over him but they were all inside and he wasn't going to ask Neelie. Mindful of the damage she could inflict, he half-sat and leaned against the rough carved pole holding up the shading, roof. "I ain't seen North since, a couple a months I guess. Reckon college is changin' him."

"That's what college does, Key, that's why you go. At least those who know they need changing." Neelie let the rocker swing her, forward and back and forward again until Key felt she was a prize dangled in front of him and removed again and again to remind him of who he was exactly. And where he didn't want to go, where he couldn't go, where he never belonged.

"Neelie?" His good hand was on the plank floor, palm up; he let the fingers roll in sequence. "Neelie." She laughed. "I told you, you're asked only for the day. Clean up is my best advice." He let the hand fall quiet and leaned back, felt a throb in the broken wrist and considered getting the truck to the McKendrick place.

"You forgot about Thanksgiving, didn't you, Key?" He grinned without looking up, seeing her legs and ankles, the down on her skin, freckles in the oddest places, above her knee, along her thigh, disappearing under the bunched skirt. Holidays made no difference to him, nor to the mama cows and their babies he was nursing.

She wore a thick sweater and ankle socks and sturdy boots but showed her lovely legs to him and he couldn't reach them unless he put weight on his busted wrist to caress them with his good hand and that had already dumped him so he leaned on the porch step and grinned at nothing while Neelie kept at him about not knowing the day of the week and the time of day and how to behave in public. He wondered what had got to her, had her talking and ranting when all they ever wanted to do with each other was to do it to each other. The world had crawled inside her and displaced him, started its worm-like burrowing where beauty and sex and pleasure were destroyed and all that was left was guilt and sorrow and obligation.

Key finally interrupted the vindictive flow, bored with the constant useless chatter. "It's why I live here, Neelie. Cause I can't live in your world down there." He changed direction and turned serious. "Don't know what I'll do this winter. Ole man Rushton ain't talked 'bout keepin' me on."

That comment, the core of his own private worry, went past her like nothing. She harped on her own ruffled feathers; "Thanksgiving is in two days. You think you can clean up and come in? We'll eat about noon, Mama says."

"Yes, ma'am." He tugged his unruly hair, made a mock half bow from the waist. "For certain, ma'am, you say so, I'll do just what I'm told." He tried to lighten up for her, tried to set her free. She would have none of his charity. "Key, you've got to do better'n that or they'll guess. Please, we can't be caught. Oh please."

I don't know if I was beginning to grow up or just getting mean but I wanted to hit Key, stomp on his busted arm or slap his face until he fully comprehended the serious nature of a day shared with my family. We had no history of being in public except that once with Mickey long before our affair. A silly word but I can't think of how to describe what Key and I were doing with each other. It wasn't love, it wasn't happiness or romance or a future with commitment; it was raw sex in anyplace we could find and with all parts of our bodies.

I didn't tell him that Mickey would be joining us for the celebration. Mama insisted and Papa didn't seem to care.

When I went to ask Mickey, I tried very hard to put the invitation in a bland, uninspired way so he could easily and with a clear conscience decline, stating family obligations of his own. But he smiled that dazzling smile and said he looked forward to sharing the meal and could he bring some of his mama's posole and green chile, since they were from near Velarde in New Mexico and it was a tradition among their family.

What a combination: we had North coming in from college

with a girl none of us knew anything about, my mother and father were sniping at each other, a behavior I had not witnessed until now. For me, well, I had my boy friend and my lover sharing me at the dinner table. It promised to be an event worthy of Blanche DuBois or from the imagination of Margaret Mitchell. I kept up with my senior reading on Blanche, and Scarlet was long a favorite with my friends and even I admired her spitting courage while hating her deceit. And I was practiced in what I did not like; I guess I wasn't yet grown, only trying out the boundaries.

Chapter Eleven

Ray forked out more hay to the sorrel and the brown while he glared at the paint mare. She might belong to Rushton but that didn't make Ray approve of the flighty mare; too bad Key rode her down from the line camp. Too bad Key had to show up at all.

Claudie was mad at Ray, and everyone else in her house, and Ray didn't know why. Should be his wife would be pleased with the holiday; North and his girl come visiting, with Neelie setting next to Mickey Herrera who was nice enough, seemed bright, and was going someplace other than a dead-end ranch job. Now North's girl, Sylvia, was a plain quiet thing who couldn't keep her eyes off North, whose hands strayed near his arm or hung above his shoulder, but never quite touching him. The boy was in his second year in college, in a family where most had barely finished high school. Ray was proud of him, close enough he'd been his son. And he still had no idea why Claudie was cross. It showed in her tight eyes, the pull at her mouth, never mind she talked nice and kept offering seconds, especially to North.

It was easy to see she favored North. Walking behind

him to the stove she patted his back or touched his hair, gestures a momma would make, even if North was no longer her pup. Her pup.

Maybe it was jealousy running around the house. Ray saw that more in Neelie who looked at the girl North brought home but didn't talk to her. Asked questions from North that separated him from his Sylvia, about the way Ray figured Neelie would act the first time North brought home a girl.

So Claudie's fuss belonged to something else and he wanted to blame it on Neelie bringing her Mickey into the house. Ray shook his head, in any case he was glad to be outdoors, away from the crowded house. Doing what he knew best, feeding hay to the brown and North's sorrel and the damned paint mare.

Mickey Herrera wasn't bad after all. He was quiet and polite and Ray liked the taste of his mama's posole dish mixed with the peculiar green chile of New Mexico. Mickey sat in the middle of a quarrelsome family and remained easy, and gentle, but Ray'd seen his hands, taken a good long look. Those hands'd once bucked hay and tamped fence posts, and Ray was curious how he got from there to his salesman's job.

He meant to ask a lot, about Mickey's family, where they lived, did he have a place of his own, was he fixing to be a salesman all his life. It was easy to see Mickey was taken hard with Neelie. Maybe she felt the same, but it was Ray's job to find out what he could about a possible suitor. She was young, but Claudie had been a year younger when Ray first loved her.

He stopped, easing himself upright, rubbing his belly. He shook his head. Claudie could be mad about his not eating much of the fine dinner she put out for the crew. He tried to taste everything but couldn't look at her when he didn't finish the apple pie and refused the peach short cake. Eating gave him pain lately, nothing to worry 'bout. With North here three more days over the weekend, they could get fire wood stacked, the rest of the hay moved. Without the two boys, he hadn't been able to finish the early winter chores. Charlie Rushton said something about that but Ray put him off, counting on North coming home to help.

Key wasn't worth much with the broke wrist. Soon enough he would have to ride out, bring down Rushton's cows but it was late this year, grass still good, no snow yet. It was too bad Larkin didn't have that particular chore right now pressing on him, it would take him out of the McKendrick household. Ray couldn't account for his discomfort around the boy this time; he knew Key well enough, had welcomed him into the house, but today it didn't feel quite right.

These weren't charitable Christian thoughts, Ray accepted it. The boy wasn't bad, just it made Ray edgy to have him around. Neelie was looking too beautiful for the Larkin boy to ever get near her; it was bad enough that Mickey Herrera showed his intentions, Ray couldn't deal with the burden of Key Larkin's rep.

He walked back to the house, stopped outside and looked through the sparkling window into the big room Claudie called their dining room and saw the young folks setting round the table. Even Sylvia seemed to be giggling. Claudie sat alone, at her end of the table, both elbows resting beside her empty plate, a look of confusion on her tired face. She had been beside Ray through so much hurt and sorrow, now he couldn't even comfort her in bed, but she was his beloved and he hoped she still knew it. The words were harder and harder to say.

Key Larkin stood up, awkward from that busted arm; Neelie looked at him and the light to her eyes shamed Ray into thinking wrong. Quickly Herrera pushed back from the table, patted his belly lightly to let it be known it was a gesture of pleasure, not an insult. Ray could hear him through the open door. "Señora McKendrick, it is a fine meal you have allowed me to share with you and your family. I can't thank you enough."

The words did what Ray figured they'd been meant to do; Neelie turned from Key to Mickey and her face lit up in a truly beautiful smile. "Yes, Mother, this was lovely." Good Lord, Ray thought, what next. She'd call him Father if he was at the table still. He was glad he'd stayed outside, he needed to belch, and he knew how much Claudie hated any such exhibit of bad manners. His belly hurt, he'd eaten too much.

Then the Larkin boy spoke again and all attention focused on him: "Mrs. McKendrick, I know my manners'n all. Ain't had a meal like this to a long time. You did yourself proud, ma'am, puttin' out all these fine fixin's."

The look on Claudie's face startled Ray, then he knew it was the outrageous dialect which upset her. Even North laughed, while his Sylvia put a hand to her mouth to cover the giggles. Only Neelie didn't respond.

Ray walked into the kitchen, spoke into the sudden quiet; "These youngsters'll do the dishes and cleanin'." Claudie contradicted him; "Meanin' North and Key as well as Neelie. Mr. Herrera and Sylvia are our guests." Ray held up his hand; "Sure 'nough, Claudie. Neelie, you come walk with your pa. Let the boys do the work this time."

He knew Claudie would be furious, risking her best china in clumsy hands while forcing her to set with strangers, but he had things on his mind with Neelie, and Claudie would do better with the girl than the rest of them. Lord help her if Key got to teasing; she might run screaming in female panic. She was a mite of a thing though she was tall enough. She would never survive Key and North and Neelie fighting in the hot kitchen

Their walk wasn't a success. Ray was stiff with his words and this was one time he knew he needed to be careful. He tried a gentle approach first; "That's a nice young lady North brought home with him. She thinks he walks on water, guess that'll soften any man's heart." Here Neelie looked at him oddly and he talked on, fearful he'd already said the wrong words. "She sure is polite enough, easy in makin' a man feel comfortable." Not, he thought, like his Claudie, or this daughter who marched beside him and bit her lip to keep quiet while he made the usual man-fool of himself.

Still he had seen the fire in Neelie a few minutes ago as she watched Key Larkin and he needed to warn her, to coax her into admitting all the boy's faults and seeing him for what he was. But Neelie got in her words before he could get started. "Daddy, she's fine for North. You leave off picking on her." He couldn't get over 'daddy,' it made him feel older, like his time had gone past. Then she spoke what was really on her mind, and the words packed a wallop. "What is it you want to say to me? I'm not a child, you can't sneak up on me by being sweet." That hurt. Ray looked back at the solid stone ranch house, stubbornly waiting on all the repairs and modern appliances he'd been brash enough to promise Claudie when they moved in twenty years ago. For a few years he said, till he got back on his feet after selling the ranch. Lord how fast the time went.

Then he looked at his Neelie, arms folded across her chest, right foot cocked at an angle, hips slanted jut like her ma. "You know the Larkin boy's arm was busted like that?" She answered, quietly, hiding what Ray wanted to know. "He told me the mare flipped him off. Wouldn't let me do for him or tend the arm in any way."

All that could be the truth with more woven in the words than Ray liked. He wasn't one for hidden meanings and masked thoughts. His nature was too blunt, and too cautious to read into a sentence more than he could hear. His child was tall enough he didn't need to bend down far to look straight into her eyes and not glance at the smooth forehead, the wide sweet, innocent mouth that belonged once to a little baby. Now she had the marks of a young woman incidentally his daughter. She was a true woman, more of her ma than of him; and it was best he keep that in mind. He needed to acknowledge that these two women in his life shared a strong temper and stronger will.

"That the same paint mare he rode in today?" He was curious and Neelie nodded yes. Ray snorted, then held a hand up to the air; "It's beginning to snow." His daughter came in close to him then, even nudged his arm enough to let him know it was all right when he put his arm around her shoulder and gave her a half squeeze. "Rushton keeps givin' those rough broncs to the boy, it's a wonder that he's got no more than a broke arm. That mare may be pretty but she's got poor cow sense it seems to me."

He'd babbled enough, he felt rested, revived, hoped his child felt the same. For there was too much waiting in that house, the Mexican in his two-door coupe, North in with a duffel bag on his shoulder, walking easy the last mile to the ranch, the little girl struggling beside him. And Key Larkin, who appeared after all the others were gathered, one arm held close to his chest, the mare tossing her head and prancing, tail flagging, whinnying at whatever moved including Ray's old brown gelding who barely looked up from the hay pile.

Then he remembered why he brought Neelie out here, what it was on his mind he needed to clear. "Neelie, you're my daughter, I hate to...well say much against...it's your ma who knows about women things not me." His mouth was dry and he rubbed his eyebrow. “It looked strange, when you cut his meat for him at dinner. I know he’s only got one workin’ arm but it don’t set right...you doin’ such for the Larkin boy. It worries me.”

She skipped in steps that reminded him of the paint mare, but this was his Neelie, his Cornelia named after her great-grandmother and already to graduate ahead of her class, with letters coming in about scholarships and a whole future no McKendrick ever dreamed of before.

“Daddy, I was helping him. He needed help.” Ray missed ‘papa,’ gone with pigtails and white socks and the way she would grab his hand and swing from his arm when he raised it level, she and smiled at him like there was no one else in the world. “Sure, child, I know that. I could see. It’s just...I want to tell you, with that Mickey here and ah...well your ma said it when Key come in, he’s gotten prettier, that’s what she said. Me I wouldn’t notice less he cut off half his face. Just worryin’ you know, it’s what papas do.”

He risked a look and there was the fire he knew would show, just like Claudie. “Daddy, I was doing what any sensible person would do. There’d have been turkey and stuffing and mashed potatoes flying left and right if no one helped. And it looked to me right then no one was going to offer but me. He sure wouldn’t ask for help. That much we all know.”

A whole lot to say about almost nothing. “You’re right, Neelie. I didn’t think that’s all. We best get in, tell Key it’s beginnin’ that snow. Rushton will be wantin’ his cattle moved in this storm, you just bet he will.”

Claudie sat in the rocker under the ramada Ray built

when the summer sun cut in low to the windows and drove them outside with the heat. It wasn't hot now, except in the kitchen, so she brought out a shawl with her and wrapped her shoulders and wished she'd worn boots and socks instead of pretty flat shoes and thin nylon stockings like Ray used to like. She stuck her feet out in front of her, tightened her toes, saw the absurdity of the useless shoes and thought of the nonsense of her wearing them. Something had to return her Ray to her, and it would take more than silly shoes and bared legs.

Inside she heard the pans rattle along with a clatter of china and she had to remind herself not to holler or rush inside to direct the chaos going on in her kitchen. Finally she remembered, she had company right next to her and was glad of the lessening light so her embarrassment was not easily seen. Mickey Herrera spoke up for her, "I do apologize, ma'am, sittin' here in the cold and not talkin' to you or the young lady. I guess I ate too much and dozed off instead of remembering my manners."

The boy had sense. He was a man she chided herself, no high school dropout or student but a full-grown male. He kept on talking and she liked the sound of his voice. "Mrs. McKendrick, it is peaceful to sit in the cool air. I believe it is beginning to snow. How beautiful it is here. I miss this, working as I do. As for Miss Hastings, I believe she also is pleased enough with the quiet. How are you, miss, after that wonderful meal?"

North's girl said nothing, just smiled down into her folded hands and seemed to shiver a bit. Claudie began to speak; "Thank you, Mr. Herrera. I do appreciate your kind words but the turkey could be more tender and I near to steamed the beans dry." She was prattling to cover up any threat of silence. Then the girl surprised her. "Mrs. McKendrick, I want to thank you also. And you too, Mr. Herrera, for saying what I wished to. North, he's told me so much about the ranch, and you, Mrs. McKendrick, and your cooking. He says he'd blame his size on the meals but he was already this big when he got here."

Now all that was a mouthful and more than Claudie wanted to know about North and this girl and what they said to each other. But the child seemed not to notice the impact of her talking and kept on, telling Claudie how much she cared for North and how sweet he was and she hoped his family approved of her because she and North were serious about each other. Claudie sighed, let her hands rest on her tight stomach. Victim of her own cooking. Why hadn't Ray eaten more, was he tired of her in the kitchen also? The girl talked, Claudie barely heard the sounds. Her thoughts went to her daughter, a prickly subject right now.

Neelie had changed too much, never mind she was out walking with her pa. She talked different, sounded like a radio voice stead of her own folks. Schooling did that, Claudie recognized the difference but it never was important before. Like the voices in those copied poems from that Christmas. A clarity to their speech inside her head, with no sliding sounds, no lost ends, just beautiful words eased into her heart as she lay up in bed and read while Ray pushed his paper bits around, fussing over the accounts.

Claudie's head jerked; good heavens she'd almost fallen asleep. "My 'pologies to you both. Sylvia, would you check the kitchen, see if some of the good china survived? I have a few things I want to talk over with Mr. Herrera. If he don't mind."

The entire day had fascinated Mickey. The unusual collection of family and guests, himself included, the muted arguments so different from his own highly vocal family. It helped that he'd met Key Larkin once before. The man held great importance to Neelie and therefore he was interesting to Mickey as well. Still a boy in many ways despite working a man's job. And doing the work quite well, for most men now would not ride horseback with a broken arm they'd set themselves and make no fuss about the incident. On the few chances Mickey had to talk with Key, he had seen in the pale eyes a pain deeper than suspected. It worried him, for the pain was not of a physical nature.

Now Mr. McKendrick was a size and breadth that made his nephew not so much of a shock. He was so obviously a good man frayed and weathered by the years. Mickey liked him almost on sight; a good man to work for but not one to cross.

Neelie he loved, as simple as that. Knowing she was young, and half-wild herself even with her responsible job, he still loved her and would wait until she began to love him in return. He suspected a childhood fascination with the rogue cowhand but guessed it could not last, knew from the distance in Larkin's eyes which said he was ready to look over the next hill wondering what he would miss by staying in one place too long.

North he liked on general principles without having much time to speak with him. Big and slow-moving, incredibly strong but not mind-numbed as would be easy to assume. His girl, the plain one, was perfect for him, willing and needing to remain safe and secure in North's considerable shadow.

The one he most doubted was about to interrogate him as to his intentions on Neelie's behalf. Mickey forced a quiet cough, took out a clean and pressed handkerchief and wiped his mouth. Signals of his upbringing, designed to set a tone with Mrs. McKendrick, tokens needed to bolster Mickey's confidence that he could indeed handle and accept what this willful woman would say, right from the base of her heart.

"Do you love my daughter?" Claudie smiled in the dark, not caring if he heard the challenge in her voice. "Yes, ma'am." Good, he gave it right back. "Do you intend to marry her?" "If she will have me, and if you and Mr. McKendrick approve." He paused. "But only in that order, ma'am."

She laughed out loud, he knew her Neelie well. "What do you think of your chances with her?" Here was no quick retort, no collection of words meant to soothe her or deceive. "Mrs. McKendrick, earlier in the fall I would have said that in a year Neelie and I would marry. Now, I don't know. She has been...moody of late, distant from me yet not wanting me to leave. I,...have you noticed a change...anything?"

In the resulting silence Claudie felt a small tickling on her legs and saw flakes of snow. "Mr. Herrera, we must have this discussion indoors. I believe it is beginnin' to snow, and I am cold. And it occurs to me, I have not been fair in my duties, I have not asked Miss Sylvia any questions about her family and her intentions, although what she feels about North is obvious. I mean to ask how they met and where she lives, those small details on which families may come together with their youngsters, or stay separated from too much difference."

It was a formal speech, unlike her earlier style, and Mickey saw in it a possible warning about his family background, but as a true lady would, she held out her hand and smiled at him, an obvious effort. "You, Mr. Herrera, I'll take to callin' you Mickey if that's all right with you, you're always welcome to our home."

Being one-handed had its pleasures. He couldn't wash or dry so Key leaned on the counter and picked at North. Sort of having his own way for once. North was surrounded with dishes and Neelie and worrying about his girl out with the missus. He couldn't reach for Key when he hit a sore spot about school and classes and a life separate from the two boys racing through the hills, roping cactus, chasing bulls till the bulls chased them and generally living life better suited to a man than inside a school building, listening and writing and trying to learn God knows what.

Neelie he didn't need to think about at all; his body knew where she was, what she was doing. She came in from talking to her pa all flustered and ready to fight; wanting North's attention yet brushing up against Key, twisting off when North might look. A dangerous game, played willingly by both of them. Her dish-wet hands sliding by his groin, his shoulder into her breast; foolish, stupid acts that would cause one hell of a ruckus if North caught on.

It was a relief when the Hastings girl came back in, but without Mickey. Mickey, who was obviously the right man for Neelie. Not Key, he was never the right man, he wouldn't give Neelie a home and children and nice clothes and good manners; he'd take the Neelie on the dun pony, barelegged and wild, long hair covering her eyes, curling over her breasts and belly, eager to taunt him, reaching for him, opening her legs wide even when she was fully clothed.

The Hastings girl wasn't much to look at, though Key never met a 'plain' female couldn't light up with loving. This one had that look around North, and North too got giddy and love-struck when she was around, if such words could be applied to one the size of Northern McKendrick.

Then it started to snow. Key watched the beginning

flakes through the high kitchen window and shook his head. "Hell, North, pardon me ladies, I got to go. Rushton'll be mad, me not bringin' in them mamas before this even though he told me to hold off. He'll bitch, sorry, ma'am, about me wastin' a day eatin' and enjoyin' you folk's company, he'll be on my hide, dock me any cow don't make it, put me in debt for the next five years."

Key heard his own monologue and liked the intentionally rough language, saw the Hastings girl quiver, felt Neelie's anger and knew better than to look at North, the boy would say something mushy, get Key all wound up. He thought to apologize and kept on in the same manner instead. "Glad I rode that mare now, she oughta do right well in the storm, the bitch likes a good fight and she's got one comin' to her." No apologies this time.

The shock on Sylvia Hastings' face was worth the smack Key took from North across his back that sent him stumbling into the counter then sideways up against Neelie and the shock and feel to Neelie's hips almost sobered Key. "See you later, North, have fun with the chores now I'm gone." Key got out of the kitchen before North smacked him again.

Neelie let her opinion be known as soon as Key disappeared. "He can't saddle one-handed. I'll go help him, North you try to explain Key to Sylvia. I think it's a good idea, Sylvia, it's been nice getting to talk with you. I'll be back in a few minutes." No one could stop her, North opened his mouth to say that Key managed to get here with the mare saddled and bridled but he never got the chance. Neelie bolted, ignoring all propriety. She should have stayed inside and been polite to Sylvia, but she had to escape and catch Key at the corrals.

He was waiting, the mare already bridled and tied, the saddle set on the ground, its upended cantle white with new snow, the woven wool blanket draped on a sawhorse braced up to the corral poles. He reached to Neelie and held her close, she could smell the meal he'd just eaten, and that wonderful dry woods smell all his own. Still she pushed back from him, her voice low and urgent.

"We can't, Key, too many people-we can't." He countered, his voice harsh; "Then why've you been pushin' and pullin' and rubbin' on me, talkin' and flirtin' with Mickey and mad at North cause he got himself a nice girl?"

God he was smart; she'd forgotten that the dialect of 'ain't' and 'gosh' and cursing and using all those double negatives teachers warned their college students about was his way of mocking another life.

His hands went to her waist, his mouth found the tip of an ear; the snow was blinding now, the mare shook her head and the bit chain jingled. Neelie shivered as snow went down her collar, "Yes, here. Now." She leaned on the folded saddle blanket and raised her skirt while he undid his fly. He came in close and she felt him poking her belly, then sliding to the crease of her thigh, digging at the lace on her panties. Damn. Caught; she struggled while he got more impatient and jerked on the elastic until the panties tore. He lifted her with one arm, braced the other on a corral pole and entered her; a grunt from her, a gasp, hips moving together, she reached backwards, arced herself from the fence railing and raised again, trusting the strength of Key's one arm. A short gasp and the pain on his face changed into a long silent cry then they ended together.

"See, anything's possible, especially in a snow storm. Gotta go, the ole man'll be lookin' for me." Then Key kissed her even as he raised the saddle over the mare's wet back with one hand. Inevitably he had to pull his mouth away from hers to lean against the mare and tighten the cinch. With a quick pat to the mare's snow-drenched neck, he climbed aboard and was gone into the heavy snow.

It was Rushton who brought the news; he was blunt about the incident, taking on full responsibility as he related the events to Ray. "Damn, it was me told that boy no hurry 'bout bringin' them down. Guess I got a cowhand to winter, can't blame him for half-freezin' or wreckin' on the mare. I never did think that mare'd make up into a good cow horse. He brung all but three head down off the mesa, sure can't fault a man rides like that for the brand."

Ray looked at Rushton, half inside his Chrysler, belly taut against widespread legs, a large hand resting on each knee. "Yeah, Ray, that boy took my word, rode in the snow and brought down every last cow cept those three. Lost the mare, broke her leg in a fall he said, busted him up some, guess the folks to the hospital gonna keep him two, maybe three weeks, maybe more."

Now that's a story, Ray thought. Busted up and on a half-wild mare and he brings down over two hundred mama cows and their babes. What the old timers called loyal to the brand, though a man might get fired once he was hurt riding for the brand, left on his own to recover or not. But that was the old days, now it seemed Charlie Rushton had some loyalty to his own.

"Hell of a note, Charlie. Good to know the kid's got that much to him." Rushton rubbed his face, still white above the eyes after all those years of shade from his hat. Red veins burst across his nose and cheeks, the big hand covered most of his eyes and brow as he wiped away some whiskey damp. "Yeah, guess he stays put for awhile. Why I came here, askin' you and the missus to put the boy up once he gets out a that place. Heard tell your daughter's livin' to Trinidad now that she got out a school early. Smart girl, that child a yours. Now she's gone, I can ask you a favor like this 'un."

Both men, wise enough to accept certain behavior, nodded at this sideways comment on Key Larkin's character. Ray thought a moment, rubbed his eyebrow to give himself time. "I'll ask Claudie but I can't see her sayin' no. What'll you pay for the boy's care?" Bold and unlike Ray but he knew Claudie would ask that question first. It costs to feed an extra mouth, uses up time tending a man come out of a wreck.

Rushton hesitated a bit, rubbed on his mouth before speaking; "Oh, seems the boy might lose a toe or two, already lost the little finger on that busted hand to the frost bite. He ain't gonna be as pretty as he was. Won't hurt the rest of us none, him bein' ugly as we is." Rushton coughed, spat, laughed at the foolishness. "That boy ain't wore out his looks yet, not yet but they'll go, he'll be down to wishes and memories 'fore long, the way he's goin'."

Ray answered quickly; "I'll ask my wife, Mr. Rushton. See what she says, Good thing Key got most of the cattle, it could be a hard winter startin' like this." In this way he got Rushton on to a rancher's best topic, weather, and Ray had time to figure out what he would say to Claudie. Then Rushton named a high figure; "Tell that to your wife when she asks, it's $10 a week for feed and some care. I'll send someone bring him to the doc's when they want to see him. Other than that, he can stay in the 'dobe, good enough place, it's got a wood stove. Give him a chore he can handle, keep him busy." Then Rushton continued in an uncharacteristic way and Ray was surprised enough he said nothing back. "Thanks, Ray, it's a big favor I'm askin'.

Maybe if I believed more in God's plan or destiny or something that gave dimension and logic to events, I would never have gone to see Key in the hospital. I knew full well what would happen, wanted it, had come to need it and him more than I could ever dream. All the magazines and stories and talk among the women around me, the older ranch wives worn down and doughy, plumped from their endless cooking of huge meals, sleepless from long hours and too many children, the town girls thin and angry, sifting through the small local choice for husbands, none of these females ever said within my hearing or to my knowledge that they liked sex, that they craved a man, that they were as obsessed and consumed as I was by the sexual act in itself.

Conversely I cannot imagine sex with Mickey at that time in my life, or with any of the men who populated our small community. It was Key I needed, and it was I, in return, that he fed on while his body betrayed him. The small bits of gossip about Key were now usually dull. He hadn't been chased through a bedroom window or shot at by an irate husband for quite a while, This lack in his usual method was laid to the fact that he worked at Rushton's line camp and no woman was foolish enough to go up there pursuing him, which would be the only way Larkin could carry on his mindless rutting.

Thankfully my comings and goings, on my pony or in the truck, were not of interest; I had always been a rebel and most of my acquaintances thought they knew I was so in love with Mickey that a man such as Key would not stand a chance. The facts were simple to those around me: I had graduated from high school just after Thanksgiving in a simple ceremony for there was one other student who also graduated. Because of the time and distance, and money involved, it was decided I should live in town, for although I received some financial aid from the university where I was to go in the fall, I needed to save as much money as possible.

A relative of Mama's, a distant cousin, had an extra room

she would let me have for $3 per week; another cousin was more generous, agreeing to feed me two meals a day for nothing, her part, she said, in getting at least one member of the family into college, having had five children none of whom finished high school. It seemed odd to me that she didn't count North, but I guess his undetermined father and his recent entry into our family group made it difficult for her to accept him as a McKendrick. So my family rallied and I worked long hours at the five and dime, spending more and more time with Mickey in the evenings, well chaperoned of course, and while we sat and talked, or read to each other, and on occasion listened to radio programs or watched the one television set on the entire street, I was thinking of Key, knowing there was no possible way I could get to him.

A week of living this way and I was about to go crazy, when the news concerning Key and his accident spread through town. The women dreamed as they speculated and you could see it in their eyes. It was almost possible to pick out those he had bedded from those who only fantasized. I said nothing, no one except Mickey thought I would be interested, and it was on Mickey's suggestion that I wrote to North. Mickey was genuinely concerned, having expressed a liking for Key from their two meetings, and at that I almost had an attack of conscience. But thinking of Key in town, so close, pushed that acceptable, responsible thought from my mind; my body ached at night, I had dreams that are unprintable, I was so aware of my body that one night when Mickey did touch me in a place more intimate than my wrist or elbow I came close to jumping him. My hands reached out involuntarily towards his belt, my mouth opened in reflex and thankfully Mickey was turned away, the gesture which unnerved me meant to draw my attention to the antics of a clown on television. I shuddered then out of raw hunger. I shudder now to think if I had followed through with my desperate attack I would have lost Mickey and thus lost the best part of my life.

How can I put two such mismatched and opposing needs

on one piece of paper. How can I keep these separations of my soul and body inside without going mad amazes me. I love Mickey, and yes of course we have fought and there have been times when I hated him, times I wanted to tell him in detail about Key and the madness of our couplings. And he knew, at the end, about Key and that Key had seduced me which is the way Key presented the situation and blackmailed me into allowing this misrepresentation. I never told Mickey, or anyone, the real truth until now

North made the trip from Pueblo to visit Key. He came in by bus which got him to the hospital well after visiting hours. A nurse tried to prevent him from seeing Key but for once North used his size, scowled at the woman, raised a fist and said he was family come a long distance to see his kin and there wasn't no one going to tell him what he could and couldn't do.

Key was propped up in the narrow bed, lights low, his face turned towards the curtained window. He was sleeping and North sat himself in the visitor's chair, much too tight for him so he kept one side of his butt on the edge and held himself quiet with both hands clamped to the steel and vinyl padded arms, and simply watched.

His friend had lost even more weight, the fine-boned face was drawn, most of its high color faded to sallow gray. North stared at the left hand and arm lost in a wad of bandages. Uncle Ray told him the little finger was gone, the wrist might never heal right, he would lose some use of the hand. Pity cause the boy was good with horses. But a few missing parts of this kind wouldn't bother him with the ladies.

Reddish patches high on each cheekbone were frost-bite; North recognized the signs, even in Texas once in a while a drunk would sleep out in the bitter cold and if he survived to morning he carried that tinge in his face for a long time. Only a light blanket covered Key. North glanced at his charts, checking over his shoulder so no snooping nurse would catch him. There were no other visible bandages but some ribs were more than likely busted. A bottle hung from a silver stand, yellow liquid dripped down a long tube into the back of Key's good hand. Pinned that way in bed, the boy looked like a monster bug in a kid's collection.

Key's head rolled; a grimace tightened his features as his eyes opened. "Wondered when you'd get here. North." That last word was a whisper but it said enough. "Never have been inside a hospital," North said, speaking as if he and Key were having a two-sided conversation. "Ma didn't hold with them, said too many people died once they got inside." He waited a beat, grinned. "Maybe I shouldn't have said that."

Key's slack mouth moved in a shadow grin. "Me too, but this time I ain't dyin'. Just damn tired." North nodded as if what Key said made sense. Shorthand, reaching between the years with thoughts and stories and feelings only spoke of to one other person.

"I reckon Uncle Ray's been in, and Mrs. Claudie. Now Neelie, she's not likely to come, ain't too fond of you when you're healthy, but I'll set fire to the girl, make her at least pay some respect to you, oh great savior of mama cows. Lookin' like this, there ain't much you can do to her anyway."

Key nodded off to sleep so North sat in the miserable chair for another hour or so, once even taking Key's good hand, holding it in his own, wondering at the thin tubing run in a vein, scared of the strength he knew lay within those fragile bones and how close his friend had come to dying. About four in the morning, North took the milk run back to Pueblo. It was three weeks until Christmas.

This gets complicated yet it is really simple. My family wanted me go to the hospital to visit Key; they and all my friends encouraged me, and Mickey was the worst, saying that he would drive me and wait outside if being in a hospital made me too uncomfortable. How could I tell any of these well-meaning people why I stalled my visit, why I had written North in the first place asking that he come see Key?

How do you tell the man you most likely will marry that you are waiting until the invalid is on the mend and healthy enough to fuck? How do you explain in detail the erotic pull of sex on a hospital bed or in the bathroom or anyplace you can find privacy for a moment or two? It could be under the bed for all I cared, never mind that he most likely would have a roommate or be in a ward. Somehow we would manage, and since my dislike for Key was so well known, I could not risk going back twice to visit, I could not say that I was worried or wasn't he such a hero or such drivel to make a second visit palatable. I had some sense at least in the matter of keeping our liaison private.

Consequently it made sense for me to wait until Key was on the verge of being released before stubbornly, reluctantly visiting him and sitting at his bedside, politely exchanging conversation while a student nurse hovered around us. Like most of the female population, she was half in love with Key already, although he was much less beautiful than when I first saw him in our house, charming and sad then, a pretty, lonely boy. Now he wore the battle scars of a hard-working man, no longer a child, but still as appealing, still giving off an aroma of pure sex which aroused me to instant readiness.

The damage Key had endured on his maniacal effort to bring in the herd would in time give even more character to his face, which he did not particularly need. His bout with misplaced bravery caused a change in me I am at a loss to express or understand; he became more than a lover, more than my obsession, he was a hero who I now could adore and I was angry at him for risking himself so foolishly and loved him as well as desired him. It was not a healthy change but one I could not alter. Inside me grew the torment which I had avoided when I was simply having sex with Key; the urge to tell those around me of our involvement, our love, our incredible passion. These emotions wore out my heart, that they had not simultaneously occurred in Key never entered my mind. What a fool I was then, but I was a teenage girl with her first love.

To even the most careless reader it must be obvious that in our sexual encounters birth control was never mentioned. Today, with the overload of information available to active teenagers, my innocence would be unconscionable. What I knew then about reproduction and pregnancy is frighteningly little compared to what my grand daughter must already know.

As a farm child of course I recognized the physical act of impregnation. But I also believed that unless we had sex exactly when I was ovulating, like the cows and mares we teased to make certain they were ready to be put to the bull or stallion, then I could not get pregnant. I also believed that sex during my period, which to my initial horror we tried and I learned that Key liked the blood, would also prevent conception.

Since all but the inattentive reader already knows that I become pregnant, and marry Mickey instead of Key; it is of no surprise that my theories about birth control were terribly wrong. What is more surprising is that given Key's moral character I did not catch some horrible disease. I did believe that during our involvement he was faithful to me, and thus I was at much less risk than could be expected.

I hope I have not betrayed any ending to my tale by the discussion of my eventual pregnancy; after all I have a daughter and two sons, and a granddaughter, a husband to whom I have been faithful for more than thirty years. But in the time before our hasty marriage, I was faithful only to Key.

Chapter Twelve

She missed her daughter. She was living in town, moved there right after that miserly ceremony the school tried to call graduation. She'd come home only one day at Christmas while North was with his Sylvia to her folks. They were gone from her life. Claudie's world had shifted and changed and she had been left behind, stayed at home, and she didn't like all these things in her children's lives that moved without her.

It should have been simple to live with only Ray but they got in each other's way too often, with no soft touch or pat to lessen their tempers. There was no warmth in the nights, no close sense of his body as she drifted into sleep. The days were too quiet with no slammed doors or questions yelled from another room. She wasn't needed anymore.

Last week Charlie Rushton through her husband Ray asked her to take in the injured Larkin boy. She couldn't find the energy to say no. The thought of him in the house again was disturbing. And yet the words to explain this to Ray were lost in the kindness in Ray's eyes as he asked for one more favor.

She would put the $10 Rushton said he would pay

into Neelie's bank account, to be there in the fall when she needed books or clothes or whatever girls need when they go off to college and leave their mamas behind.

Claudie found herself singing a small ditty, one her own pa taught her. 'Comin' round the mountain when she comes.' She pinned up the last of the laundry. Ray was out by the corral, fussing over a first-calf heifer looking to birth in January, a full month before her due date. No matter, it felt good to sing a bit and feel the warm sun on her back and know that when she took down the shirts and undergarments and pressed them to her face, they would have that chilled sweet aroma of cleanliness and love.

Key had the room to himself, since the man in the bed next to him died in the night, and though the staff came and cleaned up the sheets and pillows, and pulled the curtains, the man's lifeless form stayed in Key's mind. They even put a rolled up blanket at the foot of the bed, as if the next occupant might catch cold before they got the dead man put away, wherever it was they put the dead.

He was bored with the hospital, until Neelie came in the room and then he was glad the old man had died, though he didn't even know the man's name, never really saw his face. He and Neelie could be alone in the barren, sunless room, unless one of the dull-witted orderlies decided to come in ahead of schedule and pull and tug at Key or mop the floors and make a nuisance of himself.

Neelie's voice was magic, taunting Key with how lonely he'd been. "All those stories I heard, they must have been lies. You look fat and hardly a scratch on you." He recognized the tactic, using that sass to tease him, get him to make a fool of himself. This time he'd get to her first.

He reached for her with the hand missing its little finger, the bone at the wrist still red and prominent and hurt like hell. He tugged at her elbow, she had to look down and see his maimed hand. She stepped back, off balance enough that he wrapped his good arm around her waist and pulled her to him and kissed her. At least that's what he tried to do but she leaned down on top of him and her weight drove the breath from his lungs.

Their bodies touched top to toe, and his exploring hand quickly learned she wore no underpants beneath the demure sweep of her full skirt. "Ah," he breathed out hard into her mouth, and got stabbed for his trouble by a rib that wasn't quite healed.

Feeling him twist under her, Neelie laughed. "Thought you had me, huh? I know better, I've been told, hell everyone knows exactly where you got hurt. You can't lie on that side, there's three ribs busted there and one bruised lung. Here, it's my turn to push and twist and put you where I want."

She was triumphant and joyous and Key laughed; what he'd always desired, a woman to know what she wanted and eager to take it. From him. He gestured to the shrouded bed, she helped him swing his legs around and stood back while he shifted to the other bed. Parodying what they were about to do, she held the curtain back and curtseyed as he passed close to her.

It was a different and difficult act of love, a slow dance of desperate coupling. Mending ribs and the damaged hand immobilized Key; penetration was deliberate, Neelie's body settling in inches down Key's erection until they connected groin-to-groin, Neelie's legs wide over Key's hips, her arms braced on the scratchy hospital linens. It wasn't a high rush into deep warmth but careful and tender sliding, a melding of deep breaths, hands rubbed over exposed skin, as if it was desire and not infirmities which inevitably dictated their pace. Neelie lay wide open to him, wanting him deeper but not frantic, not laughing or crying or on the edge of explosion. She stayed calm and at peace, willing to receive as well as take. His first words as she lifted herself off him, into the stillness, were "I'm sorry, that wasn't much." Neelie rolled her head and looked at her lover; he didn't seem to notice any difference in what they'd just done. She was in pieces, removed from the ache of wanting, touching some part of him in the way his need had finally touched her. There weren't words for the peace inside her. She disagreed with him; "Key, that was lovely."

He didn't answer. She risked a second glance, saw the perfect profile of brow, nose, mouth, chin, the brow marred by fading scars, a bump on the nose, a small tear by the lower lip which she had felt but not seen. If she said too much, he would suspect her and buck against the compliment. "You could say the atmosphere here isn't up to our usual standards." He laughed at that and immediately put a hand to his ribs. His other hand, fingers bandaged, rested on her shoulder, its weight a comfortable presence.

Ray parked the truck at the entrance. He was picking up a patient, no one would question him. At the desk there was only one paper to sign; Charlie Rushton had paid the bill, no fuss, no confusion, a check given over once he read in detail each item on the bill. Ray had to sign he was taking Key from the place, nothing more.

The boy was in a wheelchair. Ray thought to make a joke but the sunken eyes stopped him. "Be home soon enough, boy. Claudie's got stew and cobbler waiting. And a fire in your room. Neelie came out yesterday, stacked up enough wood you won't have to do a thing for a week or so. About when you'll be wantin' to get out a the house, I reckon."

It had been a surprise, a nice one, when Neelie had turned up to the house. Claudie went crazy baking up brownies and making pies for her daughter, anything to keep her visiting in the kitchen. Still Neelie was moody, quiet even, and volunteered to go and stack the woodpile. Ray and Claudie had exchanged looks but said, 'sure, child, go ahead.'

Planning anything around Neelie's temper lately had been impossible, add that to Claudie's moods and Ray found he was looking forward to Key being in the adobe, give him reason to go check him in the evening to get away from Claudie and her sulks. It wasn't her fault, he guessed it was that woman thing happened about now. Claudie was nearing forty and her own ma went through the time just shy of thirty-five. It kept the families small and drove the husbands crazy her own pa said.

Ray scratched at his chest, watched the nurse push that wheelchair out the door. He wished the boy would make some wisecrack to the nurse who wasn't pretty but wasn't ugly neither. And young enough, hell, they were all young enough for Key.

"Come to break you out, boy." Still nothing, so Ray took over guiding the chair and the nurse walked alongside and still the boy didn't flirt or even look up. Going to be a hard winter Ray thought. He wished North was coming home today instead of a month when there was a break at school. Graduating this spring, big doings, ideas too about that girl Sylvia and wanting to have a family of his own. The mess Key got himself into was nothing North and his size could fix, but still Ray wanted the boy home.

My parents had no idea what they were bringing back into their lives. Key with North to guide him was a stabilized, steadied force; alone, even injured, he was loose and directionless, in constant motion despite being confined to a chair near the wood stove, trying to get warm, trying to mend. When I think of it now, that period of four weeks with a wild animal barricaded in their yard must have been the most uncomfortable, most difficult time for my parents in their married life. And I say this knowing of the dead first-born, the week Mama spent hospitalized and close to dying. These were occurrences which were shared among neighbors and friends; there was information and knowledge available on how to deal with the sadness of their loss. Women knew instinctively how to heal my mother. Men knew to gather in silent circles, shuffling the earth with their boots, talking mindless words about cattle and weather and crops, holding my injured father among them, healing him with their intentional closeness.

Having Key living in the old adobe with no guidelines, no rules, must have been the closest to hell my parents ever came, in this life certainly. Although if I believed in heaven or hell, I know with a strong certainty that both my mother and father would be safe in heaven, it would be me who inhabited hell alone.

He got to the house for supper. Walking wasn't easy, bending over to shove short lengths into the wood stove no easier. But both were necessary. Five minutes after he'd finished with the meal he couldn't remember what he'd eaten. He made no attempt to do the dishes, or offer any of the social politeness deemed necessary in the company of others.

He was done with them. The McKendricks sat at the table and looked at him like he was a bug specimen, he knew better but it's how he felt, studied, heads cocked at one time to the same angle so he almost laughed but it hurt to even think such so he put a hand to those darned ribs and coughed most politely, turned his head and tried to stab a second piece of the pot roast the missus made. He knew it was a meal he liked.

Eating hurt, like doing most other things, but the worst hurt was looking at this momma and poppa and seeing the weight of their daughter, knowing the intimacy of her open body while keeping his stare calm as they prattled on, asking no questions or demands that might over-extend him or set him back. If he could tell them that by agreeing to take him in they were hurrying his recovery, they might relax but the urge carried too much explanation and he didn't want to face the questions and tongue on the missus; she could smart a man with her voice.

He was in hell, placed there deliberately, meant to reschool him to living with human beings who weren't drunks or wild or pounding on him for what they wanted. The McKendricks were decent folk, nothing more. Mr. McKendrick was polite, asked Key to call him Ray again; Key nodded, they shared scars from working for the same boss.

The missus was different, woman always were. Angry at him, and at her husband, maybe extending the anger to all men, she barely was civil the first night except to press seconds on Key who could barely get the food to his mouth. "Tastes good., ma'am, but I can't take in 'nother mouthful. Ain't done much to work up the need." He had to say something nice to appease her.

Getting to the adobe room and lying down was as much fun as the trip to the main house for the meal.

Hell, he thought, I ain't worth nothing. Then he fell asleep on the bed fully clothed.

When he didn't appear for breakfast, Ray suggested Claudie look in on their boarder but Claudie didn't want to bother. Boy was tired, that's all, she argued. She could see it last night. Now that there was a sink and toilet in the house, the boy more'n likely was using the old outhouse and wanting his privacy. He liked being alone, Claudie recognized that in the boy, he liked alone more than was good for him. It was North who liked company and dragged Key along, but given a choice, she knew Key would seek out a lair and hole up, the wounded animal he was, and come out only when he was fully healed. That was good enough for him, Claudie told her husband. They would leave the boy alone then, let him decide when he needed help.

By dinner at noon she was worried but said off-hand to Ray that maybe Key hadn't heard her call, maybe he was sleeping, maybe he wasn't interested in her cooking. So she pestered Ray into going to check. He came back worried. "He looks at me and I don't see myself in those eyes at all." That was more poetry than Ray spoke in the past ten years, Claudie looked sharp at him, concerned about the flight of fancy, but he had nothing more to say. She heated up soup, buttered a slice of bread and went to the adobe.

The smell hit her first; acrid sweat, sour heat; the boy was quiet, his face flushed but dry. He looked to be sleeping, the bedclothes bunched up underneath his back, his good hand grabbing for fistfuls of sheet. Claudie rested her hand on his forehead but he didn't stir or speak up. Unwilling to confront him, she plumped up the pillows and moved him around enough he had to react. His eyelids fluttered and warned her so she stepped back and folded her arms, waiting for him to come fully awake. "I'm okay, ma'am." It was all she could drag out of him and it wasn't satisfying but Claudie stood and waited, hands on her hips, until he gave in; "I'll eat later, ma'am." Claudie snorted, "You sit up and I'll feed you, no argument." He simply closed his eyes and went limp and there wasn't much she could do. "You need food and Rushton's payin' us to feed you. Eat, damn you."

Even she was shocked by the cursing. The boy's eyelids flinched but the eyes remained closed. It was difficult not to touch the still handsome face where she had stitched him and the scar remained, or to push back the greasy hair off his forehead and set herself down to the side of his bed, maybe treat him for a bit like a small child or beloved member of her scattering family. It was odd, she thought, to miss taking care of others, to need that sense of being important to them by cooking and tending to their hurts.

There was no movement from him, no suspicion he cared that she had stayed in the room. She didn't bother to pick up a spoon. "All right, I'll leave the food. You take care to eat before it gets cold, the bread is still warm, I know you can smell it. It'll bring back memories." Instantly she hated her foolish tongue, but still he didn't move.

"Sorry, boy, you set up and eat when I'm gone. Leave you to yourself with no prattlin' woman to bother you."

He was somewhat improved the following day. Through the kitchen window Claudie watched him wander to the outhouse like she knew he would. Ray laughed when she told him, said it was just like the boy, stomping over frozen ground to keep from talking to folks inside where it was warm. Shy, he said, backwards around people. Claudie countered with no manners or good sense.

It became a routine for five days. A plate of food left inside the adobe, on the banco near the cold fire. Dirty dishes left half-full and outside in return, a shadow headed to the outhouse, water pumped from the old well. When the plates began to be wiped clean, Claudie heaped the next with more food.

Finally Key appeared at the back door, lightly bearded and ragged but walking better. "Out of firewood, ma'am," he commented, while selecting from the half cord Ray put up for emergencies. It had been mild since the Thanksgiving storm, another irony in the boy's life; almost freezing to death one day, weather kind enough for a light jacket by mid-January.

Because of the weather, Ray was able to pull the Dubble Wells pump again and he spent three days cursing, turning up worn and greasy at night after working on the ancient Aeromotor. It needed a different wrench or a cog welded in the shop, a small part from town. Claudie was glad, for Ray seemed to thrive from the activity. He wasn't so tired, didn't rub at his chest or sigh so deep and then break wind and try to make a joke of it. Like he was younger and stronger and could handle what was coming at him.

One night while Key was still with them, Claudie rolled over, half awake from a terrible dream, and found Ray's hand waiting for her, his body hard, pushing at her belly, dividing her thighs and she welcomed him, the first time in well over a year. It was brief and sweet with no great passion but when she woke in the morning, she felt the dried semen between her legs and knew her nighttime pleasure had not been a dream.

Key was there only a week when the stacked wood ran out completely and he volunteered to go with Ray up-canyon to bring in downed juniper and broken piñon. His fault, he said, using up their firewood.

Ray took the boy at his word. Claudie sputtered that he wasn't healed enough to be of use and that they should wait. Both men looked at her and Ray asked the obvious question. "Wait for who, Claudie, ain't no one comin' up here by magic to say oh let me drag in a cord or two for you, please, just for fun." She stood there, hands folded across her chest, angry at both men and with nothing more she could say.

She was right, of course. Ray knew that in the first stand of juniper when he bucked the tree into chunks and it took Key a long time to pick up each piece. He was hampered by the one bad hand but he rolled those fingers into a ball and used it to stack the short pieces up his arm like a busy waiter. But it took him a long time, he couldn't turn and throw a chunk into the truck bed but had to walk, real slow, still he didn't quit, didn't complain, kept walking from the truck to the wood and back, endlessly, while Ray cut and watched. And admired the boy's grit.

By mid-day they had less than a truck-bed of wood. Claudie had made up sandwiches and a thermos of coffee for noon. Ray ate hungrily while the Larkin boy chewed as if the effort hurt too much. He wouldn't talk, not even to answer dumb comments Ray made. Finally the sullen air exploded inside Ray. "Boy you're here doin' your work, ain't no cause to make it worse settin' all miserable and ugly."

Key's shaggy head, hair chopped short in the hospital and growing wild, all which-way, turned carefully, those pale eyes looked at Ray and the older man got hot and uncomfortable. Trespassing, he thought, going where the boy didn't want him. "Mr. McKendrick, Ray.

I'm too wore out to talk."

The words left Ray feeling dumb, "Sorry, boy, I'm a bit shot myself but it sure ain't the worst day I been out cuttin' wood." He tried making amends, a gesture he learned maybe too late with Claudie. Say what you feel first, don't let it build. Like last night. He needed to kiss her this morning, tell her how wonderful she was in the dark of their marriage bed, but instead he went off cutting wood with their maverick. Ray shook his head, silent in his thoughts. He'd loved Claudie the moment he saw her, forgot to tell her that, forgot in the work and sore and misery of these past years. He still loved her.

"We're goin' in, got enough wood to hold you for awhile. Me, I'll get Charlie to hire on a boy from town. Ain't no cause for you to worsen yourself. Me, I got other things need doin'." What he wanted was to see Claudie and maybe this time be man enough to tell her. How much he needed her, just what she meant to him.

Living between folks like the McKendricks was rough. They demanded every day, kind words, thoughts to be shared, comments over a meal, thank-you and yes, please, and all the courtesy Key never got taught as a kid. He was a quick learner, the teachers always told him that, so he'd known how to shadow what people did in company. But there were times when the devil in his gut wrenched clear of the teaching and poked at others, picked at sore spots and traded on weaknesses. Key sat there grinning, knowing what he was doing and liking the pleasure of it.

He couldn't do any of this with the McKendricks. No hurt and soothe, kiss and tell. His memory stored up sensations of Neelie and he watched the mother and knew how badly she was betrayed. It was worse when they spoke of North. Yet here he was having coffee with the missus while Ray was up to Dubble Wells again. Key thought he could hear the cursing and complaints from a distance and when he told the lady about his pretending, she looked sideways to him and laughed. Then shoved the last bit of sweet roll onto his plate. "You need this, Key. Even if we get more meat on you, you still look like a plucked chicken." He tore a bit off the corner, let its sweetness melt him, licked his mouth clean of the cinnamon sugar.

So when Neelie came in the kitchen, what she found was her lover and her mother sitting together, each looking secretly pleased. The first words out of her mouth bit into the air, sharp with jealousy. "You look like that cat licking up the last of the cream. You're the son of a bitch I was warned about, Key Larkin."

Mama's head snapped around, her usually quiet eyes tightened and Neelie felt the reprimand in her gut. "You will not speak to anyone in this house that way, child. Ever." She had not heard her mother speak so formally; while the words settled between them, her mother's back stayed erect, her shoulders high, both hands flat on the table. Neelie did not lift her eyes to see into her mama's face, instead she focused on her own hands, reddened fingers, knuckles swollen, spotted skin, a thin cut mending across the base of the right thumb.

Key didn't move, barely noticed Neelie, didn't put the last of the sweet roll in his mouth. One hand remained near the bread, the other lay in his lap, still lightly bandaged and always sore. His eyes were down, angering Neelie even more. But she dared not speak again, fearful of exposing herself to the over-quick response of her mother's heightened senses.

"Ladies, I best be gettin' to my place." That was a

mouthful said and realized, Key thought. "Ma'am, thank you for the coffee and the treat." He rose from the table, halfway out of the chair he stopped, vulnerable to Neelie's closeness. "Neelie, it's nice to see you too." He straightened up, and walked out, frightened of what Neelie still might say, or do.

Before he got back to his room he was soaked through, his good hand trembled, his bandaged hand ached and his stomach churned so he changed course to the outhouse, barely making it, shamed and vaguely amused by his downright pitiful condition.

Neelie sat down where Key had sat. "Mama." She deliberately used the childish term. "I am sorry but he looked so...settled, so much of where North should be. Do you remember, when North brought him home and I cried when you and Papa said he could stay?"

As she spoke, the familiar words drew out more memory. Neelie wished for Key, his mouth anywhere, his hands all over her, his body pinned inside her, his legs wrapped with hers. Yet she could see and hear and feel these wants and still be clear-eyed and plead with her mother for forgiveness. And something more.

"I came to tell you that Mickey asked me to marry him. I guess that's why I got so upset, please forgive me? And I said yes to Mickey. Please be glad for us too."

How these two souls inhabited my body at the same time scares me. I never felt unfaithful to Mickey before we were married and I did not desire to marry Key, not until everything changed. I gladly accepted Mickey's proposal knowing that I would try and bed Key as soon as I got the chance. Our times together were severely limited by him living with my parents but even that reminder of my sin, of our lusting acts, did not deter me.

Finding him seated in obvious contentment with my mother set off an indecent, irrational fury. Accepting Mickey, living in town, owning my own truck, a good job, going to college in the fall, all those matters were shoved aside by jealousy and it was with my own mother that the monster became a threat. It had not occurred to me until that very moment, a picture I can visualize without a photograph, that I would kill another woman if she threatened my pleasure with Key.

It took a great deal of discipline for me to sit down at the table and in a normal tone apologize and then ask for her blessing. I am glad and surprised that I was able to achieve the deception for it proved to be of some importance later on. As I sat down, I could smell Key's scent, feel the warmth of his body still in the chair. I pushed back the plate smudged with crumbs, avoided the flat knife used to spread butter. I was insane in my feelings at that moment, and fought wildly, internally, to remain my mother's child, retain some sense of my own life.

What I wanted was to spin out the door and jump Key, plow him to the bed and roll under him, take him, breathe in his scent of fever and fresh bread and dirty clothes, damp skin. Male skin. Key, no one else at that moment mattered to me; I heard my own words about marrying Mickey and could not believe it was my voice that spoke them.

Now, in the attic of our house, remembering what I never expressed to another person, I can feel the strength of my ancient obsession and wish desperately that Mickey were down stairs, home, near our marriage bed where I could consume him instead of being eaten alive by memory.

I heard a voice, looked down at my hands: the fingers curled through the faded picture, the face and body of the unknown friend were punctured by my fingernails. My granddaughter's voice asked again, "Are you all right, Gramma?" Slowly I was able to return to the story, editing continually as I told of the two boys and how it all ended.

"Are you sure this is what you want?" Claudie was very careful, too conscious of her daughter's unexpected outbursts and the fragility of her own barely remembered feelings when her ma and pa asked the same question about Ray all those years ago. "What will you do about college? Will they give you a scholarship if you are married?" Be careful, Claudie admonished herself, don't scare her until she becomes what you are, consumed and confused and uncertain of the future.

While the litany of want and prediction raged through Claudie, she sat calmly at her kitchen table, dishes and crumbs scattered on its surface, a tendril of damp hair floating above her right eye, a tremor so unnoticeable that even her once beloved Ray would not guess what surged through her in a powerful second warning. Here was her chance to do it right, to have and share in family and affection. To bring her Neelie back home once more.

She liked Mickey and knew Ray respected him. There were small things she wished would change but if Neelie was happy...Claudie saw the tension as Neelie waited for her mother's opinion. "Child, I am glad you and Mickey will marry." There, said out loud, approval sought and given. "Let me cook up your favorites, your pa'll be back soon enough with that motor." It was easy to slip into the expected role of wife and mother, the cook and mender, the healer of bodies, the washer of souls.

Her words came roughly, scattered around a sudden panic. "Tell me all, what date do you have in mind or haven't you got that far, and what about his family, when will we meet? Tell me the details, the plans you've made."

It was of little surprise to her father when Neelie told him. He nodded and said of course and that he expected the formality of Mickey asking for her hand even though they all knew he was delighted and did approve. Neelie laughed. This man was her father, not the somber, gray-faced man of the past year or two but this light quiet teasing meant to jostle and disrupt and never, never, hurt.

Key didn't come in for the supper. Ray stuck his head inside the adobe and saw that the boy was on his bed, feet hanging over the side, unmoving even when he called out his name, so he told Claudie he'd take a plate in later, that tonight it was just family and wouldn't it be fun to call North at the dorm, if they had a phone, and tell him the news. That telling would be done tomorrow from town but for tonight it was only the family to celebrate.

It was the sixties and we didn't have a phone or a television. But not to have a phone then was the mark of living far from town. It cost so much per mile to put in the phone poles so if there weren't enough folks on the line, the individual had to pay and Charlie Rushton was cheap. Being semi-retired and a widower of thirty years, there was no way he would put out good money for what he called the new-fangled invention. He liked playing the buffoon at times, the old cowboy who remembered when horses rode out longer, when cattle put on better weight and even when automobiles and trucks were better made. His pose got tiring but in the end, there were places in which he was right. Such as the character and morality of men and women he hired, and since he paid the bills my father didn't argue with him about a phone.

It might have been fun to call North that night, with the

entire family talking to him, Mama and me and then Papa, talking and giggling and listening and spelling out plans in which he would always be included. But then, if we'd had a phone and called North, we would have had to include Key and this was one celebration he should not attend.

As I see it now, Key's non-appearance at supper indicates what I only suspected then, that he was sensitive to his standing within our ranks, that he cared about our involvement, that he knew he was getting close to hurting me. I was not so perceptive and was furious he refused Papa's invite, but there was little I could do except sulk, which quickly wore off. The pleasure and relief in my mother's eyes and the teasing from my father made that night, around our table, mirrored the way we had been years earlier before the turmoil of North's arrival and Key's interruption into our family.

Chapter Thirteen

The winter thaw came in early February, the same week that Mickey Herrera got his best suit cleaned, washed and polished his car and checked its tires, filled it with gasoline and oil and took the long drive out of town on the back road towards old Trinchera Plaza and Branson, but he turned left down a dirt track at the bent gate and small rusty sign.

His coupe fitted in nicely between the battered GMC and the old Ford truck. As Neelie had promised, she was home, but there was no sign of Charlie Rushton. In a small box held in his vest, Mickey carried a ring, a thin gold band set with a small diamond; his mother's mother's ring, with which he would formally ask for Neelie's hand in marriage. After Mr. McKendrick had his say, Mickey would present the ring to Neelie.

Despite his fears, despite the sweat on his palms and the tiny core of worry that Neelie would at the last moment turn him down, the talk with the McKendricks, first the father and later both mother and father, went well, as far as Mickey could read their tight faces.

There was little to be read from McKendrick's expression as he invited Mickey into a small room scattered with papers and broken ranch gear. The older man took time clearing a space where Mickey could sit, then he sat in the sprung chair and rubbed his chest and his jaw, and asked Mickey how the drive out was, mud and all from the thaw and did his car do well on the bad roads. It took Mickey several minutes to realize that Raymond McKendrick was nearly as terrified as Mickey himself. Finally they got to their business.

"She's our only child. The missus ... well we lost our first one, didn't expect to have another, so Neelie, she's more than special to us. Any child is special to the parents, guess you two will find that out soon enough."

It wasn't said with a leer but Ray McKendrick's words opened up the delicate subject between two men who saw the same woman in a differing light. McKendrick let the chair fall back to upright and braced his hands on the crowded desk. "Mr. Herrera, you come to ask me something?"

The date was set for August, before the fall gather. Time enough for the women to do their arranging and give the scattered relatives a chance to set their schedules so they could attend. Neelie watched more than participated in the preparations, and she was glad for her mother's excitement. She seemed to come alive daily, eyes glowing, existing within a hurried walk, as if there wasn't enough time for all the things she wanted done.

The dress would be made by a cousin living in Denver, who sent down bits of fabric for Claudie's inspections, and patterns too, a list of the right measurements and how exactly to take them so the dress would fit perfectly. Neelie felt she had little part in all this, as if it were another's wedding, not hers. Mickey too was bowled over by his chattering mother and three sisters several aunts and a great-grandmother who had ideas and opinions and expected everyone on both sides of the marriage to listen to them.

Neither of them had much chance to be alone; there was always a friend, busy and excited about the upcoming marriage, or a customer in a distant town wanting a bigger order. Mickey felt compelled to widen his route so he could support himself and a wife who would be going to college in the fall. Not to Denver where she had been accepted but to the same two-year institution where North was about to graduate.

Neelie came home every chance she could, to help her ma, talk with her pa, and ride her dun pony. The agreement wit the neighbors had been changed, the pony would go to them as a babysitter for their grandchildren until he was needed for Mickey and Neelie's offspring.

She rode up to the line camp one day on purpose. While it was March and warm, the higher elevations still had lots of snow melt and it was a cold ride. It would be a long time before Rushton would hire a man to push his cows to their summer graze.

Key had disappeared shortly after Neelie's announcement and no one had seen him for over a month. There was no report on a unruly, lame hitch hiker, or a man getting in brawls over women, there were no ladies with smiling faces in town, he'd gone and disappeared and after a while even Rushton gave up thinking on the boy, he had others things more worth the worrying.

Neelie found him where she thought he'd hole up. Like a wounded cat, he'd gone to ground. In the line camp, leaned down more from living off game, hair gone wild and thick at his neck, hanging low across his eyes, beard soft and curling, darker than she would have thought. His eyes were the same, pale and electric in his copper face. He appeared as she approached the cabin, before she had a chance to call out. He stepped up to the pony and cupped its muzzle, crooned to the animal who rested his head on Key's shoulder and rubbed gratefully against him.

He spoke first, his voice raspy and low; "Neelie, congratulations." She couldn't bear the stupid civility. "You son of a bitch, where have you been when I need you?" He winced, and she was glad. "Come on, Neelie! This's too much even for us. I like Mickey, and your folks, they were good to me." Then he said the words they rarely shared, the thought that would always divide them. "North is a friend, Neelie. I owe him something besides fucking his family."

She kicked her legs out and the pony shied. One foot reached Key's chin, she let her boot run up almost to his ear until he shied like the pony. In a better time he would have pulled her from the pony, this time she slipped off on the side away from Key.

Wordless, slow and deliberate, Key took the pony by the bit, knelt and fastened the old hobbles left hanging in a tree, slipped the bit free and hung the bridle on the same tree branch, and turned the pony loose to graze. Practiced movements from a long habit. Neelie watched, fascinated as always by his beauty, and overwhelmed by the urgent need which had brought her to this place.

He was ahead of her when she climbed the cabin steps, holding the door for her, looking away, body withdrawn as she went in past him. His reluctance sparked a buried greed. As he was busy with the door she came back and rubbed against him, kissed him, found that perfect fit of their bodies which invaded all her dreams. She kissed him on the ear and then the neck, which tasted of dirt and clean cold air, then to his mouth while her hands went down his back, careful of his ribs when he inhaled sharply and she remembered.

"Neelie, we're wrong, damned and wrong." She kept still, knew that he protested without meaning as his body responded to hers. "One more time," she promised. He spoke into her mouth, past the tangled hair around their faces; "Yes." His hands were deep into her now, unbuttoning her blouse, pressing his roughened fingers on the soft skin, the rising flesh. She smiled around his mouth, and tilted her hips to get even closer into him.

They lay together breathing each others' rhythm, quiet and close without need to move or speak. It was a moment Neelie wanted forever. Then she spoke; "Key, I'm pregnant. You're the father. Not Mickey. You."

His body pulled away from hers at all points of contact. He did not move or respond but he no longer touched her. She kept on; "I know exactly when, I knew the moment it happened. In the hospital that time." She waited, he did not respond. "Key?"

Sudden raw words spilled from him, what she expected but not what she wanted to hear; "I won't never marry you. Don't tell Mickey, just get him in your bed, he'll want to believe it's his." Harsh and cruel and what she had already thought of and discarded. She would not give Key up, she would have this child with him as their dowry.

"It's not right, not to a good man, or to the child. Or you." She had unintentionally separated him and wondered if he heard the sentiment. "I know you don't speak of love and I don't use the word around you but it's changed, this is our child, you and me into one. You can't not love your baby or want another man to raise it."

Her thoughts were mangled, the words not what she had rehearsed but his touch had opened her unexpectedly, confusing her with specific wants. She tried again; "If I tell Papa he will make us marry." The anguish showed deep in Key, and dug into her heart but he still said nothing, did nothing but stare at the ceiling, his unblinking eyes refusing the pain evident in the white ring around his mouth.

"North, too, I'll tell North." Blackmailing him into love, and marriage. She hated herself, the words, the thoughts, the deepening need that soured in her mouth and overflowed into such abuse. She had known from the very beginning yet she wanted to try, she wanted Key. And she would do anything, say anything to make him agree to her idea.

"Help me." Her voice broke, she felt the tears. Key Larkin did not respond.

I remember the days which led to my challenging Key all too clearly. I sat at the Royal typewriter Mr. Kopeski let me bring home from the store and tried to clear my demons by typing thoughts and snippets of my being into the night. Until my cousin began to complain each morning. Resting my head on the black typewriter roller and crying, I sought a release and a solution that wasn't there.

There were no definitions or rules where I now was, only deep pain had a recognized value. Looking at facts didn't help my desperation. I had grown up hating a boy who fooled with any woman, who said to me from the start he did not care what flesh he lay between, what skin and bone and mouth gave him pleasure. And I had grown to love a gentle man professing love for me. One of them was father to my child, the other held my promise in marriage.

I knew without hospital tests or examinations that I was pregnant and Key was the father. Mickey Herrera deserved better than this and so did the child. But I loved Key and yet had promised to live with Mickey's hands and body and love. I did believe that Mickey could make me happy. But it wasn't fair to him to unknowingly become a parent to Key's child. So it was for me to make the choice. And I chose Key.

The searching, tearing, rendering emotions were enormous; alone in the room, aching, torn apart. I was told by my boss at the store that if I didn't come to my senses soon enough he would have to fire me. I was losing regular customers, I was weepy, perhaps it was the upcoming wedding and I was nervous.

As Cornelia McKendrick I had come to a point of impossibility; I could love and create a family with a good man or chase a man who did not want me and suffer the indignities and rewards of this pursuit. I needed North to talk to then, but he wasn't coming for a few more days. I felt the pressure inside, it increased daily, pounding within me until I thought and hoped I would die. I understand better now; then the whole world was against me and I had no place to go but to find Key.

This story began as a tale of two young men standing close, smiling just past the camera to another person, innocent young men pleased with each other and their new friendship. It was about North and Key, about answering my granddaughter's question.

Now it has turned into a story about me, about my inexplicable behavior and the trouble it caused my family. I have no excuse or real explanation for what I did so many years back, I only know how the extreme need inside me felt, the despair at the idea of not being with Key, or more correctly not being with the person I had built up using his face and body and forgetting that he had his own soul.

If marital, consensual sex has not been important in a woman's life, then she will have no understanding and compassion for my youthful actions. I am not asking for forgiveness from anyone; the only forgiveness I received was from Mickey who healed me slowly, over the long years of our marriage, knowing what I had done and accepting me and the child into his heart.

My parents never forgave me, or at least we never discussed the situation, for the final revelation was far worse than anything I had done and it tore my parents apart in a manner which was unredeemable, irrevocable. Even now I cannot recall what occurred without the demeaning and paralyzing shame which kept company with all those events. My family shut out reality and settled on a more conventional though publicly shaming version of a truth.

But all this is the future; at the time I went hysterical and Key had to deal with me and my fantasies and get me safely off the mesa, back to where I belonged, with those who loved me.

He would put both hands over his ears and squeeze his eyes shut if he thought that would block out the sound of her, the crying that didn't stop, the gasping for air, the open mouth, mucous flooding from her, weeping more than he thought possible.

No matter what he did or said, she would not calm down. It was to force him into the marriage, he'd seen his own ma try that ploy and it was as unsuccessful as Neelie's attempt.

There had never been a promise from him, never a word of love or wedding. He had been relieved when the announcement of her impending marriage to Mickey became common knowledge. His conscience was saved, it was good, he could leave her well cared for. She was wild and beautiful, creative with her hands and mouth, open to him, hot underneath him, eager to experiment but he would not marry anyone, especially Neelie, for any of those reasons. He had seen too much the end result of mating to wish the responsibility. He knew too well not to commit that folly.

"Neelie, no...I'm takin' you back to your folks. They'll clean you up, I can't. Damn it, I won't." She made no effort to help but did not hinder him as he pulled on the opened blouse, not bothering with the bra, and slipped on her jeans, stuffing the flimsy panties in a back pocket. There would be no disguising her condition, or his part in her despair. As he tugged on her jeans, he could not stop his hand from cupping the slight bulge of her belly, more than her usual female roundness, a hint of what lay inside, growing, becoming more a part of Neelie than he would ever be.

Her sobbing was reduced to hiccups by the time he bridled the pony. She even climbed up unaided onto the dun's back but did not ask the pony to move and Key knew he would have to go with her. She could manipulate him to that degree. It meant facing the McKendricks but that too didn't matter. It would be done, and then he could leave with no more ties, no hopes that he could ever deserve a family.

He gave her his jacket and put on an extra shirt. It was March and chilly but they wouldn't freeze. The trip down was difficult, Key's ribs still ached and his balance was uncertain, he reached out once with a hand and found the fingers didn't bend right and when he hit the barely-healed stump on a scrub oak he couldn't stop the curse. It was the first time Neelie spoke rationally to him. "You all right? Runnin' into things in the dark?" That bit of teasing, a very small joke, helped him feel better though the stump bled some and he turned his ankle on a miserable rock and this time kept his mouth quiet.

It was a long three hours before they saw lights at the McKendrick place. More lights than usual; ah shit, Key thought, North must be home from college. He volunteered to put the pony in the corral, after leaving Neelie directly at the back door, no place for her to duck out, nothing for her to do but go inside and face her demons. He was the coward, taking the reins to lead the pony to the corral, where he wasted more time by rubbing the pony as it ate hay until the pony snapped at him for interfering and he knew he was extending the time he gave Neelie to talk it out with her folks and North.

When he walked into the kitchen he hung back at the door, its warm familiarity a distraction. The family sat around the table. No one looked directly at him, Neelie half-jumped from her seat, head high, defiant, eyes glistening. "I told them I'm pregnant Key." He was relieved, the worst was done. They didn't want to kill him so Neelie be dammed he was leaving her with her family. "But I didn't tell them all the truth." He held in his breath, already knowing and getting ready to duck. "That you are the father."

No movement, not a twitch. No raised fist or harsh curse, only a subtle shift among themselves, a lowered gaze, a draw of deep breath. Both McKendricks parents looked at their daughter and then in unison looked at Key. Still no word or action from them, but it must have been that tandem move which loosened North's rage.

He stood up so quickly the chair flew back from under him. His big shoulders bunched, his fist doubled and Key saw the blow and did not move; the crack of his cheekbone told him it was broke again. He was spun backwards, all the time watching North's face, knowing he put that killing rage in the quiet eyes. It was all his, the fathering, the family's pain, and North's immense strength was a blessing for it obliterated everything in Key except the need to stay alive.

He sprawled over a chair, fell with it, lay entangled and made no effort to rise. North stood over him; Key did not move. North picked him up and held him close; Key felt the spittle from each word. "You son of a...I was told you were like this and didn't...I know better now. You bastard." The last word was singled out, spat from North's mouth and it hurt more than the broken cheekbone or the blood running into Key's mouth or the loosened teeth, the reawakened pain in his bad wrist. "Bastard." It was the truth. Then North hit him again, full on the mouth, hard enough Key's brain went black, and as he drifted, he spoke softly to his friend; "Thank you." But he recognized that North could not hear him.

Then Neelie was pounding at North, crying and hitting and calling him terrible names. North dropped Key, who fell loosely, without muscle or bone. North turned and grabbed his beloved cousin, held her close and tried to quiet her. Key stayed down, awake enough to wipe at the blood from his nose and kept his thoughts to himself. The room closed in on him, it felt as if all those in it took a deep breath in unison.

Then Neelie erupted; "I love him, do you hear me, North. We're getting married." Then she stopped, seemed to realize that her words had frozen both her parents, and North. Now she had their complete attention. "I am going to marry Key Larkin."

Lying on the kitchen floor, Key looked at the pattern of drying blood on the back of his hand, felt the pounding weakness in his bad wrist; she'd refused to hear him, no one could make her understand. North would turn around now and kick him to death and

Key accepted that he would do nothing to stop the killing.

North picked him up with one hand, held him close, slapped him hard with the other hand, splitting Key's lower lip. "North. You're right. A good beatin' is the only thing that'll make me pay attention." He had to mumble, his mouth hurt something fierce. North drew back his hand, readying a new strike. Key cleared his throat, spoke out clearly; "You stop, North, or I'll have to fight back."

The absurdity of his statement cracked something in the room. Ray McKendrick choked on a dry laugh, the missus was silent. North, however, got the message and set Key down in a chair. "You don't move you miserable bastard." His sigh had the weight of a hurricane. Key winced in spite of the settling calm . Neelie got in the way again; "None of you may like Key being the father but he is and I love him and he loves me and we're going to marry. Mickey is a mistake." Only then did she begin to cry. "It's Key's child. We've been lovers for months now."

Platitudes and logic had no meaning. Neelie's blind declaration would not be changed. North, however, had to try. "You want to marry him? Not Mickey? But Key? Loving this worthless piece of... he's betrayed us all, Neelie. How can you talk about love? What kind of love can that bastard give a child?" Key felt each word dig through him, bury him in a private grave. He had lost this time, lost everything that ever could have been good.

Neelie fought hard; "You can't tell me how I feel, Northern McKendrick. You don't know about this kind of love. I bet you and Sylvia, why you hold hands and maybe kiss and she lets you touch her breasts above her clothing if you're good but you know nothing about love."

There it was, girl still had it all wrong. Key clenched his hands between his legs. Sex ain't love, he wanted to say to her. Sex feels good, yeah, and it gets you close and held for a moment but it ain't love.

Ray McKendrick's face went deadly white, as if the situation finally hit him. His daughter, in bed with a viper, a renegade taken into the family on good graces. Touching and poking and doing all those things a man did with a woman. His child, his beloved baby girl. She wanted that poking, needed that particular man, a man her father and the whole damned community knew was no good.

McKendrick put his head in his hands and Key watched the tough, stringy shoulders heave up and down, tremble, shiver. He feared the man's pain more than he did the depth and strength of North's immense fists.

Claudie McKendrick finally spoke. Her voice was soft and clear, commanding that they all listen. "Neelie child, you can't marry Key." His name was said hard in contrast to the love in Neelie's name. Neelie grimaced; Key steadied himself. Wondered just how the woman would say what was coming next. Neelie tried; "Mama, you haven't listened. He's the father of my baby, I love him. I need him, not you and your words."

The older woman's face was relaxed, untroubled, her eyes distant. Key knew what she was about to do, and admired her inherent courage. There was no rise of emotion or threat in her tone as she voiced a fact to stop all hearts in the closed room.

"Neelie, since that Christmas, remember it? When your pa and North shot the turkey and Key joined us? I've been bedding Key since then, whenever your pa's not around, whenever I can find him or he can find me. You can't marry a man who's bedded your mother." Claudie McKendrick made her choice.

Ray McKendrick's head lifted, his eyes went wide and blank. He wiped tears on his sleeve, stared at his now quiet wife. Her words echoed in the room, around and around, destroying all those who heard them.

Neelie sat down hard, the chair creaked under her sudden weight. Both hands went to her mouth, her eyes were shut. She cried out once, then was stilled.

North went straight at Key who raised both hands in surrender but Ray McKendrick spoke up and North stopped. "Don't. Not now." Key didn't like the promise in that 'not now.'

This is when North lied to me. I can't prove it since the situation was never discussed or mentioned again. Any attempt on my part to ask North met with silence. But circumstance points to violence, and the one time I could get him to speak at all about that evening and its aftermath, North said he had done nothing he felt ashamed of concerning Key. I believed him, and I also believed that my father and North took Key out somewhere and beat him very badly. And I am certain that Key did not resist.

There is no kind ending to this story, and I have not told my granddaughter all the elements, especially the last bits. My mother was right, I could not marry a man who would fuck me and bed my mother and smile to us both, lie to me about how special I was, how tender he felt towards me, how much I meant in his life, while he spoke some of the same words to my own mother.

It took several days to realize the extent of the destruction.

My father was extremely quiet for a long time, North could barely stand to be around us and spent most of his time riding fence or pulling the motor on the Dubble Wells pump, and my mother baked madly, sewed until her fingers bled and her eyes ached, and when I came out of my own misery I began to see the terrible consequences of my thoughtless actions.

I don't think I ever saw my father smile again, or heard him laugh or tell a joke or even seem pleased by what went on around him. He never healed. For within the year he had a series of strokes and then a big one which put him in the hospital where he died. He came to my wedding to Mickey, which was an enormous effort for him. I could see it in his face, in the stiff, horrible manner in which he moved, and the ugly grimace which had to pass as his smile when he spoke to the members of the wedding party. The depth of his love for me was in that enormous gesture of support and convention.

He sat with Mama, held her hand while the vows were spoken, but I knew, even as he observed the social aspects of the ceremony, he did not believe that a marriage could be held and kept in trust.

It was his pain which forced me to tell Mickey the truth before the wedding, to give him a chance to back out of his promise. It was not as difficult as I suspected. He nodded as I talked, turned pale but made no sound when I spoke in too great length about Key's attraction for me, and when I was finished, said he would marry me and the child would be ours. Not a child to be abandoned but one to love and cherish.

From there I began to heal from the wildness of my aberration which cost so much. I know my father's death was mine, I accepted my guilt and tried to make amends, mostly with North since Mama and I stopped talking after that night, after those few words which bared her soul and shattered mine.

What drove her to it? In the later years, when I was mother to three children, two of them boys who looked just like their father, I asked her bits and pieces, and she haltingly, in abstract terms with never a defined moment or intimate fact, agreed to tell me. I believed she tried to warn me, using her adultery and her hasty marriage as examples.

She loved my father from the start, from the moment they met when she was in high school and he was a rancher. My father married late after he fell in love, my mother married early for the same reason. The years between them held no difficulties until my father became an old man before his time and my mother was unfulfilled and restless. Key Larkin was there, thrust into her care by oblivious people such as my father and North. And me. Somewhere around always, at the adobe with North, up to the line camp on Rushton's orders. Living alone in the adobe and needing physical care. She tended Key too often when he was hurt and her husband no longer had the desire or the ability to seduce her.

She turned to a boy twenty years younger to give her peace, and pleasure, and to keep her marriage in order.

I hated her for her needs until I saw they were my own. I hated my father for his weakness, until once, as an afterthought, my mother told me that as a child he had rheumatic fever which kept him out of the army and limited his physical durability.

Perhaps now I can accept her actions, but it took years and all that anger and hurt before I could sit up here and hold on to the picture and not cry, but tell bits of the story to my grandchild, Key's grandchild. The rest I might tell her when she becomes a woman and is curious about men or seeks them out in a dangerous and promiscuous way, needing to understand the history of her own creation. And the true identity of her grandfather.

North died when he was forty-five, of a cancer the doctors called 'inoperable' and sent him home. We all loved him, Mickey and I and our boys and the girl, Connie. They worshiped their uncle, for that is what they called him. He and Mickey had gone into business together, running a series of hardware stores which were successful enough that recently they were bought up by a large chain. Which is where Mickey is now, settling the deal and finishing up the business.

North's wife, Sylvia, although not the Sylvia from college but a woman he met three years later at church, still lives four doors down from us in town. We are friends but not close, not calling every day, yet conscious of our mingled history and knowing we remain connected by the memory of a special man.

I hoped for years that Key was put on a train or bus and let back into the world unscathed. Then I went through a period when I hoped North did lie and that he'd beaten Key to an unrecognizable pulp where his pretty face could not be repaired and he could no longer destroy the women who wanted him with that deep ache only he seemed able to erase.

I will never know what happened to Key. Which is why, when I labeled these photos one rainy afternoon while waiting for the birth of my first grandchild, I put North's name on the back, with the afterthought of 'unknown friend' scrawled across Key's fading image.

Claudie McKendrick's Statement:

I was delighted when my child decided to write this memoir. To me, each word is filled with the bitter truth I once tried to avoid. My conscience is eased by knowing that my act of confession so many years ago, selfish as it was in motivation, gave her the chance she needed, to move from her own obsession with that beautiful, terrible boy to marrying a good man who has provided well for her and filled her life with love. Mickey has his faults, we all do, but he has a heart almost as big as our beloved North's.

It is important that I begin this apology with the explanation as to how my bizarre affair had its birth. I did not seek Key out; to be courted and bedded by a young man was not something I would ever come to on my own. These are the only words I will offer in my defense.

The Christmas we invited Key to join us, he gave Neelie a book of poetry and he hand-copied three poems for me. Now I know they were very specific poems in their order and intent. Then I had no idea of their significance as I read the first one to my gathered family. Robert Frost's "The Road Not Taken" is a simple, deliberate, beautiful poem of great delicacy.

Even my Ray, with his limited education, could understand the symbolic nature of those two roads.

Key gambled on my family's attention span and won. They did not want to hear two more poems, so we moved on to the excitement of other presents, and only later that evening did I read the remaining poems to myself, in the special quiet which comes after a holiday when all the dishes are washed and put away and the family is fast asleep.

It took a while to see beneath what I first considered very odd choices for a gift. The second poem was "Crazy Jane Talks with the Bishop," by Yeats, the third was "Calypso's Island" by Archibald McLeish. Both deal with women who are aging and filled with unrequited passion. At least in my analysis of them this is what comes to me. Perhaps it was my situation coloring what I gleaned from the words. This is how we all come to poetry, what makes each piece an individual revelation.

In their different ways each poem touched me on the first reading as I puzzled over them that night. I have told no one about their significance until now, not even my daughter. I know she has kept the paper with them printed on it folded in the poetry book Key gave her, but she has not looked at the individual poems and comprehended the clarity with which Key told me what he wanted and would give in return.

He was young and male, handsome, sexual, eager to create fantasy despite the difference in our ages, the loss of my physical charms through birth, death, and hard work. If you read these two poems, you will finds many disturbing lines; their words and tone were foreign to me then, speaking in harsh flat syllables of age and its physical manifestations. The descriptions were too close to me, my body had given up its hard, firm youthfulness and my husband didn't want me. Here in front of me was proof others lived this same life, others suffered for their age and their undiminished and unfulfilled needs. The poems spoke of losing self in the duties of bearing children, marrying a good flawed man, and then, further down in one of the most poignant statements, the poet had mouthed out loud my inner feelings. I had a choice, to hold on to my daily life, my small tragedies and let the world pass me, or I could go out and take what was needed, what was now missing in my life before even that choice, that chance, had passed me by. You do understand that it has taken me years to fully understand the poets' words, but they struck me even then with their power, their deep insight into my confusion. I did not know until that Christmas, reading those particular poems, that others could feel the loss and the age and the unfairness as I did in those terrible, lonely moments.

These hand-printed, slightly smudged words were not the traditional lover's plea, but in context with my child in the process of leaving home, my husband's growing disinterest in my aging body, once beautiful like my daughter's but now gray and tired, worn out through duty, the words were sharp and almost physically penetrating. Key knew just how to touch me without putting hand to flesh. He was far too clever for the obvious. In rereading the three poems I gain a great insight into the lost depth and brilliance of Key Larkin's mind.

Yet what drove me to respond? Now it is accepted if a woman near forty takes a younger man to her bed. She is applauded for her lewd courage. I never did love Key. I loved only my husband. Who for unspoken reasons of health could not come to me in bed. I did not know how ill he was, nor did I comprehend the effect of his growing debility.

If Ray had told me of his illness and we had gone together to our family physician, who knows, perhaps we might have saved both him and our marriage. The fact is, my husband could not tell me, or anyone, how badly he felt, how much a struggle it was for him to keep going, and why he had no sexual interest in me. I forgive him now. All these years later, I forgive him for not talking to me, but I do not forgive my own actions. Nor do I truly regret them.

To diverge from the subject at hand: if you think you detect a change in my voice and manner from my persona in my daughter's story, you are correct. I have taken classes at the local university extension for several years now, and even have begun to write my own poetry.

So to return to the issues. Except for the effect it had on my husband and my marriage, I would take the boy again for the pleasure of him even as I sit here rocking, hands rubbing each other against arthritic pain, legs weakened by too many hard years, flesh sagging, breasts turned to wasted dugs, body hairless as a child's.

There was no pretense of love between us; it was simply lust, hot and fulfilling. Giving me the selfish strength to climb into my marriage bed and hold my beloved husband hear his night cries, feel the empty weight of his flesh. I would lie there, tears cold under my eyelids, his shoulder close to me, I would lie there and want him with no thought or memory of Key. I substituted mechanics for what Ray and I once had and it became enough. In my mind, I had no choice.

There is little more to add. Neelie has written the story well but it is from her point of view. My decision to speak at the crucial time destroyed what remained of my life yet gave my daughter a final opportunity. For her, marrying the likes of Key Larkin, even if he had agreed, would have ended any life she might possibly have. It was a mother's choice: without Key I would not have stayed strong those past years. As it was, I had the remaining strength to nurse Ray while he died, then helped tend his nephew, our beloved

North, until his own sad, premature death.

Now I am married to a man six years younger than I am and he too is dying. I will care for him better than I did for Ray, and thrive on the physical necessity. I have come to the conclusion that, for women like me, it is the need of our loved ones which defines us, gives us our meager chance to reach beyond our own mortality and become more than we ever expect of ourselves. I will nurse Forrest and when he dies I will bury him and mourn his death, another death in my long life. Yet I am thankful for my life, and for the gift of acceptance and even love that Key Larkin once gave me.

Printed in the United States
1140500001BC/176-178